# A SPOONFUL OF MURDER

Also by Robin Stevens:

MURDER MOST UNLADYLIKE
ARSENIC FOR TEA
FIRST CLASS MURDER
JOLLY FOUL PLAY
MISTLETOE AND MURDER
CREAM BUNS AND CRIME

Available online:
THE CASE OF THE BLUE VIOLET
THE CASE OF THE DEEPDEAN VAMPIRE

Tuck-box-sized mysteries starring Daisy Wells and Hazel Wong

Based on an idea and characters by
Siobhan Dowd:

THE GUGGENHEIM MYSTERY

# A Spoonful of Murder

A MURDER
MOST UNLADYLIKE
MYSTERY

## ROBIN STEVENS

PUFFIN

## PUFFIN BOOKS

UK | USA | Canada | Ireland | Australia
India | New Zealand | South Africa

Puffin Books is part of the Penguin Random House group of companies
whose addresses can be found at global.penguinrandomhouse.com.

www.penguin.co.uk
www.puffin.co.uk
www.ladybird.co.uk

First published 2018

006

Set in 11/16 pt ITC New Baskerville
Typeset by Jouve (UK), Milton Keynes
Printed in Great Britain by Clays Ltd, Elcograf S.p.A

A CIP catalogue record for this book is available from the British Library

ISBN: 978–0–141–37378–2

All Correspondence to:
Puffin Books
Penguin Random House Children's
80 Strand, London WC2R 0RL

MIX
Paper from
responsible sources
FSC® C018179

Penguin Random House is committed to a
sustainable future for our business, our readers
and our planet. This book is made from Forest
Stewardship Council® certified paper.

To Nat and Gemma,
the other mothers of my books.

# A Spoonful of Murder

Being an account of

The Case of the Jade Pin Crimes,
an investigation by the Wells and Wong Detective Society.

Written by Hazel Wong
(Detective Society Vice-President and Secretary), aged 14.

Begun Monday 24th February 1936.

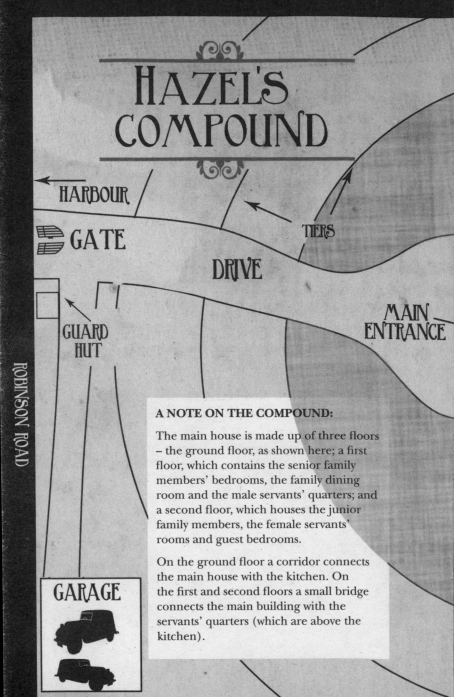

# HAZEL'S COMPOUND

HARBOUR

GATE

TIERS

DRIVE

MAIN ENTRANCE

GUARD HUT

ROBINSON ROAD

GARAGE

**A NOTE ON THE COMPOUND:**

The main house is made up of three floors – the ground floor, as shown here; a first floor, which contains the senior family members' bedrooms, the family dining room and the male servants' quarters; and a second floor, which houses the junior family members, the female servants' rooms and guest bedrooms.

On the ground floor a corridor connects the main house with the kitchen. On the first and second floors a small bridge connects the main building with the servants' quarters (which are above the kitchen).

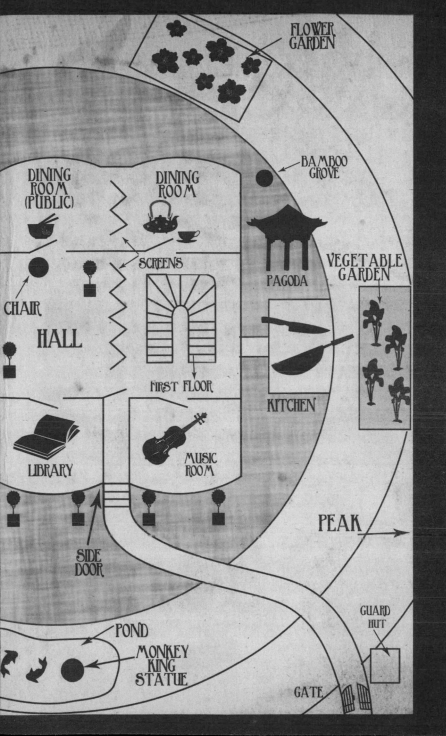

FLOWER GARDEN

BAMBOO GROVE

DINING ROOM (PUBLIC)

DINING ROOM

VEGETABLE GARDEN

SCREENS

PAGODA

CHAIR

HALL

FIRST FLOOR

KITCHEN

LIBRARY

MUSIC ROOM

PEAK

SIDE DOOR

GUARD HUT

POND

MONKEY KING STATUE

GATE

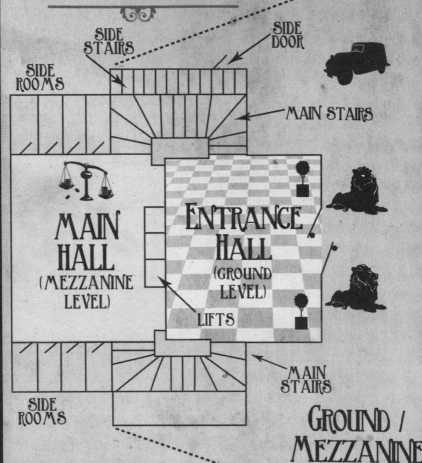

# HONG KONG & SHANGHAI BANK

**SIDE STAIRS**

**SIDE DOOR**

**SIDE ROOMS**

**MAIN STAIRS**

**MAIN HALL** (MEZZANINE LEVEL)

**ENTRANCE HALL** (GROUND LEVEL)

**LIFTS**

**MAIN STAIRS**

**SIDE ROOMS**

# GROUND / MEZZANINE FLOOR

← **PEAK**

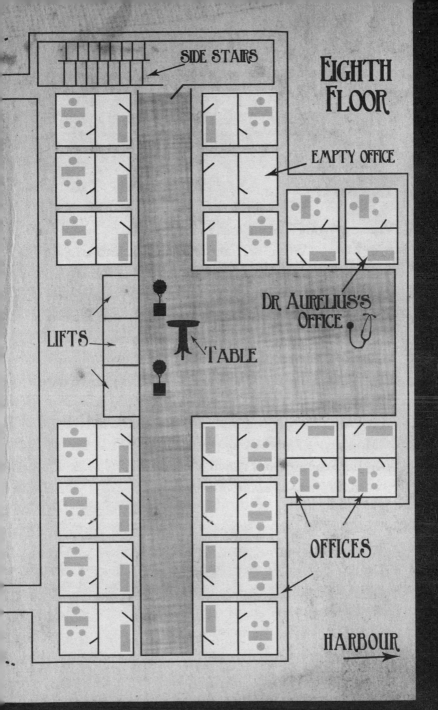

# CHARACTER LIST

**THE WONGS**

Vincent Wong (Wong Lik Han 黃力漢)

June Wong (Wong Ka Yan 黃嘉欣, also known as
Ah Mah) – *Mr Wong's first wife*

Jie Jie (Wong Min Su 綿素) – *Mr Wong's second wife*

Hazel Wong (Wong Fung Ying 黃鳳英, also known
as Ying Ying) – *Vice-President and Secretary of the
Detective Society*

Rose Wong (Wong Ngai Ling 藝玲, also known as
Ling Ling) – *Hazel Wong's half sister*

May Wong (Wong Mei Li 美麗, also known as
Monkey) – *Hazel Wong's half sister*

Edward Wong (also known as Teddy)
– *Hazel Wong's half brother*

## THE BIG HOUSE

Su Li 素李 – *Teddy's maid*
Ping 萍 – *Hazel's maid*
Wo On 和安 – *Hazel's chauffeur*
Assai – *Ah Mah's maid*
Ah Kwan 阿昆 – *May's maid*
Pik An 袁琵安 – *Rose's maid*
Ng 吳兄 – *A cook*
Ah Lan 阿蘭 – *A gardener's boy*
Thomas Baboo – *A guard*
Maxwell – *Mr Wong's secretary*
Daisy Wells – *President of the Detective Society, a guest of the Wongs*

## HONG KONG

Mr Peter Svensson (known as Sven) – *A businessman*
Mrs Kendra Svensson – *His wife*
Roald Svensson – *His son*
Mrs Bessie Fu – *A businesswoman, owner of the Luk Man Teahouse*
Mr Kai Wa Fan 啟華燻 – *A businessman*
Wu Shing 胡城 – *A lift operator*
Dr Crispin Aurelius – *A doctor*
Sai Yat 細一 – *A Triad gang leader*
Detective Leung 梁 – *A private investigator*

# PART ONE

# SAILING TO ADVENTURE

# 1

Somehow, even though Daisy and I had seen the body with our own eyes, I did not quite believe that the crime was real until we came back home from the doctor's office this afternoon.

Before that moment, it all just seemed like a bad dream, the very worst sort – like the one I have sometimes where we're investigating a case and I realize, like a slow shiver going up the back of my neck, that the murderer is after Daisy, and there is nothing I can do about it.

But, unlike those dreams, this time I cannot wake up, no matter how hard I pinch myself. And I know that I ought to have been able to stop what happened.

Daisy says that this is nonsense. She says, wrinkling her nose, that I could not have stopped anything – and, in fact, if I *had* been on the spot, I might have ended up murdered too. Like much of what Daisy says, this is true, though not particularly comforting. But all the same I cannot shake the feeling that I've failed.

You see, I have come back to Hong Kong. Here it is beautiful and bright, the air is warm and heavy and I am at home. No one looks at me oddly. I'm not strange, and that is a wonderful feeling, like opening up your hand and realizing that you have been clenching the muscles of it for far too long.

But, all the same, some things have changed in uncomfortable ways. I have been in England for almost two years, and while I was there I learned how to be not only an English schoolgirl and a best friend but also a detective. That is what the friendship between Daisy and me is all about, after all. We are secretly detectives, and have solved five murder cases so far, and, although it is not exactly true to say that we helped the victims, we did at least find out the truth about their deaths when the police could not.

But in Hong Kong I am with my family, who remember me as the smaller, younger Hazel I was when I stepped onto the boat to go to Deepdean. It's harder to be brave and grown-up and sensible when all I'm expected to be is dutiful, a good daughter and a good older sister. It's particularly hard to be the second, because— But I am getting ahead of myself. Daisy says to tell things in order as much as possible, and she is right. At least I have not forgotten how to lay out a case in a new notebook, the one Daisy gave me for Christmas.

All I will say, before I go back to the moment when everything started – this journey, this crime – is that a terrible thing has happened, a thing that the Detective Society must investigate. And we will – but this time I am stuck in the very middle of the case. I am not just a detective, I'm a witness. And I think that I might even be a suspect.

# 2

It all began with a telephone call in January, during the first week of our spring term at Deepdean School. There was snow on the ground, and my head was still full of Cambridge at Christmas, and the rather shocking thing that had happened at Daisy's Uncle Felix's wedding in London on New Year's Day. So, when I was summoned to Matron's office to speak to my father one morning, Hong Kong seemed very far away indeed.

The line crackled and boomed. 'Hello?' I said, and heard my voice echo away from me, halfway across the world. There was a pause, and then my father began to talk.

'Wong Fung Ying,' he said, and his voice sounded hollow even through the telephone. 'Prepare yourself.'

Wong Fung Ying is my Chinese name. To everyone in England, and usually even to my father, I am Hazel

Wong. He only uses my other full name when something very serious has happened, and so my stomach dropped in anticipation.

'It's Ah Yeh. Your grandfather. Hazel, you know he has not been well. I'm afraid he has passed on. It happened yesterday. We did not think – we did not think it would happen so soon, but it has.'

'Father!' I said. 'Are you sure – *really*?' I clutched the telephone, and the mouthpiece trembled against my lip. I felt a rush of impossibility. I could smell my grandfather's pipe, the tobacco on his breath, feel his hand heavy on my head.

'I would not lie to you, Hazel. Now, listen to me and be calm. You must come home. You'll miss the funeral, of course – that will happen next week – but if you leave in the next few days you'll be here for at least part of his mourning. Do you understand? You can't miss that.'

'No, of course I can't,' I whispered. My throat was full of things to say, but all that came out of my mouth were those words. I remembered, so clear and strong I could taste it, sitting next to Ah Yeh, watching him peel an orange into segments and pass me every third one. He was too big and important to have gone. It could not be. 'What does Ah Mah say?' I asked.

'What? Your mother agrees with me, of course. You must come home,' said my father, sounding confused. I knew it had been an odd thing to say – but I had to ask.

'Now, Matron will arrange your transportation. You'll catch the boat at Tilbury Docks, and it shouldn't take more than a month—'

'I want Daisy to come,' I said. I was rather surprised at myself for being so bold. I had almost not known what I was going to say until it was already being said. But, as I spoke, I realized how much I meant it. If I was to come home (if I was to face my mother, a voice whispered in my head), I needed Daisy with me.

'Hazel!' said my father, sighing. 'It's always *Daisy* with you. A more unsuitable friend for you I couldn't imagine, even if she does *appear* to be a lady. Do you think she'll be able to manage Hong Kong?'

He did not think so, but I knew she could. Daisy adapts to wherever she is, like a brightly coloured lizard. So I took a deep breath and gathered all the bravery I had found on the Orient Express to overcome my father's will. 'I'm not coming without her,' I said, and my hand holding the telephone receiver trembled even more.

My father sighed again, and made an impatient noise. 'I shall speak to the school,' he said. 'If they agree, and if her family does too – well, I suppose you may bring her. But, Hazel, I do not want you to be silly about this, do you understand? Don't let Miss Wells put any of her wild ideas into your head. Your Ah Yeh was old. Old and tired. It was his time. He is not another *case* like – well, like the one last summer, or any of these other ridiculous things you've got yourself mixed up in. Do you understand?'

'Yes,' I choked out, wiping my eyes. I *did* understand, and that was not why I wanted Daisy there. I did not need her for detection. For once, I simply needed her because she was my best friend.

'Good. Now, hand me back to your matron. I need her to put me on the line with that headmistress of yours.'

I handed the receiver back to Matron, and went stumbling out of her study. Daisy was waiting in the echoing, chilly House hallway outside, her blue eyes wide and her nose wrinkling with curiosity.

'What's up, Hazel?' she asked, but I pushed past her without a word. I went rushing up the threadbare carpet of the House stairs and along the narrow, dimly lit corridors to our fourth-form dorm. The window was open, even though there was frost on the grass outside, and I wrapped my scratchy grey wool blanket around my shoulders and lay down on my bed, shivering.

I knew Ah Yeh had been ill. But he was not supposed to die with no warning, when I was not even there. I was supposed to be with him – and anyway he should not have died at all, because he was Ah Yeh. He was as much a part of our house and Hong Kong as the columns in our hall, the pond in our garden, the steps up to our front door. He could not *die*.

I wrote Daisy a note. Sometimes, when I cannot say something, I write it. This was one of those times. I wrote it in several different codes, because Daisy and I have been practising (and she is fearfully bad at sticking with it), and I folded it up and put it on her bed. Then I went to lie down again.

Daisy came in. I knew it was her because she walked softly, one foot in front of the other, like a thief. There was a crumpling as she opened the note, and then an annoyed noise. I heard her pull open her school bag and rip a piece of paper out of an exercise book, and then I heard the scratch of her pencil as she began to work on the codes.

I counted seconds, and then minutes.

'Hazel,' said Daisy at last. 'The note was unnecessary. You might have just *told* me.'

'I couldn't,' I said into the blanket. I could feel my eyes stinging, but I told myself it was just the wool making them smart. 'Not out loud.'

'I'm going to sit on your bed,' said Daisy. 'If you don't mind.'

I knew that this was her way of saying that she was sorry about my grandfather. Daisy doesn't usually ask for permission for anything. She just thumps down on my stomach or my legs and doesn't care whether it hurts me or not.

'All right,' I said.

'So,' said Daisy after a pause, 'I suppose I'm coming to Hong Kong with you, then?'

I leaped up and threw my arms around her. That was when I really began to cry.

# 3

I have never done well on boats. They always make me feel watery, inside and out – and of course I was already more watery than usual. I remember the journey to Hong Kong as tasting of salt, from the sea and from the tears rolling down my cheeks.

Daisy had a marvellous time, exclaiming over the dining room and the cabins (all as glorious as those on the Orient Express, though on a larger scale), but there are only a few days of the voyage I can properly recall now, and one of them was the morning we heard the news about George V.

'Dead!' said Daisy blankly, staring down at the five-day-old newspaper. We were sitting on the SS *Strathclyde*'s first-class deck under the Egyptian sun after breakfast, staring out at the mirror-smooth water of the Suez Canal as our tugboats dragged us forward, puffing steam. 'Goodness, we'll have to have a new king now!

Oh, I must find a mourning band from somewhere. It's all right for you, Hazel. You're already in black.'

'The poor queen,' I said. 'The poor princess and princes!' I stared down at my black dress and felt *their* pain along with my own for a moment.

Daisy cocked her head to one side thoughtfully. 'I wonder. I suppose it *was* natural causes? I mean – we don't think that there was any *foul play*? He was the king, after all. What if someone *murdered* him?'

'You know he's been ill, Daisy,' I said. I had the unpleasant feeling that I knew where this conversation was going. 'He was an old man. And I shouldn't think anyone would want to kill him. His eldest son doesn't want to be king at all!'

'Hmm,' said Daisy. 'I suppose so. Though somehow it makes me think . . . Hazel, there's no possibility – I mean – are we quite certain that your grandfather—'

'Don't say another word,' I said, suddenly hot to my fingertips with hurt. 'Ah Yeh isn't one of our cases. He wasn't murdered. He just *died*, Daisy. People die of natural causes. And what are you saying – that *his* son might have killed him? *My father?*'

'No!' said Daisy, and I was glad to see that she was blushing pink. 'I only meant – well, wasn't your grandfather rich?'

'I suppose he was,' I said stiffly. 'But, Daisy, you can't go around saying he was murdered. And don't you

13

*dare* say anything like that to my family when we get there, all right? Grandfather died of old age, just like our poor king. He was almost eighty!'

'All right,' said Daisy, grumbling. 'But you can't blame me for *saying* it!'

'Yes I can,' I said.

There was a thoughtful pause from Daisy, and then she patted my hand apologetically. Everything was all right between us again, but, whenever I saw one of the British passengers with a mourning band over their sleeve, I felt as though the ache in my chest was doubled.

The other thing I remember is Daisy in the library.

As the ship steamed through the Strait of Malacca, and the water around it turned greenish blue, with frills of phosphorescence smoking off behind it every night, she began to behave in a rather strange fashion.

She kept slipping away at odd moments and returning hours later, her fingers stained with ink. I thought she might be making notes about the passengers without me, and was rather upset, until, as we were docking in Singapore, I went to the library to return *Tess of the D'Urbervilles* and came upon Daisy, seated at a table with a pile of books in her lap, a pen in her hand.

She jerked her head up to look at me and a blush spread across her cheeks under her suntan.

'What are you doing?' I asked.

'Studying,' said Daisy after a pause. *'Don't tell anyone.* It's just that – well – you've never told me much about Hong Kong. Which is *fearfully* bad form, Hazel. So far, I have simply had to infer, but that won't do while I'm visiting. I know I have the right clothes, I looked that up in magazines, but clothes can only get one so far.'

I blinked at her.

'Daisy!' I said. 'Are you *worried* about going to Hong Kong?'

'Of course not!' said Daisy, her blush spreading. 'I only want to make sure I'm fully prepared. Now, Hazel, tell me all about your family. You have two little sisters called—'

'Rose and May,' I said. 'They're . . . eight and five now, I suppose.'

'And then there's your father, who of course I know. And your father's, er, two wives.'

I could feel myself blushing too, at that. My father does have two wives: my mother, June, and his second wife, whom we call Jie Jie. Jie Jie is not her real name – it's a pet name that means something like *sister* – but, after so many years of calling her that, I cannot think of her as anything else. I had only mentioned Jie Jie in passing to my English friends, and I had always thought that not even Daisy had truly taken it in. It's almost impossible to explain to someone from England, where a husband is supposed to have just one wife (and if he has more it's bigamy, which is a crime), that my father's two wives know each other and actually live in the same house.

'You don't mind, do you?' I asked anxiously.

'Hazel, it doesn't bother me in the slightest,' said Daisy. But – as I looked at her – I thought I saw a little nervous twitch at her jaw. And I felt, as never before, the gulf between her idea of family and my own. I had thought that Daisy would take to Hong Kong as she has always taken to other new places we have visited – but I had forgotten that all those places were in Europe. We were beyond the edges of Daisy's world now, into my own, and Daisy had realized it, even if I had not.

Over the next few days I began to think more and more of my family. When I am in England, I try not to, because it hurts too much, but now I let myself do it. I thought of my father, looking down at me through his glasses and handing me a book. I thought of Jie Jie, catching me up in a hug and kissing my cheek. I thought of Su Li, my own *mui tsai* (this is a sort of young maid in Hong Kong), giving me cakes when I passed a test at school and tickling me until I cried with laughter. I thought of my sweet, funny little sisters, Rose and May. And I thought of my mother.

This last gave me a worried feeling. I hadn't seen my mother in more than two years, and, unlike my father, I had heard almost nothing from her. I only had the parcels with letters she made the chauffeur Wo On write, full of cakes from Ng the cook and terse little notes. Before I went away, I was always rather nervous of my mother. Although I know she's fond of me, she is so strict, and so beautiful, that she makes me feel small and dull. We have never had much in common. She didn't approve of my going away to school in England, and she let everyone know it. My mother bears grudges, and likes to punish people she is angry with. I was quite sure that she was still cross with me. That was why I had asked my father about her.

What if my mother did not want me to come home?

# 4

The SS *Strathclyde* finally pulled in to Hong Kong, Kowloon docks, on the 15th of February, thirty days after we had left England. My heart skipped to see the wide curve of Victoria Harbour, the Peak rising up green behind it under a blue sky. It was spring here, still cool by Hong Kong standards, but warmer and brighter than any English spring would ever be.

As the ship drew closer to the dock, I could smell the city floating out to meet us.

'Oh!' said Daisy, wrinkling her nose. 'Is that normal?'

I breathed in the green heat and the dirt and the cooked-bun smell that is Hong Kong to me. 'Yes,' I said, and I could feel myself smiling. 'It smells like home.'

'Not my home!' said Daisy, sniffing bravely and trying not to use her handkerchief. 'But – well, I suppose this is an adventure. I must just get used to it!'

'Do you mind being here?' I asked suddenly. I realized that I wanted Daisy to love Hong Kong – wanted it absolutely desperately.

'Hazel Wong, don't be a chump,' said Daisy. 'There is nowhere else in the world I would rather be. This place will be utterly different to England, but that makes it utterly fascinating. I would be no sort of detective at all if I turned round and went home just because I didn't like a smell! This is going to be marvellous, Hazel. All we need now is—'

'Don't say it!' I said quickly. 'Not here. We're in Hong Kong for my grandfather, Daisy, that's all.'

'Spoilsport,' said Daisy, and she stuck her tongue out at me. I tried to keep my face serious.

There was bustle all around as the ship began to dock, ropes flung between us and the land, porters bringing our luggage and piling it up around us. I remembered the last time I had been on this boat, when we docked in England two years ago. I was bigger now, inside and out – but suddenly all that time telescoped away. It didn't matter where I had been, or what I had done. I was home.

The gangplank rattled down, and all the passengers cheered. There was a chaos of shouting and shoving on the shore, men in ragged vests hoisting their green and red rickshaws, waiting cars honking, coolies with heavy loads swinging on their poles and uniformed porters with sedan chairs. I pointed it all out to Daisy joyfully. I knew this place, and I knew its people.

The first-class passengers began to disembark, their luggage carried ahead of them. Europeans in linen suits and pith helmets, Chinese in *cheongsams* and long jackets, Indians in robes and saris. I had changed out of my black Western mourning dress into a white one (in Hong Kong, you see, white is the colour of death). There was a wide white hat on my head and my hair was in a plait down my back. Daisy was all in white as well, her gold hair glinting under her hat and her cheeks pink.

Down the gangplank we went when it was our turn. I looked about for Su Li, and the car that would take us to Hong Kong Island, and my heart beat even faster as I wondered if my father would be part of the greeting party. For a moment I forgot to be sad about Grandfather. I was only excited to be back.

But what if we were being met by my mother instead? That thought made my heart beat faster for a different reason. Was I ready to face her displeasure?

Then I recognized the long black Daimler that I used, with Wo On, the chauffeur, beside it. He was waving at me, and I realized that Mother had not come, and neither had Father. The only person standing next to Wo On, bowing deeply and wearing the Hong Kong servants' uniform of black trousers and long white jacket buttoned up the side, was a maid.

But it wasn't Su Li. It was one of the younger *mui tsai*, little round-faced Ping, who blushed as easily as I did and was only a few years older than me. She was taller than I remembered, but she looked just as shy and awkward as ever. I couldn't think why she was there. Where was Su Li? If any *mui tsai* was going to be here to greet me, it should be her. I was confused. My good mood faltered.

'There,' I said to Daisy. 'That's our car. We have to get in it to go on the ferry.'

'Oh!' said Daisy. 'Where are your parents? Is that girl wearing *trousers*? Is she . . . a maid? Is she your Hetty?'

'Father must be busy. He'll be at home,' I said doubtfully. 'And everyone wears trousers here! Yes, she is a maid, but . . . not like Hetty. Remember I told you about Su Li? She must be waiting for us at home too.'

'I knew that about the trousers!' said Daisy, reaching up to fiddle with the brim of her hat, looking for all the world like a cat afraid of getting its paws wet. 'I read it in one of those books.'

Daisy nervous enough to lie was obviously a sight I never thought I would see – and yet here it was.

We walked towards Ping and Wo On, arm in arm, and I could feel Daisy's fingers digging into me.

'It's all right!' I said encouragingly. 'Come on, Daisy, it will be all right!'

'It's just so fearfully new, that's all,' muttered Daisy. 'And the day is so hot!'

'Are you nervous?' I whispered. 'Daisy Wells!'

'*I am not nervous!*' hissed Daisy. 'I am merely adjusting to my surroundings. Give me a moment, please.'

I had imagined my homecoming plenty of times – but somehow this reality was nothing like any of them.

# 5

'Miss Hazel!' said Ping, as soon as we were near enough. She spoke quickly, in Cantonese, and I could see her trembling with the effort to say the right thing. 'I am sorry for your loss.'

'Thank you,' I said automatically. 'But where is Su Li?'

Ping ducked her head, as though she was embarrassed. What was wrong? I wondered. Could Su Li have . . . *left our family*?

'There has been – that is, things have changed. Su Li has another position in the household now. I am sorry to tell you this, Miss Hazel. Your esteemed father has given me to you and Miss Wells while you are here, and Su Li – you will see. Your father apologizes that he could not be here. He is awaiting you at the house with the rest of the family.'

She bobbed her head again, her face flushed. I felt as though I was still on the ship, feeling the ground move beneath my feet. I was bewildered and rather annoyed. What was I not being told?

'Come into the car, miss,' said Ping, trying to be soothing. 'It will be all right.'

'Hazel!' whispered Daisy behind me. 'Hazel! Are *you* speaking *Chinese*? What did you *say*?'

I realized with rather a shock that Daisy had never heard me speak anything but English and a bit of French. 'Just – hello, really,' I said, blushing. 'Nothing very interesting.'

'That was much more than hello!' said Daisy, eyes wide. 'Hazel, I never knew you were so clever!'

I smiled at her, and for a brief moment my mood lifted. Daisy does not give out compliments lightly.

But then I climbed into the car and breathed in its smell of leather and the oranges that I used to eat on its back seat. I got a wave of sorrow in the back of my throat. Oranges were Ah Yeh. I could no longer ignore why I was here. I looked up at Wo On and saw him staring back at me sympathetically through the rear-view mirror.

'I'm sorry for your loss, Miss Hazel,' he said, his broad, sunburned face wrinkled up with compassion. 'It's hard, I know.'

'Thank you,' I said, and hoped as I wiped my face with my handkerchief that Daisy would simply think I was hot.

The car started up with a roar. Ping was in front with Wo On, and Daisy was in the seat next to me, her skirt tucked around her, peering out at the bustle and brightness of the docks. I reached out and squeezed her hand, and she squeezed back.

We had to drive onto the ferry with seven other sleek black chauffeured cars, and chug across the water of Victoria Harbour to Queen's Pier. I stared out of the car window as we went, breathing through my nose and trying not to be ill.

Junks and sampans bobbed around us in the churning water, their red sails like wings, and behind them, as we came closer, I could see tiers and tiers of white and brown buildings. I blinked. There were new buildings I did not recognize, and behind Queen's Pier was one that was huge, with dark stripes of windows down its front and two side wings like lion's paws.

'What's that?' I asked.

'The new Hong Kong and Shanghai Bank,' said Wo, turning back to look at us. 'Very impressive.'

It looked to me as though it ate up the skyline. And it was not the only one. All the places I knew, including the Post Office and the five-storey headquarters of

Wong Banking, seemed smaller next to these. I had grown while I was away – and so had Hong Kong.

We drove out in the shadow of the Hong Kong and Shanghai Bank, into the wild bustle of Hong Kong Central, and I leaned forward in the car as it jolted through the streets. I was grieving, but all the same Hong Kong was all around me, and that was thrilling. Chinese New Year decorations were still up everywhere, and the city looked wonderfully festive. I pointed out all the sights I knew to Daisy, and Wo joined in when I was at a loss. He also shouted at the other cars in the road, and the people in the street, in a way that I could see shocked Daisy. When he swerved to avoid a tram, Daisy gasped, and her face looked rather strained as we swerved to the right to dodge a bundle of bamboo poles that were being unloaded from a cart. I laughed out loud. I had almost forgotten Hong Kong traffic – now I remembered why I always found British driving so dull.

All around us were tall buildings, half of them unfinished, with workmen balancing on narrow scaffolding as they worked, dust flying. We drove past jewellery stores and teahouses, and pavements filled with people in jackets and robes and *cheongsams*, all in a Hong Kong hurry. It was hot in the back of the car too. I puffed air out of my bottom lip to cool my face. Everything was so familiar and yet so strange. I stared and stared, trying to learn this new Hong Kong all over again.

There was the sort of Chinese medicine store my mother loves, done up in red and gold, with great glass bottles of dried and powdered things – leathery skins and brittle shells and bones. I could smell the ginseng, even through the car window, and also the hot, full stink of rubbish in the gutter, being nosed at by two brindled pi-dogs. A group of coolies squatted on the street, eating rice out of a pot, and a rickshaw rushed by, dodging round the dogs.

We were moving away from the busy middle of the city, and now we turned right on Garden Road and climbed upwards. We were driving up the side of the Peak now, with heavy green trees above us and vines draping from them. White-and-black tiger-striped butterflies darted out of the way of the car's nose, and I could smell azaleas and see their salmon-pink blooms like splashes of paint. The car tilted upwards again, and we turned right onto our road, Robinson. We passed one wide gateway, and then another, and I saw Daisy gaping at the houses we drove past.

And then we were turning into our compound, and Thomas Baboo, one of our family guards, was waving to us in his red-and-gold uniform, his silk turban glowing white in the sun and his moustache gleaming. Up our long white drive the car climbed, bright ornamental gardens unfolding around us in tiers. We stopped at last in front of our house's white facade, the three layers shining in the sun. It has wide windows and beautiful pillars, and an open veranda with heavy granite steps up to it. Each one is so high that I could barely climb them when I was little. I remembered Su Li having to lift me up each one, laughing down at me as my face turned red with effort.

The big front doors were folded back against the side of the house, as they always are in the day, and I could see a little way into the cool dark hall, with its columns and sofas and great curving pots that the gardeners fill with fresh flowers every morning.

Daisy sat half in and half out of the car, her mouth open in a most unladylike manner.

'Hazel,' she said at last in a very small voice. 'I see that I have been underestimating your wealth.'

There is a side to me that I can never really show at Deepdean, or anywhere in England. You see, my father is not fadingly rich like Daisy's, or middling rich like Kitty's and Lavinia's, or even new-money, pin-factory rich like Beanie's.

My father is so rich that we do not have just one car, but a car for each member of the family. My father is yacht rich, eight-maids rich, mansion rich. He is even rich by Hong Kong standards, a city that is all about business. But, if I ever explained that to my English friends, I would seem boastful, and more different than ever. I never wanted to do that.

'I – I – it looks worse than it is,' I said.

'*Worse?*' said Daisy, and now she was gazing at me with her most appraising stare. 'Why, Hazel – it doesn't look bad at all. But you might have told me at some point during our years of friendship that you are some sort of . . . princess.'

'I'm *not* a princess!' I hissed at her, because Wo On was coming round the side of the car to usher us out of it. 'I'm just— I'll explain later. It's different in Hong Kong.'

'I see that,' said Daisy, and now her thoughtful look was turned inwards. I wanted to ask her what she was thinking, but at that moment someone came out of the interior of our house and stood on the veranda steps.

It was my father, with a most solemn expression on his face, and at that moment I remembered again that we were here to mourn.

# 6

Wo On had dropped to his knees on the ground, his head bowed. Ping too bowed low.

'Hazel,' hissed Daisy in my ear. 'You *are* royalty! Your father is a king! You ought to have told me!'

'No!' I said. 'It's— The bowing is for Grandfather. It's part of his mourning. We have to pay our respects to him. Er, so now we have to crawl up the steps to the door. On our knees. I'm sorry.'

Daisy blinked. 'Crawl?' she asked. '*Really?* How *spiffing!*'

'It isn't! It's serious. You can't look cheerful,' I said quickly. I knew Daisy, and I knew that this would seem like the most splendid fun to her. I wanted her to understand that, for once, this was not a game.

So Daisy and I dropped to our hands and knees and crawled up to my father's front door. The granite tiles scratched my hands, and I began to sweat at my temples and at the backs of my knees. It ought to have felt silly.

The English schoolgirl part of me was telling me it *was* silly. Except that, somehow, it was not. Crawling was appropriate, just as hard and horrible as it felt to remember that Grandfather was gone, and he was not coming back.

I climbed the stone front steps, my palms aching, and paused at the top.

'My Hazel,' said my father's voice.

I saw his feet in the slippers that he uses at home. My father always wears Western dress, even in Hong Kong, but when we don't have guests he likes to put on Chinese slippers. My grandfather would never wear Western dress at all – and the thought of that made me gulp with tears again. I stood up quickly and bowed to my father, and then he put his arms around me and kissed the top of my head.

'Welcome home, Hazel,' he said. Then he put out his hand and took Daisy's. 'Welcome to the Big House, Miss Wells. Thank you for coming home with Hazel.'

'You are most welcome, Mr Wong,' said Daisy and, though her legs were streaked with dirt and her white dress was quite ruined, she managed to drop into the most perfect curtsey. 'Thank you for having me.'

'Hazel,' said my father, and when I looked up at him I saw that his eyes were full of tears, but he was smiling. 'I am sorry for your loss. Ah Yeh was a wonderful man.'

'I am sorry, Father,' I said. 'I am so sorry.'

'It is good to have you here,' said my father. 'I am sorry I could not come to meet you from the ship. But now we are all here, waiting to say hello.'

I smiled. So it was all just a mix-up. My father would have been there to greet me if he could. It didn't matter, really.

And then I saw my sisters, Rose and May. They were standing on the smooth white tiles of the hall floor, shuffling their feet. Rose, in a new white jacket, smiled shyly, her hands behind her back. She was so tall now, and still the prettiest of the three of us, with long eyelashes and a little mouth that was screwed up in a grin. May, though, when she saw me looking at her, hurled herself on me like the monkey we nicknamed her for, squealing. She had been three when I saw her last and now she was five. Secretly, I hadn't been sure that I would recognize her, but her face, with its strong jaw and little button eyes, was as familiar as ever. I threw my arms around her and buried my face in her soft, rather dirty-smelling hair.

'You've got fatter!' said May. 'I like it lots. You look nice.'

'I like your hat, Big Sister,' said Rose, scuffing her feet.

'Thanks, Ling Ling,' I said, calling her by her nick-name as I reached out to hug her. 'And don't be rude, Monkey.' May made a face at me.

'MEI LI!' my father said to her. 'Be respectful to your big sister! Miss Wells, these are my other daughters, Rose and May. They are *mostly* good girls, hmm?'

May giggled.

'And here is my first wife, June.'

My mother stepped forward, taking the little dancing steps that she has to with her bound feet, and bowed to Daisy. Her hair was cut in a new style, a fashionable, wavy bob, her face was carefully painted and her curved lips were red. In her white *cheongsam* she looked very lovely – and very forbidding. My heart beat fast.

'Hello, Miss Wells,' said my mother to Daisy. 'It is good to meet you.'

'It is very good to meet you too, Mrs Wong,' said Daisy, impeccably polite, looking anywhere but at my mother's tiny shoes.

Then my mother turned to me. 'Hello, Ying Ying. Goodness, you are so big now,' she said in Cantonese, flashing me a glance from the corner of her kohl-rimmed eyes. 'So much cake in England, hmm? Now, what have you learned at that school of yours?'

'History,' I said, in English again so that Daisy could understand. I knew that my mother can speak it perfectly well too, although she hates doing so. 'I know all about the English Civil War now. And in Maths we're learning algebra.'

'Hazel is the second-cleverest in our year,' said Daisy eagerly. 'I am the first, of course, but that can't be helped. Hazel does very well, considering.'

'Hum!' said my mother. 'You are looking very brown, Hazel. Did you not use a parasol on the boat?'

'I – I forgot,' I muttered. I could feel myself shaking. I felt so small; smaller than Rose. My mother has always had this effect on me, and after two years it was as bad as ever. I looked at her face carefully. I thought she did look angry – I had clearly not been forgiven. I had to bite my tongue to stop myself apologizing.

'And this is Jie Jie,' said my father, gesturing. 'Hazel will have explained our family to you, Miss Wells.'

Jie Jie bowed her head. 'Hello,' she said quietly. 'Miss Wells, hello. Ying Ying, I am glad to see you again.'

Jie Jie is taller than my mother, with a little mouth like Rose's and May's button eyes. They are usually wrinkled up in a smile, and she smiled at me now, although rather more shyly than her usual head-thrown-back beam – she is always a little nervous when my mother's around. I smiled back.

Jie Jie is Rose and May's mother. Although she is part of my family, to the rest of the world she is not as important as my mother. Although she is my father's wife at home, when he leaves the house, my mother is the only wife he speaks of in polite society. I had tried to explain it to Daisy on the boat, but she had got stuck on the fact that in public my sisters are my mother's children, but in private they belong to Jie Jie. It simply makes sense to me, but of course it's not British at all.

What I did not tell Daisy – what I have not told anyone – is that sometimes I wish that I didn't belong to my mother at all, but to kind, warm, smiling Jie Jie.

'Now, the next introduction will be a surprise to you, Hazel, as well as Miss Wells. I wish it was under happier circumstances, but – well, you'll see. Su Li!'

And then, out of the shadows of the columns came Su Li. I jumped, and I could feel my smile growing. Su Li was here at last! Now she would turn to me, laugh, hold out her arms and say, 'Miss Hazel!' I had not quite been able to explain it to Daisy, but Su Li was not just Hetty to me, but Mrs Doherty too. She was almost my third mother.

It had all been a mistake. She would become my maid again, and everything would be all right. Ping was nice, but she was not my Su Li.

'Su Li!' I cried. 'Hello!'

But Su Li did not look at me. She kept her head bowed, focused on something in her arms: a bundle that she was hugging close to her chest.

Suddenly the bundle wriggled, and I stepped back-wards in alarm. I thought for a moment that it must be a puppy – or a real monkey, like Rose used to ask for before May was born. But then the blanket the bundle was wrapped in shifted, and I saw that it was not a monkey or a puppy.

It was a plump, sleepy baby, swaddled up so that only its face was free. It blinked at me, and then its forehead wrinkled, as though it was just as puzzled about what was happening as I was.

'Gah!' it said.

'Hazel,' said my father behind me, his voice booming with pride. 'Miss Wells. Meet the newest member of the family and Su Li's new charge, your little brother, Edward Wong.'

# 7

'No,' I said.

The word echoed around the big hall.

'No?' asked my father, frowning.

I took a deep breath. The baby blinked up at me, and then Su Li looked up at me too. Just for a moment her eyes met mine – and then they widened, and she flushed and jerked her chin back down.

'Take him, Hazel!' said my mother crossly. 'He's so fat, just like you. Su Li can't hold him for long.'

'But,' I said. 'You – he – how could you have had a baby?'

'It wasn't anything to do with *me*,' said my mother in Cantonese, crosser than ever. I knew I had offended her. She nodded her beautifully made-up face at Jie Jie, who grinned proudly and then covered her mouth with her hand.

I looked back at the baby in Su Li's arms. I am not

stupid – I know how babies happen (although Kitty has told us some things that I am sure are lies). But I could not understand how this one could have appeared without my knowing anything about it. Babies take a long time to be born, months and months – and I had seen my father in the summer. He hadn't said anything about a brother then. I had even spoken to him on the telephone, only a month before, and he had not mentioned a baby at all.

But then I remembered what he had written on the parcel he had sent me at Christmas: *Your real present is at home*, and I got a sinking feeling through my body. He had, in his own way, told me that Edward had been born, but I hadn't understood what he had meant. I had thought I might be getting a new car, or a set of bookshelves in the Library. Not *this*.

'We weren't certain until after I came home from the Orient Express,' said my father. 'And then we weren't certain he would be a boy. He was born in November, and he was rather ill at first, so I decided to surprise you when you next came home. Are you surprised, Hazel?'

'Very,' I said numbly.

This was the moment when Su Li finally tipped the baby forward into my arms, and I found myself holding Edward Wong. He was indeed very heavy. He pursed his lips at me and blew a bubble.

'We had firecrackers,' said May. 'Hung up all down the front of the house, just like there were for me, only I wasn't a boy, remember? I helped set them off and it was SO loud. It made him scream and scream. It was funny.'

'*I'll* take him, Hazel,' said Rose, and she pulled Edward out of my arms. 'You're going to drop him. Look, you hold him like *this*.'

Edward beamed gummily at her.

'He likes everyone,' said May. 'We call him Teddy.'

'Su Li is his maid now. Don't argue, Hazel,' said my mother, as if reading my mind. 'Your father says so, and so that's just how it will be. I think you'd like to be shown to your room now, wouldn't you? Ping, take them both upstairs.'

I was stunned. This was all wrong. I reached out my hand to Su Li, and she took a step backwards. She was still refusing to look at me.

'Su Li, the baby needs his afternoon tonic,' snapped my mother.

'Teddy is going to grow up into such a strong boy!' said my father, his face softening. 'He must take his medicine. Attend to it, Su Li.'

A hole seemed to have opened up in my stomach. I had been nervous about coming home because of my mother. It hadn't occurred to me that I might have been worried about the wrong thing.

# 8

As the eldest daughter, my room always used to be between my mother's and my father's on the first floor – but now Ping led Daisy and me to a room close to the bridge over to the servants' quarters. It was not a little girl's room but a guest's. Everything in it was blue and silky – the counterpanes on the matching teak beds, the soft rug on the carpeted floor, the paintings on the walls of English skies and seas, and the sprays of flowers in the blue-and-white vases. I ought to have felt pleased at how lovely it was, but it only made me feel empty.

'Teddy is in your old room, miss,' Ping said to me, bowing very low – with a quietly sympathetic look, I thought, that showed she knew what I felt. 'But here is nice. You'll see.' I knew it wasn't Ping's fault, not a bit of it, but all the same I could barely look at her.

At last Ping had tidied away our things, patted down

our beds and pattered apologetically out of the room, closing the door behind her.

I sat down on my bed. It gave thickly under me – the mattress was soft and padded, like the whole room.

'Hazel,' said Daisy.

'I'm all right!' I said.

'You aren't,' she said. 'If you were, you wouldn't be telling me so. And you have had the most dreadful shock.'

'It – it wasn't supposed to be like this!' I cried. 'I know that Grandfather is dead. But everything else was supposed to be the same! It's not fair!'

I heard how childish I sounded, and I didn't care.

'Hazel, I quite understand. It's always frightfully annoying to have relatives, isn't it? If I could, I'd have come out of an egg. And babies are a horrid surprise. Why do grown-ups seem to like them so much? It's utterly unfair that they always assume that you'll get along with your sibling. Squinty and I hated each other when we were little. Once he tried to push me down the stairs, only Mrs Doherty stopped him. Mummy spanked him for it. It was the first time we'd seen her in weeks, so I remember it perfectly.'

'I don't hate *babies*,' I said. 'I never hated Rose and May when they were babies, and I don't hate them now, either. Only—'

*Only*, I thought to myself, *they're girls, like me. Only, when they were born, I was still my father's favourite. Only, the reason why I was allowed to go to school in England was because I was the oldest girl – because Father didn't have a son.*

*What will change now that he does?*

'Only it's different in Hong Kong,' I said, stumbling over my words. 'Having a boy matters. Boys are . . . boys are more important than girls. I mean, of course they're not *really*, but that's what people think.'

'That's just the same as in England!' said Daisy dismissively. 'No one cared a pin about me when I was born, because Bertie already existed. And he's still the one who's supposed to do clever things, even though *you* know he doesn't have *half* the brains I do. He'd be much happier being a society wife than I ever would.'

I sighed. Daisy was quite sure that she understood, but I knew that she didn't. A boy was everything in Hong Kong. A brother would *change* things. I tried to explain again.

'Teddy is Jie Jie's,' I said. 'My father's second wife, not his first. If Teddy had been a girl, he would have been just like Rose and May – not as important as me, because I'm my mother's daughter. But he's a boy, the first one in the family. Which means that it doesn't matter who his real mother is. He's my father's heir. Everyone will pretend that he's my mother's real son, and he'll be treated as though he's more important than any of us. It's already begun. He has the room next to hers.'

'Hazel,' said Daisy. 'That is very odd.' She put out her hand and patted my shoulder. 'But – it's still not so different from England.'

'It *isn't* like England!' I cried. 'It's no use pretending it is. You don't understand.'

I was getting so tangled up that I realized I hadn't even mentioned the truly dreadful thing. Yes, Teddy threw the order of my family into chaos. But it was not just that – or, rather, that was not what was important. Teddy already seemed to have taken Su Li away from me.

What if he was taking my father too?

# 9

I was here to mourn Ah Yeh – and, I was discovering, to learn the new shape of my family – but, despite all that, the very fact of being in Hong Kong was still joyous. And there were holiday moments during our first week, like deep breaths between the sorrow.

It was funny, though, to notice how closely watched Daisy and I were in Hong Kong. In England I have become used to hours when Daisy and I are alone, without a mistress or another grown-up near us at all. But here there was always someone walking behind us, usually Ping, hurrying along with little panting steps. I tried not to resent Ping for not being Su Li, and usually almost managed it, but all the same her presence sometimes felt rather like the mourning dresses my mother had chosen for me – just a little too tight for the person I was now.

On Saturday Daisy and I and Ping and Wo On went up the Peak Tram. My father was supposed to come, but at the last minute Teddy developed a cough, and so my father stayed home to watch him and dose him with medicine. I told myself I didn't mind.

I sat pressed back against our padded first-class seats as the carriage jerked upwards alarmingly, too fast for my stomach to keep up with it. I looked out and got a juddering, sideways view of Hong Kong, green and blue and brown and white. I turned my eyes forward and kept them fixed on the two empty chairs that are always reserved for the Governor and his wife.

'Has the cable ever broken?' said Daisy quietly in my ear.

'I – don't – think – so,' I managed, feeling my bones jumping about with every tug upwards. I clung to the wooden seat and tried not to look as though I was praying. I have never liked the Peak Tram – but I do love the view from the top. When we emerged and turned to look, Daisy put one gloved hand to her lips in amazement, and I felt a proud flutter in my chest. When I was little, I used to think that Britain was the most perfect place in the world. I spent whole days wishing myself away from dull, ordinary Hong Kong and into an English storybook world. But now, coming back, I finally understood that Hong Kong had magic about it too.

There was my city, so far below that it looked as though I could reach down and touch it. The thick green of the mountainsides was dotted with white mansions, and there was ours, way below and to the left. From up here we could see the lines of roads, like the ribs of an open fan. Across the harbour was Kowloon Island, the windows of the Peninsula Hotel glinting in the sun. I pointed right, to where the Peak Tram had started out from, and further along to show Daisy my father's bank, near the gleaming new Hong Kong and Shanghai Bank we had seen from the car ferry. Then I pointed left again, to a place that I knew would please Daisy. 'That's the prison,' I said. 'There, near the police station. That's the beginning of Western, the district where all the gangs are.'

'Ooh!' said Daisy appreciatively. Ping had come to stand behind us, holding up our parasols against the yellow morning sun, and I nodded at her in thanks.

'And there – that's Man Mo Temple, the one Grandfather used to go to,' I said, pointing to the little green roof gleaming up at us. Saying it, I felt a stab of sadness. I was always being reminded of him. It felt as though I should be able to reach out and touch him too – only I could not.

After that I took Daisy to the Russian bakery on Queen's Road, where they served Black Forest gateaux, with chocolate melting off them in the heat, and dainty fruit tarts (covered not in strawberries and raspberries, but lychees, mangoes and Chinese gooseberries – for we were still in Hong Kong, after all). I ate yellow cake, *mah lai goh*, and I was utterly happy.

We went to the zoological and botanical gardens too, where a monkey threw a peanut at Daisy, and she threw it straight back. It was all enormous fun, until a rather odd thing happened. When I think back on it now, I realize that Daisy and I ought to have recognized how important it was. But we didn't, until much later – until now.

We were walking back to the car under a cool grey sky when a woman rushing past us in the street stumbled in front of me.

I instinctively stepped forward to catch her (Wo said, 'Miss Hazel!' warningly), and as I did so I saw a little scar like a half-moon of dots on her neck, underneath her neat bun.

'Are you all right?' I asked. The woman didn't respond. She looked at me, her face calm, and then she suddenly seized my elbow and jerked her arm, so I was pulled close to her, her lips by my ear.

'Beware, Miss Wong,' she whispered – and then she stood up and ran away, into the press of the crowd.

I stared after her, my heart beating. Ping rushed over and began to pat me down. 'Are you hurt?' she cried. 'Do you know that woman?'

'No,' I said. I saw Ping and Wo – and Daisy – all looking at me, and I got a funny feeling in my stomach. I did *not* know her – so how had she known *me*?

# 10

It hurt that I had missed my grandfather's funeral. He was already buried high in the Chinese Cemetery, out by Happy Valley. But I was there for the reading of his will, which took place on Sunday, the day after our zoo trip.

My father sat in the largest chair in the big main hall to receive the lawyer, with his secretary Maxwell at his side. It gave me a strange feeling, for the chair, lacquered black and gold, and padded with a fat red pillow, had always been my grandfather's before. He had sat there in his silk jacket and wide trousers, knees far apart and one heavy hand pressed down on each. But now here was my father, in his neat three-piece suit, with a look of concentration on his face and his legs crossed at the knee.

The rest of the family (Daisy was in our room) stood in a carefully arranged semi-circle behind him. My father nodded up at the lawyer, once, to instruct him to begin.

'My honoured family,' began the lawyer.

The doors to the garden stood open, and warm spring air breathed in. Flowering orange trees had been brought into the pots in the hall, and their sweet, delicate scent floated around our heads. I let the lawyer's voice wash over me – until something he was saying pulled me back to reality.

'And, to my honoured family, I say this: remember that it is important to be united. Do not waste time in argument, but cherish each other. My son, love your wives and your children. And, my son's wives, obey your husband.

'My granddaughters, I give to you each a token of my love – a jade pin, carved especially for you. Wear them and remember me.

'And to my grandson. It has been one of the joys of my old age to see you come into this world. My son, I thought this day would not arrive, and I was sorrowful. But now I am proud of you, and of my grandson. I bequeath a portion of my wealth to be held in trust for him when he becomes a man. All else is yours, my son, to use to care for your family – I only ask that you deal thoughtfully, choose your partners wisely and remember that the good name of the family is sometimes worth more than money.'

My breath caught. I had loved my grandfather for years. And I had been given a pin. But Teddy – even though he was only a baby, who Grandfather had known for only a few months – had been given far more than Rose, or May, or me. I looked over at my father, and saw him beaming at Teddy, who was, as usual, nestled in Su Li's arms.

She was cuddling him, letting him suck on her fingers, dangling his silver rattle above his head to make him smile. She was smiling too, so proudly – just the way she used to smile at me. I remembered how she would boast to the other maids that I was reading more, thinking more cleverly than their little girls were. But what if she had only been proud because I was Mr Wong's eldest daughter, the most important child? What if she was proud of Teddy now, not because he was growing fatter and happier every day, but because he was my grandfather's heir, my father's long-awaited son?

Su Li had still not really spoken to me, apart from polite, empty pleasantries, since I had come home. She seemed afraid to look at me, and her face, when she did so, was always stiff and correct. It made me feel as though I hardly mattered, as though she hadn't missed me at all, whereas I had missed her far more than I had my own mother.

I shook my head and looked away, at my mother, who was standing up very straight, although I knew her feet would be hurting her. Her lips were pursed.

'It is good to hear Ah Yeh honouring Teddy,' said my father, blinking rapidly.

'Hmm,' said my mother icily.

'He was so kind,' said Jie Jie, smiling. 'We must honour him, for the good of our children.'

'Yes,' said my mother, no less coldly. 'Our children. Indeed.'

Teddy suddenly made a whimpering noise, and wriggled in Su Li's arms. We all turned to look at him.

'He's hungry,' said Jie Jie.

'I shall have him fed, and give him his tonic,' said Su Li. 'He needs to keep his strength up!'

'Take him away, Su Li,' said my mother, sighing. 'Do whatever you have to.'

'Yes, madam,' said Su Li, and she walked out with Teddy nestled in her arms.

Jie Jie let out a long breath. My mother rolled her eyes. 'That baby is always needing something,' she said.

'Teddy is a good baby,' said Jie Jie stubbornly. And I saw the way my mother glared at her.

# 11

I ought to have been thinking like a detective. I ought
to have been watching everything. But all I cared about
was that my father and Su Li seemed to be moving
further away from me all the time.

That is why I was excited when I heard that, according
to my father, I was finally old enough to go to grown-up
parties with him. We had been invited to one that evening
at the Svenssons' house. I had a vague memory of Mr
Svensson – a large, cheerful Swedish man with whom my
father sometimes did business – as one of many grown-
ups who used to pass above me on their way to drinks
parties in the Library. It was very odd to think that I was
now someone who was old enough to be noticed properly.
Growing up, I thought, seemed to be something that
mostly happened when you weren't looking.

I was also pleased about the party because it meant
that I would have my father all to myself for an evening.

It's funny to remember that now, when I know that what I should have been feeling was absolute dread.

We went in a large black Rolls-Royce, my father, my mother, Daisy and I. Jie Jie stayed at home with Rose, May and Teddy. When my father goes out to Western homes, or invites Westerners to visit, my mother is shown to them as his only wife, and tonight we would be as close to a Western family as we could be.

We drove through the scented streets, the darkness heavy and thick, trees electric with the noise of insects. Daisy leaned against my arm, staring out at the houses rolling by, their windows glowing. Up a gravel drive we purred, to an open door lit up inside like a torch, with servants on the steps bowing to greet us. This was the Svenssons' house.

It was new – so new that it smelled freshly painted. It looked almost comically like an English country house, one that had been picked up and dropped down in the middle of the Hong Kong jungle. Music floated out of the open front door, as did grown-ups' laughter, and the bright pop of champagne corks.

Daisy, who was wearing a gorgeous pale blue dress, her hair in a most grown-up twist with a glittering diamond clip, smiled at me.

'Come on, Hazel,' she whispered in my ear. 'You look awfully pretty.'

I had on a white silk *cheongsam*, and my hair was up

too, held in place with the pin my grandfather had given me. Its jade head was in the shape of a rooster for my birth year. Despite my feelings when I heard I had inherited it, I loved it. All in all, I did feel quite pretty – perhaps because, for once, I wasn't wearing a dress that looked like Daisy's only less interesting.

My father led the way down the hallway, and my mother followed him gracefully, taking tiny steps. We came out into a wide, well-lit room, and a short woman with round, flushed cheeks, curling blonde hair and a purple dress came sweeping towards us.

'Vincent!' she cried. 'June! Welcome!'

My mother's name is actually Ka Yan – but to Westerners it is June.

'Mrs Svensson,' said my mother, bowing.

'Oh, do call me Kendra, June, I keep on telling you!' cried Mrs Svensson. I saw a flash of annoyance in my mother's eyes, but she nodded politely.

'This is my daughter, Hazel!' said my father. 'You might remember her? And her friend, Miss Daisy Wells.'

'Daisy, Hazel, you must call me Kendra too. I'm Mrs Svensson now, Kendra Gilbertson before I married Sven,' said Mrs Svensson. She spoke with an English accent, and her little, snub-nosed face was slightly freckled by the sun. She smelled purple too, a light, summery, lavender scent wafting off her. 'And how is your baby?' she asked my mother and father. 'My Roald is doing very well. Six months next week!'

'Oh, Teddy is very well too,' said my father, beaming. 'Very healthy indeed, since he began to take his tonic. A spoonful a day, doctor's orders. We were worried at first, you'll remember, but he's become such a bright little fellow. He has his monthly appointment with Dr Aurelius tomorrow, at noon, but I'm sure he'll find nothing wrong.'

'Marvellous! Now, Daisy Wells, I know that name. Didn't your father—'

'And I'm sure I know the name Gilbertson!' said Daisy, very fast. Her nose was wrinkled up, and there were two red spots high on her cheeks. Daisy hates any mention of her parents, or Fallingford, of course. 'Was your father the mathematician Professor Peter Gilbertson, at Cambridge? My great-aunt speaks very highly of him!'

'Why, yes!' said Mrs Svensson, clearly delighted. And she and Daisy began to talk genealogies, in the odd, involved way that wealthy British people always seem able to.

I turned and smiled at my father. I thought that this, at last, might be the moment when he noticed me. We could go back to being as close as we'd been before. But his eyes were still far away, and he had a soft, fond look on his face. And I realized that, even here, he could think of nothing but Teddy.

I turned away, hollow with disappointment.

'Mrs Svensson, please excuse me,' said Daisy smoothly. 'I do believe— Why, isn't that Lord Pallister? Hazel, come along . . .'

Before I could even draw breath, she had pulled me away from my parents, and we were halfway across the patterned parquet floor.

'Father—' I said, gulping.

'I know,' said Daisy briskly. 'But you must just stop expecting things to be the way they were. Forget about your silly family for a moment. Sit down in this chair next to me' – she lowered me into one of a bank of plush red chairs – 'and let us hone our detective skills by observing the room. Now, I do believe that this Hong Kong party essentially follows the rules of an English one. For instance, that lady there outranks that one, but the other won't acknowledge it. They're both quite furious.'

I gave her a rather wobbly smile, and looked where she was pointing. There were two women, one in a blue sari and the other in a pink Western dress, smiling and raising their glasses to their lips.

'But they're talking!' I said.

'Of course they are,' said Daisy, beaming. 'They're being very secret about how much they loathe each other. Oh, it is nice to remember that, wherever you go, people don't really change!'

'But they do!' I said. 'Or at least the little things about them do. You only think they don't because here everyone Chinese is pretending to be Western. My father's pretending he's only got one wife, for a start, and my mother's pretending that Teddy is hers. That could never happen in England.'

'Well, of course, *customs* are different,' said Daisy, waving one dainty hand. '*Traditions* are. But *people* are the same. They may behave differently, but they have the same feelings.'

I did not quite agree with her. There are some things that cannot be translated.

I was trying very hard not to look at my father, but my eyes were drawn across the room to where he was standing. He was with a tall blond man, who had broad shoulders and piercing blue eyes. They knew each other well: I could tell from the way their bodies were angled towards each other. But the expressions on their faces told me that they were not exactly friends. My father was frowning and shaking his head, his feet set apart on the floor, and the tall blond man was gesturing excitedly with his hands, his eyes flashing and his face twisted with passion.

I watched my father. He's very good at staying calm, even when he really isn't. I could tell that this was one of those times.

'Who is that man?' asked Daisy. I could feel her sharp curiosity. 'Do you know him?'

'Yes,' I said slowly. 'That's Mr Svensson.'

'Tonight's host?' asked Daisy. 'Goodness! He oughtn't to be rude to his guests! That's a terrible faux pas.'

'Oh bother,' said Mrs Svensson, coming up to us and sighing. Her purple dress drifted around her becomingly. 'They're at it again. I do wish they wouldn't talk business at a party.'

'What are they discussing?' asked Daisy.

'It's the same old thing,' said Mrs Svensson, rolling her eyes. 'Sven wants Mr Wong to invest in his latest venture, but Vincent won't do it. Honestly, men are so dull. They can never have *fun*. Now, girls, please do take some canapés.'

She pointed at a plate that was being carried by a Chinese waiter, looking rather uncomfortable in tails and shiny Western leather shoes. I was doubtful – but then I peered down and saw what he was carrying.

They were tiny, dainty little fish balls, just like the ones Su Li used to buy me from street vendors in Central, only done up for a party. I reached out for one, beaming, and nudged Daisy. 'Try it!' I said. 'Go on.'

I could see that Daisy was unsure – but of course she is nothing if not polite. She reached out and put one into her mouth.

I watched her, and saw her face change from confusion to delight. The canapé was warm and rich and spicy, English on the outside, but perfectly Chinese inside, and I smiled at it, and at Daisy.

'They are rather good, aren't they? Cook is clever,' said Mrs Svensson. 'Daisy, how are you enjoying Hong Kong?'

'Oh, it's simply splendid!' said Daisy. I beamed even more to hear her say that. It mattered that Daisy loved my home.

'Yes, so it is!' cried Mrs Svensson enthusiastically. 'It has its own odd set of rules, of course, most of which I ignore. I'm quite a trial to my servants. I'm always rushing off on my own with Roald – I can never bother to wait for the maid. I think it's far more fun to do things for oneself. That's the boarding-school girl in me, I suppose. I came here three years ago, when I married Sven, and I was quite trepidatious when I arrived – the heat, you know, and the people – but I think it's marvellous now, especially since the new house is finished (only ten months behind schedule and double the budget, like everything dear Sven manages), and we don't have to live in the Peninsula Hotel any more. It was lovely, of course, but not very homelike. Now, do excuse me. I must go and be a hostess,' and she rushed away again. She always seemed to be on the move.

'I like her,' I said to Daisy.

'Oh, so do I!' said Daisy. 'She's right about Hong Kong, you know. It's lovely, even if it is fearfully foreign.'

'Hong Kong is no more foreign to me than England is to you!' I pointed out.

'Goodness,' said Daisy, blinking. 'What an odd, Alice-in-Wonderland thought that is! I suppose you're right. This isn't foreign at all to you. I always forget that.'

# 12

We watched as Mrs Svensson swooped down on my father and Mr Svensson, standing on tiptoe and kissing her husband. He laughed and put his arm round her, and whatever the mood had been vanished. But it had been there – and I could tell that Daisy was as curious about it as I was. But, of course, the grown-up thing to do was to pretend we didn't care. It was terribly annoying.

'Come on,' Daisy said. 'Let's tail two of the guests and see if they notice.'

'No!' I said. 'We can't, Daisy. We're at a party!'

'Of course we can!' said Daisy. Then she stopped and stared at another woman who was making her way across the floor to my father. She was an older Chinese lady with a broad, determined face and clipped, short hair, wearing a silver *cheongsam*. I knew her too – this was Mrs Fu, a businesswoman whose father and husband had been very important, and who now owned our family's favourite teahouse, the Luk Man. I knew that my grandfather had been her investor, in memory of her father. She began to speak to Father – and her expression changed, to become just as unexpected as Mr Svensson's had been. She looked upset, almost pleading – and my father, replying to her, set his jaw all over again into his calmest annoyed expression.

'Whatever is going on now?' hissed Daisy. 'Who is that?'

'That's Mrs Fu,' I said. 'She's – well, she runs a restaurant now. I thought that she and my father were friends . . .'

I was a little unnerved. I had known Mrs Fu for years. She was kind, if rather fierce, and I liked that she was a woman who did business with the men. I couldn't understand why she should look at Father like that – I had never seen her even the slightest bit cowed. She held up her head no matter who she was talking to.

'I can't read their lips!' said Daisy, frustrated.

'That's because they're speaking Cantonese,' I said. 'Hold on – let me try.'

My lip-reading is not as good as Daisy's, but I managed to pick up a few words. 'Can't help!' said my father.

'. . . ridiculous,' said Mrs Fu. 'Remember Father.'

'Business!' snapped my father. 'Things have to change now!' Then he turned away from her, towards my mother, who was talking to Mrs Svensson, and looking unhappy about it.

'Miss Wong!' said a voice. I turned and saw Mr Wa Fan walking towards us. He had been one of my grandfather's oldest friends, a fellow member of the Tung Wah, the Chinese local government organization that my grandfather had been part of for years. They had their headquarters in the temple my grandfather visited, Man Mo Temple, and they seemed to organize every part of Chinese life. Seeing him now, without my grandfather by his side, gave me a pain in my chest. He was wearing gorgeous robes, a silk cap with a peacock feather on his head, and his white beard was as long and luxurious as ever, but somehow he seemed smaller than I remembered, more wrinkled, half lost in his outfit.

'Good evening, sir!' I said politely, bowing. 'May I introduce you to my friend, Daisy Wells?'

'Hm,' said Mr Wa Fan. 'So, you are back.' He spoke to me in Cantonese, ignoring Daisy. Out of the corner of my eye I saw Daisy's ready smile falter. She wasn't used to being overlooked.

'For Ah Yeh's mourning,' I said, nodding. I had to speak in Cantonese as well, of course, otherwise it would not have been right.

'Good girl,' said Mr Wa Fan. 'You are a dutiful granddaughter.'

My stomach twisted. 'But I ought to have been here,' I said. 'When it happened.'

'Nonsense,' said Mr Wa Fan, frowning at me. 'It was not your fault you were away. It was your father's.'

I blinked. 'Oh,' I said. 'But—'

'Your father thinks that Western school is the answer to everything,' said Mr Wa Fan, his face wrinkling up more than ever. 'But it is not. Your father ought to think harder about what he really owes to his community and his family. If he does not, there will be consequences.'

I was puzzled. I didn't know what to say to that. Hearing my father calling to us that it was time to leave was the most enormous relief. I gabbled my goodbyes to Mr Wa Fan, who was glaring between me and my father fiercely, and backed away, tugging at Daisy's arm.

'We must get home,' my father was saying to the gathering. 'My son has his appointment at the doctor's tomorrow at noon!'

*Teddy again!* I thought, frustrated. I couldn't bear it. I rushed out of the room, so quickly that it was almost not polite. Daisy had to hurry to keep up with me, and I knew, with a feeling that was both delighted and nervous, that my father would not be pleased with my behaviour.

It was not until we were out in the warm night, my mother's maid Assai bringing us our wraps, that

I noticed my hair falling down against my collar in a thick coil. I reached up and patted my head – and felt nothing. My pin was gone!

It was a horrid realization. I had only just been given it, after all, and by Ah Yeh. How could I have lost it already? I knew I could not tell my parents. I hated the thought of disappointing them any more than I already had this visit.

So I kept silent about it, all the way home. But as I walked into the main hall and Ping came out to meet us, she exclaimed, 'Your pin!'

'Shh!' I hissed. 'I dropped it. It must be back at the party – please don't tell Father and Mother!'

'Oh, Miss Hazel!' said Ping, looking distressed. 'Wo can fetch it tomorrow.'

'Thank you,' I said, simply desperate to stop talking about it.

And that was the last time I thought about the pin until the next afternoon. If only I had remembered to get it, things would be very different now. But I did not know that yet.

# PART TWO

# DEATH BY APPOINTMENT

# 1

It was raining on Monday morning – Hong Kong rain, which is as warm and thick as blood compared to thin, cold English drizzle. I opened our bedroom window and leaned forward, reaching my hand out, palm up to catch the drops. Laughing, Daisy leaned beside me, so far out that she almost toppled over. Ping, folding our clothes, looked up and gasped.

'It's all right!' I said. 'She won't fall. She has good balance.'

Ping opened her mouth, closed it again and looked flustered. 'Please make her stop it, miss,' she said. 'I don't want her hurt.'

'Daisy,' I said, nudging her. 'Come back in.'

Daisy sighed, and drew her shoulders back inside. 'I never would have thought that in Hong Kong you have to be even more ladylike than in England,' she said. She had noticed the tight-dress feeling too.

At breakfast that morning, everyone seemed on edge. I don't think I'm simply remembering it that way because of what happened later – everyone really was jumpy and out of sorts.

Daisy had tried *congee* for the first time and was not enjoying it. She stared at her bowl, muttering, 'This is absolutely not like rice pudding at *all*,' with a betrayed expression on her face.

My mother had a headache (which she often gets when it rains, or when my father has done something she does not approve of), and was sipping tea with a most sour expression on her face.

May was sulking in her chair, because she had been caught throwing oranges against the hall ceiling to soften them and her *mui tsai*, Ah Kwan, had made her drink castor oil as punishment. Rose was teasing her about it. I poked Rose with my chopsticks.

'Hazel!' said my father irritably. 'May! Rose! Control yourselves!'

I felt cross. I have always been the big sister and they the babies. We are not usually lumped together. But now, of course, we were all the big sisters, and Teddy was the baby. We all had to behave better, because he could not.

'Where are the farms here?' asked Daisy. She said it innocently, but I knew she was doing it to distract my father. 'I mean – why isn't there more milk?'

'This isn't England, Miss Wells. There isn't much need for it. But there's a farm in Pok Fu Lam, and on Lantau the monks make cheese. In fact, talking of Lantau, I have been thinking that it might be almost time to take Teddy there. He hasn't been on the yacht yet, after all.'

My heart sank again.

Yacht visits to the island of Lantau are something that my father and I share. It is unusual for a girl to go. I know I am very lucky (so lucky that I swallow my hatred of boats, cling on tight and pretend to be enjoying myself). I cannot go into the monastery itself, for I am a girl, but the journey across the blue and green water to the great green hummock of Lantau Island is a time that is just for my father and me, with no business, or little sisters, to worry about. The two of us sit side by side beneath a canvas awning and read our books (or at least my father reads, and I try to hide my seasickness). The air smells salty, and there is salt on my top lip when I lick it, and the sun strikes up from the water onto the pages of our books. When we come home, my mother is always annoyed, because the sun on the water makes me brown.

But now my father wanted to share that with Teddy? It wasn't fair. No matter that I used to wish my father would take someone else. Lantau had been mine, and now I was losing it. I glared across to where Teddy was sitting on Su Li's lap. I wished him anywhere else in the world. I wanted him gone from our house.

Writing that now makes me feel ill.

Teddy beamed at me, showing pink gums. 'Teddy is quite young for a boat journey!' said Su Li quickly.

'I believe I give the orders,' said my father coldly. 'And I would never do anything that might harm my son.'

Su Li ducked her head until it was almost touching Teddy's. 'Yes, sir,' she said. 'Apologies, sir.'

'Now, Hazel, it's Teddy's appointment with Dr Aurelius today,' said my father, turning to me. 'As your mother is unwell, I thought that you might be able to accompany him – you and Miss Wells.'

He was peering over his glasses at me, eyebrows drawn together, and I knew that this was the sort of request that was not a request at all.

'Hazel does not need to go! Su Li ought to be able to do her job without supervision!' said my mother crossly.

'Hazel ought to begin behaving like an older sister! She should want to accompany her baby brother!' said my father at once.

'Hazel, I am glad you are home, to help like this,' said Jie Jie. She spoke quickly, looking between my father and my mother.

It is often Jie Jie who has to act as the peacemaker. I understood that she wanted me to help her, and so it was for Jie Jie, not my father, and certainly not for Teddy, that I said, 'All right. I'll go.'

'Excellent,' said my father, nodding at me. 'Maxwell, do we have those papers for the Liu contract? Bring them over to me.'

And that was the end of the conversation.

# 2

In Deepdean, the doctor's office is the San, where Mrs Minn is always waiting to soothe you and bandage you up and give you a biscuit. At Fallingford, Dr Cooper comes whenever he is called with his little leather case and his round, bald head. But in Hong Kong the Western doctors are kept away from the rest of the city, high above the busy streets, on the upper floors of banks and office buildings that are cool and pale and polite. They are the other side of life from the Chinese doctors my mother goes to who smell of gingko and liquorice, where things that you do not exactly want to look directly at float in bottles.

I used to be dragged back and forth by my father and my mother, between the Western doctors who tapped my knee and pressed their cold, round stethoscopes against my chest and told me not to hold my breath, and the Chinese doctors who stuck me full of needles like a pincushion and told me that this remedy would stop me blushing so much. I know both sides, and now that I have lived in England they feel like a perfect metaphor for the different parts of my upbringing, English and Chinese.

I had thought that we would be going to the doctor's office where Rose and May and I had been taken for years – but we were not. Our family doctor, Dr Aurelius, had moved to new offices on the auspicious eighth floor of that huge new white building I had seen from the ferry, the headquarters of the Hong Kong and Shanghai Bank. I got a nervous feeling as I realized that, although I didn't quite know why.

At 11:40 Teddy's car, another gleaming black Rolls-Royce, was brought up to the front door of the house, driven by Wo On in spotless livery. Su Li, looking immaculate as usual, carried Teddy (wrapped in fresh white swaddling clothes) to the car. Daisy and I followed her, and Ping followed both of us, puffing rather. That morning, Su Li once again would not look at me. She gazed down at Teddy, adjusting his blankets and cooing at him. I told myself that she was only doing her job – but that made me realize all over again that, if this was true, *I* had only been a job to her as well, one that was now over. I had adored her, but I must have been wrong about how much she loved me back.

It had stopped raining just after eleven, but the air was still damp. I felt little beads of moisture at my temples, under my hair. I looked back up at the house as I was about to step into the car and saw my mother's face staring out of one of the upstairs windows. She was watching us, and when she saw me she jerked away suddenly. I could tell she was still angry that I had agreed to accompany Teddy, and my stomach crawled. To make my father happy, I had disappointed my mother even more.

'Hurry, Miss Hazel, or we'll be late!' said Wo On from the front seat, and I scrambled into the car.

Down the hill we drove, past the guarded gate and out into Hong Kong. The big houses of Mid-Levels gave way downwards to the steep, busy streets of Central, pawnshops and fishmongers' and furniture stores and warehouses with coolies going in and out, sweating in the sun, heavy loads weighing down their bamboo poles. The sea was to our right, and, as we drove, the buildings around us became more ornate, their colours brighter, their signs more beautifully painted. We drove parallel with the main tram route, and for a while with one of the trams itself. It rattled along, dinging brightly, its windows crammed with hot, tired-looking people in the white and black clothes of servants, and the vivid colours of shopkeepers and housewives.

Su Li was bouncing Teddy on her lap, singing him a nursery rhyme.

'You used to sing that to me,' I said, unable to stop myself.

Su Li's head snapped up, and she stared at me. 'Yes, Miss Hazel, I did,' she said quietly. 'I remember fondly.'

I didn't know what to say to that. It seemed almost kind, but I did not believe in Su Li's kindness any more.

Then the car made a right turn at the seafront, sweeping round to face the Peak. I saw that we were pulling up to the bank building at last. It rose above us like a white pyramid, a mountain in front of the real mountain, cutting out the sun.

# 3

'Oh golly!' gasped Daisy. 'Isn't it impressive up close?'

Wo helped us out of the car. I could smell the sea behind us, and feel a breeze stirring my hair. We walked into the shadow of the bank. Like most Chinese buildings the closed brass doors in front of us were flanked by two enormous brass lions, glinting in the sun. One, on the left, was yawning wide, while the other's mouth was closed politely. They made me smile, for they were so unexpectedly sweet and Western, although they were in Hong Kong.

'Stephen,' Wo On said to me and Daisy, pointing at the yawning – or roaring – one. 'And that is Stitt. You rub them for luck.'

I got rather a jump at that, and tried to hide it.

Teddy peeped out from Su Li's arms, his eyes crinkled up as he stared about at the entrance. 'Ah!' he said, and he forced one of his small, fat hands out from his swaddling blankets to make a fist at Stephen. Su Li carried him over, and he paddled his fingers against Stephen's metal mane. He was only waving his hands, as babies do, and I was annoyed to see Su Li look delighted, as though he had performed a trick.

'One day you will own a bank just like this,' said Su Li, laughing down at Teddy.

I hung back next to Wo. He turned to me and in Cantonese said, 'Go and pet them too. You need some good luck, Miss Hazel. It is difficult for you. You know that Su Li—'

'She's very proud of Teddy,' I said through gritted teeth.

'That isn't quite what I was going to say,' said Wo. 'But it is true. He is a good baby, Miss Hazel.'

'Miss Hazel, are you coming up with us?' called Su Li. 'We must hurry, or we'll be late for Dr Aurelius.'

'I won't,' I said. She had sounded hopeful, and I suddenly wanted to spite her. I knew that my mother would not have gone with them, if she had been here. 'Miss Wells and I will stay downstairs.'

'If you wish it, miss,' said Su Li, sounding almost sad. 'We'll only be twenty minutes.'

We all walked through the main doors, past the liveried doorman. To our left was a great curving staircase that led up to the main hall of the Hong Kong and Shanghai Bank. In front of us were three lifts, their golden doors open, that went up to the doctors' floors. Their three operators were waiting for passengers within.

Coming out of the middle one was someone I recognized. Mrs Fu, the teahouse owner, went rushing towards the main stairs. Her head was turned away from us as she stuffed something into a slim handbag, her shoulders set.

The lift operators, in red uniform with gold trim on their lapels and smart caps on their heads, all bowed to us as we approached. Two were rather old, scrawny men, but the middle one was younger, with a twinkle in his eye and a handsome jut to his jaw. 'Come on in!' he called to us. Wo On motioned Su Li towards the middle lift, and the lift operator bowed and gestured.

Su Li had paused. I turned and saw her face change. For a moment she looked . . . nervous? Afraid? I wasn't sure, and it vanished too soon for me to catch properly. She walked slowly to the lift.

'Eighth floor, if you please,' she said to the operator. 'The child has an appointment.'

The lift operator nodded back politely – but there was a funny look in his eye too. It was almost eager. He stepped aside to allow Su Li and Teddy into the lift, then closed the metal grille and the door after them. The dial above the lift began to tick upwards. Second – third – fourth – fifth—

'Come on, Daisy,' I said, shaking my head. 'Let's look around the bank.'

# 4

Together, Daisy and I climbed the stairs and stepped through the arched doorway. With Ping following us nervously, we found ourselves in the main bank hall. I had to hold back a gasp. It was so grand – so unbelievably high and big and gold. On both sides of the room, men in neat black suits worked busily at rows of imposing, marble-topped desks, and above their heads, far above, hung an enormous gold mural.

It was beautiful, I thought. Hong Kong was beautiful and exciting and important. If only – if only Teddy wasn't here. If only I could enjoy it.

Why *did* he upset me so much? He was not ugly the way May had been as a baby, all screwed up and raging. He was not sickly like Rose, who had been born early and little. I had sat outside her nursery for weeks, pretending to read, listening to what the nurses were saying to each other. But Rose and May had not changed the shape of my family the way Teddy had.

I felt a nudge in my side, and came to myself to see that Daisy was nodding towards one of the desks.

'Hazel!' she hissed. 'Mrs Fu just came past us again from one of those tellers. She rushed out of the bank as though it was on fire. And now there's Mr Svensson as well, coming out of one of the side rooms! Isn't that odd? We saw them both last night – and here they are again! I thought Hong Kong was a big city?'

Daisy sometimes has a tendency to see mystery where there is none. We were in a bank. It was natural that businessmen and -women should be here.

'Daisy!' I said. 'Don't point, or it'll be obvious.'

'Why shouldn't I be obvious?' said Daisy, with a very obstinate look on her face. 'I've nothing to hide. I'm simply in a place I have been sent to by the father of my best friend, Hazel Wong. I wonder what Mr Svensson's excuse is.' She raised her gloved hand, waved it frantically and called across the echoing space, 'Mr Svensson! Hello! Fancy meeting you here!'

Mr Svensson turned with a start, his large attaché case swinging and his big shoulders and chest making his expensive new suit strain against him. His face flickered. He seemed alarmed – which could, I told myself, be simply because he hadn't expected to be accosted by his acquaintance's daughter in the middle of a working day.

But there was something in his expression, quickly buried, that the detective in me noticed. He looked – briefly – concerned. Almost as if he didn't want to see us here. But that was silly, I told myself. I was being silly again: what I had seen in Su Li's and the lift operator's faces had simply been my imagination, and so was this.

When Mr Svensson came towards us, he was beaming.

'Miss Wong,' he said. 'Miss – Wells, was it?'

'Yes – I am the *Honourable* Daisy Wells,' said Daisy. I saw the little twitch in her cheek that told me she had noted the order we had been greeted in yet again. In England we are Miss Wells and Miss Wong, but here we were both realizing that I was the daughter of Vincent Wong, and Daisy was simply my friend.

'Yes, of course,' said Mr Svensson, smiling almost all the way to his eyes, and he took us both by the hand and shook enthusiastically. His grip was strong enough to make me wince.

'We are waiting for my . . . brother,' I said. 'He has an appointment at the doctor's upstairs.'

Mr Svensson twitched.

'And what are *you* doing here?' asked Daisy, polite but sharp.

'I've just had a meeting with my financial adviser,' said Mr Svensson, shrugging with exaggerated boredom. 'Business, you know. Money matters. Not for little girls.'

I felt Daisy bristle at that, but she giggled and said, 'Of course!'

'And now I must be going, if you'll excuse me,' said Mr Svensson. He looked at his watch quickly. 'I shall be late.'

He turned and hurried away. 'Hurried' really was the word, I thought. He rushed across the tiled floor of the bank as though he was being chased by a tiger.

'Goodness,' said Daisy, 'is there a fire?'

'Don't,' I said. I didn't want her being silly too.

We wandered around the bank hall for ten minutes by my wristwatch, our footsteps echoing into the large space. I looked at my watch again – it was twenty past twelve.

'Su Li and Teddy ought to be coming back now,' I said. 'Let's go and wait for them by the lifts.'

We walked away from the hollow boom of bank chatter, and down the main stairs. And there was Mr Svensson again. He was going out of the bank's entrance very quickly, his back to us.

'Didn't he leave ten minutes ago?' asked Daisy, frowning.

'Perhaps he forgot something?' I said. But despite myself I felt a little frisson of nerves under my skin. It *was* an odd thing to see. Today we *kept* seeing odd things.

Wo On came through the main doors then. He saw us standing beside the bank of lifts and looked puzzled. 'Where are they?' he asked.

'They haven't come down yet,' I told him. 'They're late.'

'Hazel,' said Daisy, nudging me. 'Look at the lift they took. I think the dial is stuck. It's not quite at the eighth floor.'

I saw that she was right. The gold arrow was pointing between seven and eight.

My detective sense never quite stops ticking. It's like an ember that only needs a breath of air to set it flaring up again. And at that moment I felt it truly begin to smoulder.

It was probably nothing, I told myself firmly. Su Li was only ten minutes behind schedule.

Except that I knew Su Li. She likes to be punctual. She taught me to be punctual too.

'We will go up,' said Wo On. He ushered all three of us into the left-hand lift, which was standing open, its old attendant waiting. 'Eighth floor, if you please,' he said.

I looked at him, and then at Daisy, and something crawled in my stomach, because I saw that whatever I was feeling, they felt it too.

The lift moved upwards. One. Two. Three. Four. Five. Six. Seven. Eight.

And then the lift doors opened.

# 5

We were in a beautiful white marble lobby. In front of us was a gold-and-black table, with elegant thin legs and an enormous arrangement of white flowers spilling out of a tall black vase on top. There was a corridor in front of me that stretched away, in gleaming white splendour, all the way to wide windows with a view of the harbour, like a living picture. All along that corridor, and to the left and right of us too, stretched closed white doors bearing little gold plaques with names inscribed on them in curlicue letters. Eight is a very lucky number, and here on the most auspicious floor of the building were dentists and surgeons and women's doctors and Freudians, every sort of doctor the wealthiest people in Hong Kong could want. Each, I knew, had a suite of rooms, a waiting room and a consulting room. If I pushed open any of these heavy white doors, I would see a pretty receptionist sitting behind a desk, looking at me over her glasses.

But that was not important to us now. We were looking for Su Li and Teddy – and they were nowhere to be seen.

Wo On went striding along the corridor that led to the window, and Daisy, Ping and I hurried after him. My heart was pounding – although, I told myself, trying most desperately to be rational, all we were likely to find was a cross Su Li, still in the waiting room because the doctor had been delayed.

Wo On pushed open the last white door on the left, which read DOCTOR CRISPIN AURELIUS in golden letters, and a receptionist in a neat white uniform and with glossy, pinned-back hair looked up at us curiously.

'We have come for Edward Wong and his maid,' said Wo On. 'Where are they?'

'Not here yet,' said the receptionist, a little dent appearing in the skin of her forehead as she drew her eyebrows together in disapproval. 'They are late.'

Next to me, Daisy made a small hissing noise.

'But we saw them go up in the lift, almost half an hour ago,' said Wo On sharply. His face was suddenly flushed with worry. 'They *must* have come here.'

'I tell you, he has not arrived,' said the receptionist.

Wo On swung round towards the corridor, back to the receptionist and then to the corridor again, looking utterly bewildered.

'They came up in the lift,' he repeated.

This time Daisy and I turned too, to look at that middle lift, the one Su Li had stepped into with Teddy half an hour before. And, as I did so, my neck prickled and my fingers tingled. There was no doubt about it. Something about the lift was *wrong*.

Its doors were shut, which meant that it ought to be either travelling between floors, or stopped on one of the floors below. But the dial above the doors was still hovering just below the eighth floor.

'The lift must be stuck. Have you heard them calling?' Wo On asked the receptionist.

'No,' she said. 'But it is hard to hear anything – these new doors and walls are thick.'

'We must get those lift doors open,' said Wo On, sharper than ever. 'There might be a baby trapped in there!'

He took off, striding back towards the lift, and Daisy and I ran after him, with Ping hurrying after us. I heard the receptionist begin to speak into her telephone handset, before the door swung closed on her voice.

My feet slipped on the smooth marble of the floor. It was odd, I thought, how sound died in this space. Our hurrying steps seemed to make almost no noise at all – or was that only because my ears were ringing?

Together, Wo On and the old lift operator who had brought us to the eighth floor wrestled with the golden lift doors, fighting to prise them apart. Wo On jammed his thick arm into the gap and heaved (the old man was too infirm to be much help). The lift doors were forced apart with agonizing slowness.

Daisy surged forward to peer inside, pushing me before her – and the spark of nervous fear I had been feeling swelled up and burst into a horrible flame.

# 6

Once, a long time ago, I walked into the Gym at Deepdean and found the body of Miss Bell, and all our adventures began. I remember thinking at first that I wasn't sure whether she was dead or not. She didn't look as though she was dead, only lying very still.

This time, I didn't have to wonder.

The lift was sunk down into the shaft, its inner grille only half pulled back, a foot below the white marble corridor of the eighth floor, so we had to peer down into it. But its electric light was still on, and in its glow we could see Su Li sprawled on her back. Her legs were twisted under her, and her arms were folded over her chest, hands covered in scratches. Her neck was bruised – and there was something else that made my breath catch in my throat.

There was a pin stabbed into her throat. It was a jade hairpin, carved into a rooster shape. And it looked just like – but surely it could not be – the one I had lost.

I reeled.

Daisy clutched my hand. 'Hazel!' she said. I knew that she had seen what I had. Daisy's memory is even better than mine, and it would not be like her to miss such a detail. Su Li and the open lift doors blurred in front of me. What on earth had happened?

'Where is Teddy?' cried Ping frantically from behind me. 'Where is the baby?'

I gasped. All I had seen was a body, and the horror of where my pin was. I hadn't seen what – or who – was *not* there. I hadn't even wondered about Teddy until Ping said his name. I had been a detective, not a big sister.

Wo On squeezed through the lift doors and opened the grille, then jumped down into the lift itself. He pulled Su Li's body to one side. I held my breath – but there was nothing to be seen. Teddy wasn't there.

Wo On was shouting for Ping to go for help, and the combination of his shouts and the cries of Ping and the lift operator were enough to rouse the workers in the offices nearest us. There seemed a sudden flurry of them. I clutched at Daisy's arm. I could see everything – the bloody handprint on the edge of the grille where it had been pushed open, in the shape of a large, square male hand, and another one on the operation panel of the lift, the patch of blood on the carpet, the jade pin shining in the soft lift light. But it was as though I was floating. I could not feel any of it. Su Li was dead. In that moment the anger I felt towards her about Teddy had evaporated. I stared at her horrified face, and all I could think was that I had cared about Su Li, and now she was gone. And Teddy was gone too.

'It must have been the lift operator,' said Wo On, kneeling in front of Su Li's body, mouth open and eyes wide. I could see his chest rising and falling in panic. 'See the handprints? He killed Su Li, jammed the lift, pushed open the grille and kidnapped Teddy!'

'He must be a member of the Communist Party!' cried someone. 'It's a plot!'

'No!' shouted someone else. 'It's the Triads. Look – look at that pin! That's their calling card! The Triads have the child!'

Ping led us away from the scene (I could feel Daisy twisting round to look back for as long as she could). The next thing I knew we were in low leather chairs that sighed as we sat in them. We were – I realized slowly – back in Dr Aurelius's waiting room.

'Here's some tea,' said Ping. Her face was red and tear-stained, which was odd, because my face was dry. It felt as though there was a stopper inside me, closing away all my emotions just as though I had put them in a bottle.

I sipped the tea Ping handed me, and sipped again, before I noticed that my mouth hurt because the tea had burned it.

'Oh, what shall we do, Miss Hazel?' Ping asked, her voice shaking.

I did not know.

# 7

Then my father arrived. I heard him shouting in the corridor outside. I sat up, and he burst through the door, his suit jacket flapping. He was still wearing his silken house slippers. He knelt down in front of my chair and put his big hands on my shoulders.

'Father!' I said, expecting him to hug me.

Instead my father shook me. He shook me so hard that my teeth really did bounce together in my mouth. I bit my tongue.

'Why were you not in the lift with them?' he cried. 'Why were you not there?'

'Hazel wanted to show me—' Daisy said loudly.

'Silence, Miss Wells,' snapped my father. 'Wong Fung Ying, *answer me*.'

'I didn't think I needed to be there,' I whispered.

'I should beat you,' Father said. His face, as I stared into it, was red all over, the blood pulsing beneath the skin. 'You deserve to be beaten. You left your brother alone, and now he has been taken by that wicked man.'

'I didn't *know*,' I whispered. I could not speak louder. The stopper in my throat was too tight.

My father's shoulders slumped, and he let go of me. I could still feel the prints of his fingers on my shoulders. 'Of course you didn't,' he said in a whisper. 'You are a child. I should never have allowed Teddy to be so unsupervised. You are correct: you are not responsible; I am. This is my fault. *My son has been taken.*'

'I'm sorry,' I choked out.

'Go home, Hazel. Ping, take them home,' he said, and that was his final word.

I wanted to ask if he had seen the pin, and what he thought it meant – but I couldn't. I was so confused about it. *Was* it the sign of a Triad gang? I knew that one particular local gang left calling cards like this.

And my father was wrong, I was *not* a child. I was Teddy's big sister, and a detective. If I had been in the lift, I might have been able to stop what had happened to Teddy and Su Li. I might have been able to save them. But I had chosen not to be there, and that *was* certainly my fault.

Whatever my father said, Teddy was gone and Su Li was dead because of me.

\*

Ping rushed us down in another lift, stumbling over her trousers in her haste. Her hands were trembling, and she was still crying, her face red and raw.

'Poor Su Li!' she kept on whispering. 'And poor Teddy!'

There were heavy black police cars pulling up at the bank as we went out of its main doors. Daisy made a cross clucking noise with her tongue.

'They're too late! They'll miss things,' she said to me. 'Half the people who were here will have already gone. How will they find Su Li's murderer now? How will they find Teddy?'

'I don't know,' I whispered. 'I – I can't think.'

'Evidently,' said Daisy.

I turned on her furiously.

'Don't look at me like that, Hazel! You don't *have* to think. Just sit quietly, and let me think for you. It'll be all right, you'll see.'

I understood that Daisy was trying to help. She was looking after me in the only way she knew how. But, all the same, I didn't think it would work. I had grown up hearing horrid stories about children who were kidnapped. It's quite common in Hong Kong, among families who are as rich as mine. That is why we always have maids and chauffeurs with us, why we are kept in the house so much. If we go out alone, we might be taken. And now it had really happened – to my own brother.

We climbed into the car. Wo On was already there, and he started the engine. It revved up, and we sped away. I saw Wo's hands clenched tight on the steering wheel. I saw how his shoulders shook.

Outside, Hong Kong scrolled by, hot and bright. But now the way I saw all the streets had changed. They were suddenly places where Teddy might be. He could be any of the swaddled babies being carried past us, their faces squashed up against women's backs. He could be in any of the bundles piled up on carts. He could be in that bucket, or being carried along in that rickshaw.

He could be anywhere.

Once before, at Fallingford, the Wells and Wong Detective Society had been confronted by a mystery that came very close to us – but it had been Daisy and her family who were affected, not me. I had only been able to watch. Now our positions were reversed, and I was lost in the horror of what had happened. *My* brother had been taken. *My* maid was dead.

*It was my fault.*


Our car drove up to the front door of my house and we ran up the granite steps to find it in chaos. The gardeners were all armed, the dogs had been let out to patrol during the day, instead of at night, Rose and May were sobbing in the front hall, being held by a white, shaking Jie Jie, and my mother was waiting for me.

'Wong Fung Ying,' she snapped. 'What happened?'

'He's gone,' I said. 'Teddy's gone. And Su Li – Su Li's been killed.'

I swallowed, and my eyes prickled. It was the first time I had said it out loud. Even though I had seen the lift, it still felt hardly real. Su Li had been alive this morning – now, suddenly, she was not. And, just like with Ah Yeh, I had not had time to say goodbye. I had been rude to her, and now I could never take that back. I was remembering again how she had behaved – how she had been kind to me on the journey, and I had ignored her. And her expression, as she walked into the lift. Had that been a clue? Could I have stopped what had happened, if I had only been a better detective? I had the horrid feeling that I had missed something. Su Li . . . *Su Li had known that man.*

Jie Jie let out a gulping wail.

'You were not with them?' asked my mother. She had her arms folded, and in the cool darkness of the hall her hair seemed to fade away, so that only her pale, beautiful face and red lips hovered above me.

'No,' I said. 'No, Ah Mah! We didn't get in the lift. We didn't know anything was wrong until we went up to look for them. Then Wo On forced open the doors, and—'

Jie Jie had buried her face in Rose's dark hair, but now she swung round to stare at me. I had never seen her look at me like that – as if she hated me.

'*You should have been there,*' she hissed. 'What sort of big sister are you?'

My tongue felt thick, and my eyes ached. It was the same question all over again, and I still couldn't answer it.

'I don't know,' I whispered. 'I don't know.'

I turned round and ran across the tiles of the hall, through the wide doorway and up the stairs.

'Fung Ying, come back here!' shouted my mother. I knew I ought to obey her – every Hong Kong bone in my body told me to stop and turn round and be a good daughter. But, as my feet clattered and my heart thumped, I had never felt less good in my life.

# 8

I slammed the door to our room and leaned against it, and almost immediately Daisy began to hammer on it.

'Hazel!' she cried. 'Hazel! This is not good detective behaviour! Let me in! Oh, Ping's here too. Hazel!'

I paused. Then I pulled the door open a crack.

'You can come in,' I said to Daisy. 'Ping – please leave us alone for a while.'

'Yes, Miss Hazel,' said Ping, her voice catching. I heard her walking slowly away – and then Daisy put her shoulder to the door and barrelled inside.

'Ow!' I said, rubbing my arm where she had hit it.

'I do apologize, Hazel, but it was necessary,' said Daisy, not looking apologetic at all. 'You're upset, which is perfectly understandable, but you mustn't be upset at *me*. I am your best friend, after all, *and* your Detective Society President, so it's treason as well as bad manners if you don't speak to me.'

'It's not treason!' I protested, but I felt myself smile. Daisy could always lift my mood.

'There!' said Daisy. 'That's my Watson. Now listen, I know you're in a dreadful state. After all, it's your brother who's gone missing and your maid who's died. I'd be awfully bothered if someone kidnapped Squinty – although I don't know who else would. He doesn't have many talents, apart from being a dreadful annoyance. And if anyone killed Hetty, why, I think I'd want to kill them. But all this doesn't change who we are. There has been a terrible crime, Hazel, and we must solve it. *You* must solve it, because you are a detective.'

'But—' I said. 'I ought to have been there, and I wasn't, and the worst thing is that I was angry with Su Li and I don't even *like* Teddy!'

'Hazel, you utter chump,' said Daisy. 'Trust you to think you're awful for not being utterly loyal. Your father sprang a little brother on you, and told your maid to look after him. It's terribly bad form, and I would be furious if it was me. I would *throw* things, Hazel. You haven't thrown anything. You've been a model of restraint, if you ask me. And, anyway, this is *not* your fault. You are not the person who kidnapped Teddy, or the person who killed Su Li. Now, you *do* care. I know you do. You'd care if it was any little baby taken off the street, and you care even more because it's your brother. And you care that Su Li is dead, even though she's been horrid to you all this visit.'

'I do!' I said. 'Of course I do. She – she was only doing her job, Daisy. And . . . she was part of my family.'

'Exactly,' said Daisy. 'It doesn't matter how horrid family are, they're still family. So, shall we work out what happened, so that we can avenge Su Li and get Teddy back again?'

'All right,' I said shakily.

'Good,' said Daisy. 'Excellent. I'm glad you said that. Now, this case seems quite straightforward, does it not? A woman and a baby get into a lift with a man. Twenty minutes later, the lift is found stopped between floors. The woman is dead, and the man and the baby are gone. What are we to assume? The woman didn't do it, because she is dead. The baby didn't do it, because he is a baby. There is a large bloody handprint on the half-open lift grille – a man's handprint – and another on the lift buttons, and the lift is paused between floors in a way that only a trained lift operator, which the man is, could manage. So what are we to assume?'

'That the man stopped the lift, killed the woman and crept out onto the eighth floor with the baby,' I said. 'Unless – what if someone else got in the lift?'

'Then where is the lift operator, if he's innocent?' asked Daisy. 'And what signs of any other person did we see? And anyway – remember, we watched the lift go up. We saw it go to the fifth floor before we turned away. It's very unlikely that someone got into it on the sixth or seventh floor. No, Hazel, the simplest explanation seems the best to me in this case. That the lift operator is the person who killed Su Li and took Teddy. So what we have to understand is *why* he did it, and where Teddy is now. And – well . . .'

She paused. 'There is *one* other thing that turns what ought to be a very simple case into a much odder one.' She looked at me, and the expression on her face suddenly made me feel cold. 'Hazel, the pin that was jabbed into Su Li's neck. I know what it *looked* like. It was exactly like the one you were wearing last night.'

'It wasn't!' I said, panicked. 'It was just a coincidence; it must have been—'

'Ah, but you don't think it was, either, do you?' asked Daisy, her blue eyes flashing. 'Before you upset yourself, let us be logical about this. What innocent, simple explanation could there be for your pin turning up at the murder scene?'

'What if Su Li found my pin, and wore it today?' I asked. 'Then the lift operator might have snatched hold of it to use as a weapon.'

'That won't wash, I'm afraid,' said Daisy, shaking her head. 'You lost it at the party last night, and Su Li wasn't there. Try again.'

'The – the lift operator might have been at the party,' I said, scrabbling rather. 'He might have another job as a waiter.'

'Only I didn't see him,' said Daisy. 'I made a careful catalogue of faces, as I always do, and I don't remember him. Did you?'

'No,' I said reluctantly, shaking my head. 'I've never seen him before. But – I think Su Li had.'

'Yes, I agree with that,' said Daisy, nodding. 'That is an avenue to be explored. But let us remain with this question. Is there another explanation for the pin?'

'One of the people at the party might have given it to the lift operator this morning!' I said. 'Daisy, that's it! Remember, at the scene of the crime, someone said that the Triads were behind it! One of the local Triad gangs uses jade pins as their calling cards. The lift operator could be working for someone, a gang – they're very common here, Daisy; most crime is organized. It's not like England.'

I was so relieved. It all made sense. One of the waiters at the party must have been Triad. They had found my pin, and given it to the lift operator, to use in the crime. A Triad gang had taken Teddy.

'Hazel,' said Daisy. 'I don't like to say this, after we have worked on so many cases together, but you are being utterly ridiculous.'

'I am not!' I said, stung. 'Triad gangs are quite real. I haven't made them up.'

'I am not disputing that for a moment,' said Daisy, raising one eyebrow. 'I am, however, saying that the explanation you have just put forward is fantastical. A member of a Triad gang found your pin *at random*, and *at random*, out of all the millions of easily obtainable jade pins in Hong Kong, decided to give *that* one to the lift operator mere *hours* before a planned murder?'

'Yes?' I said weakly.

'*No*,' said Daisy. 'I want a simple explanation, Hazel. What would we think if this was any other crime, and we found an easily identifiable clue on the body?'

'That the person it belonged to was the prime suspect,' I whispered. I felt colder than ever.

'Now, I know you didn't do it,' said Daisy, 'because you are my Hazel, and I know every thought in your head. If you wanted to murder anyone, you would have told me about it. I also know, because I was with you, that you had no opportunity to give the lift operator the pin this morning. But on paper – well. It was obvious to everyone how you felt about Teddy. You were threatened by him. And now he's gone missing, and your pin has been found on the body of his murdered maid – a maid who *used* to be yours. So if you didn't do it – which you did not – what does this mean?'

'Someone wants it to look like I did,' I said.

'Exactly!' cried Daisy. 'Someone who was at the party last night helped the lift operator plan and carry out the murder and the kidnap. And that someone – well, they're trying to frame you.'

# 9

'But—' I said. '*Why?*'

'Well,' said Daisy. 'That is what we must deduce.
Quite obviously, in solving that we will solve the case.
Now, Hazel, will you please explain a bit more about
these Triad people? What are they?'

'Triads are criminal gangs,' I said. 'Men who make
money by swindling people, and kidnapping children,
and – well, worse. They're fearsome. Everyone's afraid
of them, and they're everywhere here.'

'Ooh!' said Daisy, eyes wide. 'Hazel, how exciting – I
mean, how awful, if they've got Teddy. Do they do this
sort of thing often?'

I nodded. It was odd to have Daisy not knowing all
the facts, and me having to explain things to her. 'All
the time,' I said. 'It's one of the things we're always
taught to be on the lookout for, as children. That's why
the dogs are let out at night, and why we can't go out

alone. It happened to the Chengs – Alfred's uncle and aunt. Victoria Cheng's big sister was kidnapped when we were about May's age. The Chengs got her back, but they had to pay lots of money for her.'

'So it makes sense that the Triads might be behind this?'

'Yes,' I said. 'Triads are good at finding out about their targets. This kidnapping was very well planned. Going up in the lift to the doctor's office is practically the only time that Teddy wouldn't be guarded by Wo On as well as Su Li. Even if my mother had come, she would have stayed downstairs in the car, to rest her feet. If a gang had been watching our family, they would know that.'

'But are Triads usually vindictive?' asked Daisy. 'Leaving *your* pin in the dead body – if this was England, I'd say that it's the mark of someone who is *personally* angry at you.'

I frowned. 'I know,' I said. 'It – it doesn't make sense, Daisy. I've never done anything to the Triads, and neither has Father – not that I know of, anyway.'

Daisy blinked. 'Hazel,' she said. 'I think you just said something very useful. *Your father.* At the party last night – we were there because he brought us. Framing *you* makes no sense, but what if someone did it because they wanted to punish *him*?'

'No, that could be why *Teddy* was *kidnapped*,' I said. 'Teddy is the important one to him, not me.'

'Oh, *Hazel*—' Daisy began crossly. Then she shook her head. 'Pretend for a moment, all right? Pretend that your father is the target, not you. Who was at the party last night who doesn't like your father? Well, that's easy. Mr Svensson, Mrs Fu and that angry old man – what was his name? Mr Wa something? Get out your casebook, and let's make a proper list.'

I had Daisy's brand-new book in my bag. I pulled it out with a pang. These days I am never without a notebook, but all the same I did not think for a moment I would start using Daisy's present on this trip.

I took a deep, rather wobbly breath. 'Mr Svensson first,' I said. 'We saw him arguing with my father last night. Mrs Svensson said that he's trying to get my father to invest in something, and my father won't. He knew that Teddy's appointment was today, and we saw him at the bank.'

'We did!' said Daisy. 'And there's confusion about when he left. Why should it take him nearly ten minutes to walk from the bank hall to the main doors? It's a minute-long journey at most.'

'We saw Mrs Fu at the bank too, Daisy! She was actually walking away from the middle lift, so she had the opportunity to give the lift operator the pin. And she argued with Father last night as well – something about business. Father said, *Things have to change now*, and Mrs Fu looked so upset.'

'Excellent, Hazel,' said Daisy. 'Write that down! Now, what about— Oh, what was his name?'

'Mr Wa Fan?' I asked. 'He used to be friends with my grandfather, but last night he was so fierce. He was saying that Father wasn't doing his duty as a son, and he was angry with him. But – was he at the bank?'

'We shall have to investigate,' said Daisy. 'There, see? Three suspects that aren't Triad, all with excellent personal motives to dislike your father, and therefore you.'

'I think we ought to put down the Triad gang too,' I said. 'It could be them. It's the simplest explanation – we can't discount it. And we still can't be sure that it wasn't just the lift operator. I saw how he looked at Su Li. I really think they knew each other, and she didn't like him. What if he had some personal reason to want to kill her, and then decided to take Teddy and make some money as well?'

'I suppose,' said Daisy. 'You're quite right, Hazel: we must consider every possibility. In fact, can we even rule out Ping and Wo On being part of this plot?'

'Daisy!' I cried. 'Ping was with us all this morning, so she couldn't have given the pin to the operator, and neither could Wo On.'

'Irrelevant,' said Daisy, tossing her hair. 'We're only saying that they might have helped plan. We must interview them and make sure they're innocent. We must also discover what happened *after* Su Li's murder.

How did the lift operator make sure no one saw him after the crime? How did he get Teddy out of the building? Where did he take him? In this case we have two things to focus on – Teddy and Su Li.'

I nodded, and wrote it all down.

## SUSPECT LIST

1. The lift operator (find out his name!)

The simplest explanation is that he committed the crime. But why? We think he and Su Li knew each other, and she was afraid of him, but we must find evidence to back this up. So was this his motive, and he kidnapped Teddy almost as an afterthought, or was he simply interested in making money by kidnapping Teddy, and Su Li got in the way? Was he working on his own, or did he carry out the crime for someone else? (The pin makes it very likely that he was working with another criminal.) If so, who hired him, and why?

2. Triad gang. MOTIVE TO KIDNAP TEDDY: Money, plain and simple! The pin stabbed into Su Li's throat is the calling card of a Triad gang (we heard someone say this, and Hazel

confirms it) — but it is odd that they chose to use Hazel's pin. Were they trying to frame her? Was it just a mistake?

3. *Mr Svensson.* MOTIVE TO KIDNAP TEDDY: He needs money, and Mr Wong will not give him any. He is also angry with Mr Wong — might this give him a motive to frame Hazel for the crime? NOTES: He was seen at the bank at the time of the crime in a strange mood, and there are ten minutes where his movements cannot be accounted for. He was also at the party the night before, so could have picked up Hazel's pin and given it to the lift operator! He knew that Teddy was due to be at the doctor's the next day, because he heard Mr Wong mention this.

4. *Mrs Fu.* MOTIVE TO KIDNAP TEDDY: She also seems to need money — and she was talking angrily with Mr Wong at the party. NOTES: She was seen at the bank at the time of the crime by Hazel Wong and Daisy Wells, so could have given the pin to the lift operator. She was also at the party the night before, so could have picked up Hazel's pin and overheard about Teddy's appointment!

5. *Mr Wa Fan.* MOTIVE TO KIDNAP
JEDDY: He is angry with Mr Wong because he
thinks he is not being dutiful. But is this a good
enough motive for kidnap? He was at the party, so
could have taken the pin and heard about the
appointment. But he was not seen at the bank, and we
do not know if he is a patient of Dr Aurelius.

# PLAN OF ACTION

1. Eliminate Wo On and Ping from our list of suspects.

2. Find out more about the lift operator — who was he,
   and why did he become a murderer and a kidnapper?
   Was he paid to do it, or was it a personal motive?

3. Find out more about the Triad gang who use pins as
   their calling cards.

4. Look into all the motives of our suspects further.

5. Find out more about Dr Aurelius's office to
   understand how the crime was not discovered, and how
   Jeddy was taken out of the building.

'Now,' said Daisy suddenly, 'my detective senses are currently telling me that we ought to go downstairs immediately.'

'Why?' I asked.

'Someone new has just driven up to the front of the house,' said Daisy. 'Can't you hear the guard dogs barking?'

# 10

There was indeed someone walking through the wide front doorway of our house.

He was of middling height for a Chinese man, but he was built like a barrel – not fat, but full of muscle. His hair was cropped short, and he had a long scar down the side of his cheek that made his face look off-centre, and somewhat forbidding. His eyes were rather large too, and there was a black fleck in the white of the right one. He looked at me across the length of the hall, and I breathed in nervously.

I have met plenty of detectives by now. There are quick ones and slow ones, pompous ones and serious ones. But I have learned that you can tell a good detective at once. It is not what they look like, but how they look at you. My first sight of our English detective, Inspector Priestley (I do think of him as *ours* – Daisy and I have now solved three cases with his help), left me feeling as though I had been pinned to a board like a butterfly, and that was almost how I felt now. This man *saw* me, and I knew in one dizzy second that he was one of the good ones. He would be a formidable ally, and an even more formidable adversary.

My father had just arrived back to the Big House himself. He stood at the entrance to the Library and frowned at the man.

'Who are you?' he asked.

'I am Detective Leung,' said the man, bowing respectfully. 'I have been sent by Mr Wa Fan and the Tung Wah Foundation to help you look for your son.'

'The police are already looking for him,' said my father, scowling even more. 'I don't need the Tung Wah sticking their noses in. Didn't I tell Wa Fan before that I'm done with them?'

'The Hong Kong police are no good for Chinese people, sir,' said Detective Leung. 'These cases often do not end well while they are in charge. Mr Wa Fan thought you might need additional help, and so he chose me.'

'I said no!' snapped my father. 'Does no one listen to me?'

'What's a Tung Wah?' hissed Daisy in my ear.

'A – a sort of local government board Grandfather was on,' I whispered back to her. 'A Chinese one. They organize things like hospitals and policing for Chinese

113

people. Father says they're too meddling and not progressive, and he doesn't like them at all.'

Daisy looked at me significantly, and I felt my skin prickle.

'Sir,' said Detective Leung. 'I understand, but surely any help is useful? And it is clear that this is a dangerous crime. I have heard about the pin.'

I jumped.

'What about the pin?' asked my father sharply.

'The pin that was in the victim, Su Li. A jade pin is the sign of one of the most dangerous local gangs, the Five Jade Figures,' said Detective Leung. 'If their leader Sai Yat is involved, you are not merely up against one man, working on his own. Sai Yat's gang has power, and you will need all the help you can get.'

'Don't tell me what I need,' snapped my father. 'I am managing this. Maxwell is waiting by the telephone, and I have our guard, Baboo, on the front gate and on the lookout for any delivery of a letter.'

'Sir,' said Detective Leung. 'I understand, but let me help. It is your son.'

My father paused. For a moment I was sure he would tell Detective Leung to leave – but then he waved his hand brokenly. 'All right,' he said. 'Help if you can. But, if you cannot, I do not need you giving me false hope.'

'I understand,' said Detective Leung, bowing. 'Would you allow me to speak to your household this afternoon, to see if they know anything? Whoever planned this knew exactly where the boy would be, and when. I suspect they may have had help from inside.'

'If you must,' said my father. 'I have ordered that no one will leave the house this afternoon. I will be by the telephone.' He turned to stare at me and Daisy. I longed to tell him that everything was all right, that we would detect, as well as Detective Leung – but I knew I couldn't. After a moment my father went back into the Library. I heard his low voice speaking to Maxwell, and Maxwell replying. I knew then that nothing else would interest him until he had heard from the kidnappers. He was only Teddy's father now, and that hurt.

Daisy and I were left with the detective.

I bowed and nudged Daisy, who began to curtsey, checked herself, and bowed too.

'Good afternoon,' said Detective Leung.

'Good afternoon,' I said.

'You must be the eldest daughter,' said the detective. 'I understand you were at the bank at the time of the kidnap. Did you see anything, or hear anything, that you think is important?'

'I am Miss Wong's bosom friend, the Honourable Miss Daisy Wells,' said Daisy, moving into the centre of the conversation. 'We don't remember much, do we, Hazel? We are, naturally, distraught at this terrible event. We saw Teddy and his maid get into the lift, and then we went into the bank and looked about. Then we came back down to the foyer, and the chauffeur came in looking for Teddy. We all went up in one of the other lifts together, and then we opened the middle lift and – well – there she was!'

Her breath caught artfully, and she gazed up at the detective, chest heaving. 'It was *awful*,' she said.

'Hm,' said Detective Leung. 'Is that correct?' he asked me.

'Yes,' I said quietly. It *was* correct – except it missed out the pin. I knew I must avoid saying it was the one I'd lost. If I did, the detective might begin to suspect me. 'And it wasn't just a kidnapping. Su Li was murdered.'

'I am well aware of that,' said Detective Leung. 'To solve one crime is to solve the other, and both are crucial. That is why, if you remember anything else, you must tell me. A life depends on it.'

He seemed to be looking under my skin, in just the same uncomfortable way as Inspector Priestley does in England. But I did not respond, and finally Detective Leung bowed to us and made his way through the hall towards the stairs at the back of the house.

I leaned disconsolately against one of the large pots in the hall, and the sweet, light scent of orange blossom drifted down around me.

'Hazel,' said Daisy, leaning beside me, so that our faces were both in shadow. 'I can see you worrying. You think that Leung will talk to the servants, find out that the pin is yours and arrest you for Teddy's kidnapping and Su Li's murder before we can detect it properly, don't you?'

'No,' I said unconvincingly.

'Don't be afraid, Hazel,' said Daisy. 'Keep your chin up and be the Hazel I know you are. I know it's frightening, and terribly close to home, but you do need to buck up. No excuses. You can't simply despair. Why – if I'd despaired at Fallingford, we might never have solved the case!'

This is, as usual with Daisy, not quite the truth. I have never seen her so close to breaking as she was after Mr Curtis died, as the horror of the solution to his murder crept closer. I remembered that, and shivered.

'There's still plenty we can do to help you. I know we're in a foreign country – I mean, foreign to me – but the same detective rules apply. The sooner we solve the case, the sooner we can prove that you had nothing to do with it. Don't give up! Detective Leung is on the case, but so are we. We *can* get to the bottom of it before he docs, and prove that you had nothing to do with the kidnapping, I know we can. And this means – I hate to say it, Hazel – that I need you to take the lead on this occasion. Which is not to say that you are allowed to become Detective Society President, even for a moment. It simply means that I am delegating the responsibility to you temporarily. You know this house, and you know the people in it. You know where we ought to go.'

'Oh,' I said. In past cases I have become better at thinking for myself – often to Daisy's annoyance. But I had never before heard her *ask* me to do so. For a moment I was bewildered. But then I realized that, even though I had not been back for two years, even though it had changed now that my grandfather was gone, I knew our Big House, and I knew its people. And if I needed to lead, I could.

# PART THREE

# THE SECRETS OF THE BIG HOUSE

# 1

It was quite easy to follow Detective Leung. The Big House seemed full of his presence and his light but firm footsteps. We ducked into the shadows to avoid him, hiding round corners whenever he got too close and listening at doors as he spoke to the maids.

He was calm, he was cool – and he was as sharp as a knife. He left everyone he spoke to gasping, secrets pulled effortlessly out of their mouths. He was trying to discover whether Su Li had been part of the plot to kidnap Teddy, and whether anyone else in the house had helped. The pin, to him, was simply evidence that the Triads were involved – but this was only because he was unaware that *I* owned a rooster pin which was now missing. Every time it came up, I struggled to breathe. He only needed one person to give him the lead . . .

May's maid, Ah Kwan, her arms full of abandoned toys, said that Su Li would *never* have hurt Teddy – but all the same, she did not make Su Li sound particularly nice. 'She was too proud of him,' said Ah Kwan. 'And too proud for the rest of us, once she was given care of him! We all wanted the job, but Mr Wong gave it to her. Boyfriends? We are not allowed – but Su Li was carrying on with a boy, Wu Shing. She ended things with him last year. So snooty of her! Wu Shing was the lift operator? Goodness me! So he got his revenge. And a pin? Isn't that the sign of Sai Yat's Triad gang? Poor little Teddy, caught up in this!'

Rose's maid, Pik An, who was tidying the empty music room, agreed with Ah Kwan about Su Li's boyfriend – 'She told everyone that he was awful to her. She never could keep her mouth shut!' – but said she didn't know anything about the pin.

'I have heard that you are Triad,' said Detective Leung steadily, and Pik An cried out indignantly.

'Me?' she said. 'It's not the *maids* in this house who are Triad—' And then she stopped, and went quiet.

'Thank you,' said Detective Leung, satisfied. I heard his footsteps approaching the door then, and Daisy and I had to duck behind the big screen before he came out into the hall.

Something suddenly popped into my head. I had been thinking about Su Li and remembering her in the Big House – and I suddenly knew exactly where we had to go. I beckoned to Daisy, and we crept up the stairs. I could tell that Daisy did not enjoy being the follower. She kept up a soft, annoyed murmur: 'Hazel, where are we going? Hazel, really, *say* something!'

But I did not.

I led Daisy all the way to the second floor above the kitchens, where the maids and *mui tsai* live in small, hot little wooden rooms. 'Ohh!' said Daisy behind me. 'Clever Hazel!'

It took me a moment to find Su Li's room. It was not her old one. But then I pushed open the door to the room next to my mother's maid Assai's and saw Su Li's little enamel bird ornament on the bedside table. 'This one!' I whispered to Daisy, and motioned her inside.

Su Li's bed was neatly made, and her bedside table was bare apart from the bird. Her little wardrobe, when I opened it, contained her maid's jackets hanging up like so many pale ghosts. I shuddered. There was a box at the bottom of the wardrobe, a rather cheap cardboard one, brightly painted in red. I remembered sitting on Su Li's bed, my legs swinging, watching her carefully tuck her treasures into it. The most important ones had always been at the very bottom.

I sifted carefully through the box, past dried flowers and pretty bits of paper and ripped-out pages from my mother's old magazines. There, beneath them, were two small, worn photographs. One was of a handsome young man with a twinkle in his eye. I had only seen him once before, but I remembered his face.

'Look!' I whispered to Daisy. 'Ah Kwan said so: Su Li's boyfriend Wu Shing was the lift operator. Oh, Daisy, she *did* know him. And he killed her. This is horrible! Do you think he did it because she ended things with him?'

'A broken heart should *not* be a reason to kill another person,' said Daisy decisively. 'If that was his motive, then he was truly wicked.'

I agreed, shuddering. We've had suspects in previous cases who were jilted lovers, and I have always thought how terribly wrong it is to decide that someone deserves to die, simply because they have stopped loving you.

'So – what if this really is just about Su Li?' asked Daisy, wrinkling up her forehead. 'Oh, what an odd case!'

I turned to the other photograph. It was of a boy a few years younger than us, turning towards the camera with a half-smile on his thin face. He looked bold and mocking.

'So, we know who Wu Shing is, but who's *that*?' asked Daisy curiously.

'I don't know!' I said. I was feeling strangely sad. Su Li's life had more to it than I had ever known. She'd had a boyfriend, and she had not told me. I suddenly wondered about her family. I had never met them. I really hadn't known her at all.

But then my fingers felt something else beneath the pictures – a soft bit of cloth tied around something scratchy. I teased it out and saw that it was a little orange silk ribbon tied in a bow around a wisp of dark hair, and under that was a folded letter.

'Oh!' said Daisy. 'A love token?'

'No,' I whispered, suddenly short of breath as I unfolded it. 'It's not that at all. Daisy – this is my baby hair. And this letter – it's from *me*. It's one of the ones I sent to the Big House when I first arrived at Deepdean. She – she took it and kept it.'

I felt my hands shaking. I had been teaching myself over the last few weeks a new truth: that Su Li had not really cared about me. That she had rushed to replace me with Teddy, and had only pretended to be kind to me on the day of her death. But, if that was so, why had she kept my hair in the place reserved for her treasures? Why had she kept my letter? I had thought that she had replaced me with Teddy. But what if I had got it all wrong? She had not *asked* to be given care of Teddy, after all. We kept on hearing people say that it was my father's decision. Ah Kwan had said that Su Li was proud – but why should I believe her? Why had I not seen that the other maids and *mui tsai* might be as jealous as I was, for different reasons? I remembered the way Su Li had ignored me. What if she had been *forcing* herself to?

My face burned and I shoved the hair in its ribbon into the pocket of my trousers.

'Daisy,' I said, my voice trembling. 'I think we've been wrong about Su Li. She hadn't become cruel, or proud, or any of those things while I was away. She was just the same as ever. She was *forced* to become Teddy's maid, and so all the other maids became envious of her, and when I came home she *had* to ignore me. I got it wrong, Daisy. I . . . didn't pay attention to what was really going on. She tried to tell me, but I ignored her. And now she's dead, and I can't say sorry!'

'Oh, Hazel!' For once Daisy was lost for words. I scrubbed at my eyes with my handkerchief, and she patted my arm. 'But – well – that's useful to us, isn't it? It's becoming clear that Su Li wasn't part of this plot. She was the victim. We know why Wu Shing would want to kill her, and now we understand why she hesitated before getting into the lift with him.'

I swallowed. 'But . . .' I said, 'we didn't understand. We should have helped, Daisy. I should have helped!'

The thought was so horrid that I suddenly could not bear it. I wanted to go somewhere that felt safe and good, after everything I had just heard. And there was only one place that would do.

# 2

The kitchens are attached to the back of the Big House by a thin, quiet passageway on the ground floor, like the pinch of an egg timer. As we hurried along, I could see the bamboo grove through a window to our left, and the red pavilion, and the garden where flowers are grown for cutting. Then we emerged into the wild heat of the kitchens themselves.

I thought back to the kitchens at Fallingford, cold and empty, with only Mrs Doherty's small, bustling form and Hetty's red hair to give them life, and I couldn't imagine a greater contrast. Our Big House kitchens were full, of white-coated cooks and waiters and pot-boys, of steam and smells and the gleam of knives as they rose and fell, dicing vegetables and paring meat off bones.

There was a plate of cakes near the entrance – left there for the children, just as they had been before

I had gone away to England. I smiled when I saw that this, at least, had not changed.

I picked up one. It was fat and golden on my palm, egg-shaped and flaking gently. I took a bite of it and my mouth was bursting with sweet-tasting lotus paste, a fleck of salty preserved egg inside.

'Hazel,' said Daisy, peering inside her cake, 'I think something's gone off in mine. It's . . . black.'

'Oh, that's just the thousand-year egg,' I told her. 'It's supposed to be that way.'

'Golly,' said Daisy. 'It's . . . terribly strong. Hmm.'

She gave her cake to me, and I ate it. Then she took a step back and stood slightly behind me, staring at the bustle in the kitchens with a most un-Daisy-like hesitation.

'Miss Wong! Hello!' shouted Ng the cook, rushing up to us. His face, as always, was gleaming with sweat, and he never stopped moving. He was tall and thin and his face was shaped just like an upturned triangle. In his chef's cap and whites, his pigtail tucked away, he looked quite hairless, for his eyebrows were so fine and thin that they could barely be seen. He spoke in a quick rattle of words that were as energetic as he was.

'Miss Wong! What are you doing here? Does your father know? Should you be here after what happened earlier? Poor Master Teddy – and poor Su Li, even if she was full of herself. She didn't deserve to die. So your tall English friend didn't like the cake, did she? Hah!'

Daisy was looking quite alarmed. I have been seeing this expression on her face more and more, every time I speak Cantonese. It gives me a funny feeling, as though I have got bigger – or Daisy has been diminished.

'I miss your cakes, Ng,' I said. I felt wobbly with sadness. 'I missed you while I was gone.'

'What a bad time to be home,' said Ng. 'You came for your grandfather, which is sad enough, and now this, eh? Poor little Teddy, and poor Su Li,' he said again.

'Everyone's been horrid about Su Li!' I said in a rush. 'But she's *dead*!'

'I'm sorry, Miss Hazel,' said Ng. 'I know. This is a sad and strange crime.'

'What do you mean?' I asked.

'That pin is supposed to be Triad, eh?' said Ng. 'But it isn't. Don't ask me how I know, but I do, that's all. Sai Yat's gang has nothing to do with this.'

I squeezed my hands into fists. What was Ng saying?

'On the other hand, there are plenty of people who would want to punish your father,' said Ng. 'He's been trying so hard to be a good businessman lately that he's been forgetting to be a dutiful son, eh? Won't be a Tung Wah member, even though your grandfather was always on the council. Mr Wa Fan sent a formal invitation a few weeks ago, and your father refused to reply to it.'

'How do you know that?' I asked.

'I've got ears and eyes everywhere,' said Ng, shrugging and wriggling his thin eyebrows. 'And in his business dealings too – he ruffles feathers. Mr Svensson came to ask Mr Wong to back some new scheme of his a few days ago. I served them tea and wife cakes, but everything came back untouched. It's hard to eat while you're arguing, eh? Mr Svensson needs that money. He looks rich, but I've heard that he's spent a fortune on that new house of his. Your father knows that, and that's why he won't bite. Same when some of your grandfather's other charity cases came asking. Times have changed, eh? And not always for the better.'

I was excited. Ng had said some things that could be very useful to our investigation.

'That's very interesting!' I said. 'But have you told the detective what you think about the Triads?'

'I don't talk to detectives, Miss Hazel,' said Ng. 'If he comes round, I will be too busy to see him.'

I wanted to thank him – but I knew how suspicious that would look. So I simply bowed, turned and pushed Daisy out of the kitchen again.

# 3

As we emerged behind the big screen into the main hall, I heard Detective Leung call out in Cantonese. 'You!' he said.

I thought he was speaking to us, and flinched, then –

'You are Miss Wong's maid, aren't you?'

'Yes, sir,' said Ping's voice, sounding very flustered. I could imagine her pressing her hands to her cheeks in panic. 'My name is Ping.'

'Wait!' I hissed to Daisy, grabbing her wrist and pulling her back. 'It's Ping! Leung's found her!'

'I need to ask you some questions,' said Detective Leung. 'You were with Miss Wong and her friend this morning, weren't you? You never left them?'

'Yes, sir,' whispered Ping. 'And no, sir. I stayed with them until after – after we came home again, this afternoon.'

'And you saw the body?'

'Yes, sir,' said Ping, with a sob in her voice. 'Poor Su Li! Poor Teddy!'

'Did anything about the scene seem odd to you?' asked Detective Leung.

'It was a dead body, sir,' said Ping. 'It was awful! And the pin in the body – the sign of a Triad gang!'

'Yes, I have heard,' said Detective Leung. Was I imagining it, or was there a sharp tone to his voice? 'And Miss Wong – how is she taking this?'

I breathed in and clutched Daisy's arm. 'What's up?' she hissed at me. I shook my head.

'Miss Hazel was so upset that she locked herself in her room, sir. She is broken-hearted.' But I heard the uncertainty in her voice, and knew that Detective Leung heard it too.

'You are not with her now,' he said. 'Where is she?'

'I – I do not know,' said Ping.

'Do you often lose track of her? Does she go out on her own?' asked Detective Leung. 'Have you ever seen Miss Wong speak to any . . . suspicious characters?'

'No, sir,' said Ping quickly. 'Of course not! But—'

She stopped speaking. Suddenly I found that it was quite hard to breathe. I knew that she was thinking about the woman; the one who had bumped into me. I felt, rather than saw, Daisy looking at me, and could picture the concerned, frustrated expression that would be on her face. Daisy knew that something was terribly wrong, but, although she might guess, she couldn't understand exactly what it was.

'But what?' prompted Detective Leung.

'Nothing, sir,' said Ping, so quietly I could barely hear her. 'I have nothing more to say.'

'I see,' he said. 'Thank you, Ping. That will be all for now.'

# 4

I couldn't bear to look, but after a moment Daisy peeped round the side of the screen. 'He's gone outside!' she whispered to me. 'Ping's there alone. It's safe. What happened?'

'He asked Ping how I was behaving,' I whispered back. 'He asked if I ever went out on my own. Daisy, I think he suspects me! Come on, we have to talk to her.'

We both popped out from behind the screen, and Ping shrieked. Her face was pinker than ever.

'Miss Hazel!' she said. 'You scared me. I'm all – oh, everything is terrible! What a frightening man!'

'You didn't say anything about that pin looking like mine!' I said to Ping in Cantonese. 'Why?'

'Because I know there must have been some mistake. It *did* look just like yours, but . . . Su Li used to be *your* maid. You'd never have hurt her. And you'd never have put Teddy in danger, either.'

'Thank you,' I said dizzily to Ping. 'It's— Thank you so much.' Ping was looking at me with such a sincerely frightened, confused expression. I saw that she had weighed me up, and ruled me out – and at that moment I knew that we could rule her out too.

'Miss, I think he's gone out to see Wo now,' said Ping. 'What if he should say anything? He knows about your pin too.'

We stared at each other, in panic.

'Hazel!' said Daisy sharply. 'Hazel, what are the two of you saying? What are you going to do? You've got a terribly funny look on your face – HAZEL!'

But Ping and I were already halfway to the front door.

Wo On had clearly been polishing my father's car. The rag was still in his hands as he spoke to Detective Leung. He was shaking his head, and I heard him say, 'No. I was with the other drivers from the moment Su Li stepped into the lift until I came in to find Miss Hazel and her friend at twenty past twelve.'

'You saw the body?' asked Detective Leung.

'Yes,' said Wo. 'I pulled open the lift doors.'

'And you saw the pin?' Detective Leung went on.

I saw Wo's shoulders stiffen. He jerked his chin up – and caught sight of the three of us coming towards him down the steps.

'I saw a pin, indeed,' he said loudly. 'That's a sign of Sai Yat's gang; everyone knows that.'

'Indeed they do,' said Detective Leung. He turned round to stare at us as well.

I froze. There was a good-girl part of me that knew I ought to simply confess everything. But it was a very small part indeed. Every detective bit of me knew that I could not. I took a deep breath in, tilted my chin up defiantly and looked Detective Leung straight in the eye.

'I have heard that as well,' I told him. At that moment I have never felt more like Daisy.

'Poor Miss Hazel,' said Wo, folding his arms. 'This has hit her hard. Su Li was her maid once, and Teddy is her little brother. She was so upset to discover the crime.'

'It was awful,' said Daisy loudly, in English. 'Hazel and I simply have *no* idea what happened, and you can take my word for it. I am an Honourable!'

I knew she thought that this would sound impressive, but I saw Detective Leung's face. It was very polite, and very confused, and I suddenly wanted to giggle.

'Well,' said Detective Leung at last. 'Thank you, Miss Wong, Miss Wells. I have no further questions for you or your servants at this time. It seems the next step is to investigate Sai Yat and his gang.'

I nodded at him because I could not speak, and watched as he turned away from us and walked back up the granite steps of the Big House. It felt like being in the eye of the storm, with thunderclouds all around me. I knew that at any second the sky might crack open – but at this very moment I was safe. I breathed out.

'Thank you,' I said to Wo. 'Thank you so much.'

Wo made a face. 'I wouldn't have done anything else,' he said. 'I know that there must have been some sort of mix-up about that pin. It did look like yours, but you aren't part of this. I wouldn't be doing my duty if I didn't keep you out of it.'

'*Duty*,' I repeated. Even though I had just seen the proof that I had been more to Su Li than a duty, the word still struck me when I heard it.

'Duty and fondness,' said Wo, and he winked at me. 'I wouldn't do this for every member of the household, I promise you. And things have changed since you left, more than you understand. Teddy is a good baby but, when he was born, everyone was upset. Your mother was not pleased, and when Su Li became Teddy's nurse, the house was up in arms. Your mother and your father had one of their . . . ' He waved his hands, and in the gap between them I saw the long silences, the passing of messages through servants and children and Jie Jie, that was the pattern of my parents' arguments. '*You* know. Then your grandfather died. Things haven't been right for months.'

'I know,' I said, my throat swollen. I felt angry, suddenly, that I was not grown up. If I was, I might know exactly how to get Teddy back. I would know how to feel about the death of Su Li, who mattered so much to me, and of my Ah Yeh, that could not be fixed and solved and *blamed* on someone. I would be old enough not to need my father. It seemed as though he did not need me much these days.

'Your grandfather lived a good life, and had a good death,' said Wo On. 'But Su Li – she didn't deserve what happened to her.'

'Was there anything you saw that you think might be important?' I managed to ask.

Wo On shrugged. 'I was outside until twenty past, Miss Hazel, as I told the detective, but all I saw was that old Mr Wa Fan coming out past the car just before I came in to find you. He was clutching a bottle of medicine. Funny – he always pretends that he only trusts Chinese medicine, and then there he was at the Western doctor's!'

My breath caught. Mr Wa Fan was the only person on our suspect list who had apparently not been at the bank or the doctor's – but now we had a witness who could put him at the scene of the crime!

# 5

I suddenly had to get away. I dragged Daisy into the bamboo grove at the side of the house. As we passed through its rustling green spikes, I did not tell Daisy not to look about her, in case she saw a snake.

The pavilion in our garden is nothing like the one we have at Deepdean for Games. It is wooden and painted red, open to the elements. We sat down on the seats in silence. For a while Daisy fanned herself, staring out at the gardens around her, and did not look at me.

'Goodness. Even when it's not hot here, it's hot,' she observed.

I sat and breathed deeply until I no longer felt as though I might cry at any moment. My grandfather's death, and Su Li's, and Teddy's loss, and the pin had all crowded on top of me until they were nearly choking me. But after a few minutes they all began to melt away, and I could think like a detective again.

'Thank you,' I said at last.

'Don't mention it, Hazel,' said Daisy, waving her hand. 'Although what I would like you to do is explain what on earth just happened. I could hardly understand any of it! I do call it unfair that you can speak another language. Tell me everything! The detective didn't accuse you, did he?'

'No,' I said. 'Because Ping and Wo are protecting me. But I don't know how long they can keep it up. I'm sure Detective Leung is beginning to suspect me.'

'Watson, we'll get through it, you'll see. And if your father does find out about the pin – well, we must hope that he will simply know it wasn't you. One *knows*, about family members. But tell me what else you heard.'

'Ng – the cook – doesn't think the Triads kidnapped Teddy, either. He thinks it was someone who didn't like Father. He told me about a row that Father had with Mr Svensson about money. I think that's why they were arguing at the party – Mr Svensson needs money after he spent so much on his new house. Then there's Mr Wa Fan. Ng said that he's cross with Father because he wouldn't join the Tung Wah Foundation – it really does sound important enough to him to be a motive. And then there's Mrs Fu. Ng mentioned something about

Grandfather being charitable, and Father wanting to end that – I was wondering if that might be her, after the conversation at the party?'

Daisy was nodding her head. 'Interesting. Very interesting. All right, what else?'

'From the way Wo and Ping are behaving, I think we have to rule them out as suspects. If they had done it, they wouldn't want to protect me – and anyway they weren't at the party last night, and I never did ask Wo to go and fetch the pin this morning. So they couldn't have had it to give to Wu Shing! Wo also mentioned that he saw Mr Wa Fan this afternoon. He was coming out of the bank, holding medicine, so he must have been at one of the doctors'. We thought he wasn't at the scene of the crime, but now we know he was!

'And there's another thing,' I said. 'I know it sounds silly and made up, but in Hong Kong the Triads *are* everywhere. I think – I think Ng might be Triad.'

Daisy's face lit up. 'Oh, how exciting!' she cried. 'Triad members *here*, in your house! Real criminals – fancy that! How different!'

'It's not different, really,' I said. 'We've met lots of murderers in England.'

'Oh well, then, there's no difference,' said Daisy, and she twinkled at me. 'So, how shall we begin ruling out our suspects?'

'I think—' I started.

Suddenly May came running towards us through the bamboo. She was waving a bit of wood, a broken twig from a peach tree, and she was roaring something. Her twig whacked at the hollow stalks of bamboo, and I stood up, my heart pounding. 'May! Snakes!' I called in English.

'I'M NOT MAY, I'M CHING SHIH THE PIRATE. PIRATES DON'T CARE ABOUT SNAKES!' May bellowed at me.

Before I could even move, there was a rustling in the bushes behind us, and one of the gardener's boys appeared. He ran towards May, and dragged her out of the bamboo. May shrieked and kicked him, and tried to struggle free. It ought to have been easy, for I saw that this boy's left arm stopped smoothly just below the elbow. But his right arm was so strong that he held May with ease.

'Did you say *snakes*, Hazel?' asked Daisy. She looked rather pale. 'Naturally, I do not mind snakes at all, but—'

'There are snakes in the bamboo,' I said, grinning. 'We're in Hong Kong, Daisy.'

'So you keep reminding me,' she muttered.

The gardener's boy came up to the pavilion, still pinning May to his side.

'Miss Hazel,' he said, bowing politely. His hair was tied back in a queue, and he had dirt and green stains on the knees of his uniform. He looked our age, or perhaps a year older. I got a shock when I saw his face. I hadn't ever met him – like many of the staff, he had been hired since I left for England. But, all the same, I knew him. He was the thin-faced boy from Su Li's picture! Daisy nudged me hard, and I knew that she had recognized him too.

'Your sister. I had to make sure that she was safe.' He spoke in Cantonese.

'Thank you,' I said. 'We'll take her back to the house now. You don't need to worry.'

I had a rather uncomfortable thought. The boy must have been nearby us as we talked. Had he heard what we'd said? And why had Su Li had his picture in her treasure box? Was he somehow mixed up in this mystery? Could we trust him?

'There's a snake on your back,' I said in English. The boy's face did not change from its smile. I was relieved – it was all right. He had not understood our conversation.

I grabbed hold of May, perhaps slightly harder than was necessary (she wailed and said, 'Big Sister! Ow!').

'Miss Hazel?' said the boy in Cantonese, behind me. I turned. He was still smiling, all the way up to his eyes. 'Beware. There's a snake on your back too.'

And, quick as a flash, he ran away towards the flower garden, leaving me shaking.

# 6

When we got back to the house, we found Ping waiting for us, nervously waving from the top of the steps.

'Library!' she whispered to us. 'Quick! Something's happened!'

I imagined that, somehow, my father might have found out about the pin. I saw myself walking into our Library, which always smells of leather and of softly rotting books, no matter how my father has it aired out, and facing him in his desk chair. I could almost hear him shouting.

But, when Daisy and I crept into the Library, we found it in a sort of chaos that I had not expected at all. That is the problem with imagination – the more you use it, the more you see that the world in your head is not really the world you live in at all.

At least the Library looked the way it always had. The Chinese books are on the left, and the English books on the right, beside the big front windows. There is a huge golden globe in the middle of the floor, that you can spin and put your finger on and trace the countries sliding away under your hand. I used to love to do it when I was little. Next to the other window, the one that looks out on the side of the Peak, is my father's desk, where the telephone rests. Maxwell was sitting at this desk, his head in his hands, while my father paced the parquet floor in front of him, shouting. Jie Jie was there too, backed up against one of the bookcases, twisting her hands together, tears on her cheeks.

'What's happened?' I asked nervously.

My father spun round and saw me. His hair was disarranged and his glasses were skew-whiff. I could see the blood vessels in his eyes, darkening the whites and making him look quite alarming.

'There has been a ransom demand,' he said. My father was shaking with anger, but there was also a desperate crack in his voice that I had never heard before.

'A ransom demand?' I asked, and I heard my voice shaking too. 'What did they ask for?'

'One hundred thousand dollars,' said Maxwell, looking up at me. 'To be paid on Thursday at noon at the Kowloon docks. Three days from now.'

'They said he was safe,' said Jie Jie quietly – as quietly as I have ever heard her say anything. Jie Jie is usually as cheerful and loud as May, but now she was white-faced, and her eyes were red-rimmed.

'He is alive. I could hear a baby crying,' said my father. Jie Jie burst into tears, and my father, who I have never seen touch either of his wives, threw his arms round her. They stood leaning together, reflected in the shiny parquet floor. I was embarrassed, and looked away.

As I did so, I caught sight of Daisy. She had sidled away from me, and was now almost at my father's desk. She leaned against it – apparently caught up in the moment between my father and Jie Jie – and I saw her hand press down and crumple up some pieces of paper that were lying on the edge of the desk.

A moment later she had whisked them away into the folds of her skirt, her hand against her waist sorrowfully. But then she looked up and saw me watching her, and winked. There is never a moment when Daisy is not being a detective.

'The man had a quiet voice,' said my father, clearing his throat and stepping away from Jie Jie, who wiped her eyes and folded her arms over her stomach, staring at her feet. 'He was whispering and I could hardly hear him. And behind him there was . . . a rattling sound. Pipes, I assumed.'

My father, I thought, might not make a bad detective.

'What will we do?' asked Jie Jie.

'We will get Teddy back,' said my father, and I heard the rage come back into his voice. 'We will pay the ransom, and then we will make this man sorry he ever took *my* son away from me. Taking a child, a *baby* . . . He will pay.'

I wanted to stay there, to look after my father, but I could tell that there was no place for me or Daisy. I motioned to Daisy, and we crept away.

As we came out into the hall, we bumped into my mother. She was hovering by the pot Daisy and I had hidden behind earlier – I thought she might have been watching the door to the Library. When she saw it was us, she came forward quickly.

'Ying Ying,' said my mother. 'Miss Wells.'

'Ah Mah,' I said to her, bowing.

My mother pursed her lips at us. 'You are all right?' she asked. 'You are looking very flustered. Move more slowly.'

'Yes, Ah Mah,' I said.

'My stupid husband,' said my mother. 'You should not have been there today, Ying Ying. You put yourself in danger. They are saying the murderer was a member of a gang.'

'I didn't put myself in danger on purpose!' I said, feeling sick. 'I didn't know any of this would happen, Ah Mah!'

'You look very messy,' she said, ignoring me. 'At dinner, I want you to dress properly. Wear that white *cheongsam* that fits you best, and your new jade pin, if you please.'

I felt myself go pale, and then red. 'I – I can't,' I said.

'Careless girl!' said my mother. 'You have not lost it already?'

I stood, staring at her in terror. I watched her face change from annoyance to confusion to – quite suddenly – an expression that matched mine.

'Ying Ying,' she said softly. 'That pin—'

'I don't know how it got there!' I babbled. 'Please, Ah Mah! Don't tell Father! I lost it. I swear it's all a mistake—'

'Do not say another word,' snapped my mother. 'Do not ever speak of this again. It is forgotten. Go up to your room now. We never had this conversation.'

I turned away from her, shaking.

'What's up?' whispered Daisy as we climbed the stairs together.

'Mother knows about the pin,' I whispered back. 'And – Daisy, I don't know whether she's going to be able to keep the secret.'

# 7

Ping was in our room, piling up clothes for the sewing *amah* to mend. She had helped us, and I believed we could trust her – but I was still not sure we could let her in on proper Detective Society business.

I was itching to see what Daisy had found, but I forced myself to sit demurely with this casebook on my lap, and write up all the day's events so far. My pencil rushed over the paper, pouring out all my sorrow and hurt, until my head was left much calmer and more collected. Daisy sat next to me and tried to read *Death in the Clouds* (she fidgeted terribly, and only turned four pages). Then she went to the window and watched the gardeners as they moved about with their rakes and shears and wheelbarrows of earth.

At last Ping was called away to help Ah Kwan bathe May (it takes more than one person), and we could talk freely again.

'Hazel, we really are getting somewhere!' said Daisy, turning to me with a bounce. 'Now, first things first. Would you like me to show you what I found in your father's office? It's really rather good.'

'Of course I would!' I said eagerly.

Daisy laughed at me. 'See, now you're thinking like a proper Watson,' she said. 'Look!'

She took a crumpled piece of paper out of *Death in the Clouds* and pressed it flat across her knees.

Luk Man Teahouse
20th February 1936

Dear Mr Wong,
　Your secretary said that you were too busy to meet me, but I must ask you to reconsider your decision. Your honoured father was a good man who helped me in previous times of trouble, and a son should not ignore his father's wishes. I ask again for the money I need to keep the Luk Man open. Do not deny me.

　Bessie Fu

'Goodness!' I said, after I had read it.

'Exactly!' said Daisy. 'Look – we had motives for Mr Wa Fan and Mr Svensson already. Here is proper proof that Mrs Fu needed money, and that your father said no to her. This is a real motive for her!'

She was right. We were learning more and more about each of our suspects. They had all three been at the party the night before, and at the bank earlier – and they all had good reason to kidnap Teddy.

'Father said that the man who called was talking so quietly he could barely hear him,' I said, thinking about it. 'So we can't rule out any of our suspects. Mrs Fu might have made her voice quiet and low like a man's, mightn't she?'

'But he definitely heard Teddy!' said Daisy. 'And some rattling, which I think is far more interesting. That call is useful to us. It tells us that Teddy is safe, and that his kidnappers do want cash for him. This case may have connections to Su Li, but it *is* still about money. Talking of kidnapping, have you ever heard of the Lindbergh baby?'

'Hmm,' I said cautiously. 'Is it from a book?'

'Hazel, I am quite convinced that sometimes, when I talk, you don't listen. The Lindbergh baby was perfectly real, and one of the inspirations for the greatest novel ever written, Mrs Christie's *Murder on the Orient Express*. His father was the aviator Charles Lindbergh, and he was stolen by horrid kidnappers who wanted all his money. It all went wrong, and they never got him home again.'

'Why are you telling me that?' I asked, horrified. I realized I could not bear the idea that we might never get Teddy back.

'Two reasons,' said Daisy. 'First, because I wanted to see how you'd feel at the thought that Teddy might not be found. I wanted to show you that you *do* care for him, even though you think you don't.

'And second, because in that case ransom notes kept everyone distracted for months. All the grown-ups thought that they were the most important thing to follow, when they were really useless, at least for the purposes of finding the baby.'

'So?'

'So my point *is* that the ransom telephone call is important, but we must not fix on it the way the grown-ups are. We must continue to think logically about suspects and motives. And we need to get out of the house and investigate Sai Yat further. We can't leave that to the detective!'

'Daisy, we mustn't!' I said. 'It's terribly dangerous. You know we can't leave the Big House on our own, especially not to go and find a Triad gang.'

Daisy looked mulish. 'Nevertheless, we must do it anyway,' she said. 'And there's one more thing I want to say at this stage. We think this was an outside job. But ... we can't *quite* discount your family. Clearly, all is not entirely well at home, and we do know that the kidnapper has excellent knowledge of your household.'

'Don't even say it,' I said fiercely. 'Jie Jie is Teddy's mother, even though she's not allowed to show that in public – and you've seen how much she adores him. She has no reason to have him kidnapped. My father – well, he *couldn't*, Daisy. He couldn't pretend to be so hurt – and, again, what would he gain from having his own son kidnapped? May and Rose are babies. And my mother – no, Daisy. She knows that my father would never speak to her again, and, when Teddy came back, he'd be more adored than ever. She always knew that Jie Jie might have a son. It's *expected* here. You simply have to live with it. You wouldn't understand.'

'Hmm,' said Daisy. 'Well, I take your point in general – but, Hazel, I do think we have to add your mother to the list, at least temporarily. We'll be able to rule her out, I'm sure. But you must see that she has a good motive – although her feet don't allow her to move as quickly as you or me.'

'Bound feet used to be ordinary here, Daisy,' I said quickly. 'Most grown-up women have them. It doesn't stop you walking.' Then I heard myself, and knew that I was not helping my mother's case. 'But she liked Su Li! They used to talk all the time. That's why Su Li was my maid, because my mother chose her out of all the *mui tsai*. She wouldn't *kill* her! And she wasn't at the bank today. She didn't have the same opportunity to hand over the pin.'

'This is all very useful, Hazel,' said Daisy. 'We can use it to help rule her out.'

With a heavy heart, I picked up my pencil again.

'Good,' said Daisy. 'Hazel, you know I'm only being thorough.'

'I know,' I said. But as I closed my casebook and readied myself for dinner, I could not stop wondering. My mother's face at the upper window played in my head again and again – and so did the gardener's boy we had met that afternoon.

I remembered what he had said: *Beware. There's a snake on your back too.*

## SUSPECT LIST

1. The lift operator (~~find out his name!~~) Wu Shing. The simplest explanation is that he committed the crime. But why? We think he and Su Li knew each other, and she was afraid of him, but we must find evidence to back this up. So was this his motive, and he kidnapped Teddy almost as an afterthought, or was he simply interested in making money by kidnapping Teddy, and Su Li got in the way? Was he working on his own, or did he carry out

the crime for someone else? (The pin makes it very likely that he was working with another criminal.) If so, who hired him, and why? NOTES: We know from the photograph that he knew Su Li! He was her ex-boyfriend. So was he paid to kill her, or did he kill her because he didn't like her?

2. *Sai Yat's Triad gang*. MOTIVE TO KIDNAP TEDDY: Money, plain and simple! The pin stabbed into Su Li's throat is the calling card of a Triad gang (we heard someone say this, and Hazel confirms it) — but it is odd that they chose to use Hazel's pin. Were they trying to frame her? Was it just a mistake? NOTES: We heard from Pik An that she believes some of the servants are indeed Triad. Could this be Ng? He says that Sai Yat had nothing to do with this crime — is that just a blind?

3. *Mr Svensson*. MOTIVE TO KIDNAP TEDDY: He needs money, and Mr Wong will not give him any. He is also angry with Mr Wong — might this give him a motive to frame Hazel for the crime? NOTES: He was seen at the bank at the time of the crime in a strange mood, and there are

ten minutes where his movements cannot be accounted for. He was also at the party the night before, so could have picked up Hazel's pin and given it to the lift operator! He knew that Teddy was due to be at the doctor's the next day, because he heard Mr Wong mention this. Ng confirms that Mr Svensson is in need of money!

4. *Mrs Fu.* MOTIVE TO KIDNAP TEDDY: She also seems to need money – and she was talking angrily with Mr Wong at the party. NOTES: She was seen at the bank at the time of the crime by Hazel Wong and Daisy Wells, so could have given the pin to the lift operator. She was also at the party the night before, so could have picked up Hazel's pin and overheard about Teddy's appointment! We have found a letter from her to Mr Wong asking him for money to save her teahouse!

5. *Mr Wa Fan.* MOTIVE TO KIDNAP TEDDY: He is angry with Mr Wong because he thinks he is not being dutiful. But is this a good motive for kidnap? He was at the party, so could

have taken the pin and heard about the appointment. ~~But he was not seen at the bank, and we do not~~ ~~know if he is a patient of Dr Aurettus.~~ NOTES: Wo On the chauffeur says that he saw Mr Wa Fan leaving the bank with a bottle of medicine just before the murder was discovered. He was on the scene, and in a hurry! He has paid the detective, Mr Leung, to help find Teddy. But is this a kind gesture — or a controlling one?

6. *June Wong.* MOTIVE TO HAVE TEDDY KIDNAPPED: She does not like him, because he is the son of her husband's other wife. But, if she had arranged to have him taken, she must know that when he was recovered he would be more adored than ever. Hazel remembers her being friendly with Su Li — why would she arrange to have her killed? NOTES: She was not at the bank on the day of the crime — she had a headache. And the pin implicates Hazel, her own daughter — why would she arrange a crime that did such a thing? Her bound feet would slow her down, though they do not rule her out.

# PLAN OF ACTION

1. ~~Eliminate Wo On and Ping from our list of suspects.~~

2. Find out more about the lift operator Wu Shing — ~~who was he, and~~ why did he become a murderer and a kidnapper? Was he paid to do it, or was it a personal motive?

3. ~~Find out more about the Triad gang who use pins as their calling cards.~~

4. ~~Look into all of our suspects' motives further.~~

5. Find out more about Dr Aurelius's office to understand how the crime was not discovered, and how Teddy was taken out of the bank building.

6. Find a way to investigate Sai Yat.

7. Begin to rule out suspects.

# 8

The next morning it was raining again. I woke up, and for a floating moment felt clean and calm. Then it dropped on me, like a black weight: Su Li was dead. Teddy was gone. And I might be a suspect. I kept almost forgetting that fact, but then felt it pierce me like a stray pin poking through the hem of a not-quite-finished blouse.

I sat up with a struggle, and saw that Daisy was already awake, sitting cross-legged on her bed, staring at me.

'Good morning, Hazel,' she said.

'What are you *doing*?' I asked her.

'Thinking about the case,' said Daisy. 'I'm still trying to work out a bothersome puzzle: how to observe our most difficult suspect more closely. Sai Yat doesn't have a standing invitation to your house, after all, so somehow we must get out and go to him. And this place is far more regimented than Deepdean. Simply slipping away with a change of clothes on under our coats will not suffice. We need to be considerably more resourceful to escape.'

'The dogs are out at night,' I said. 'And the gardeners are out during the day. I told you, we'll never manage it without being seen, Daisy. It's not like England here. We *can't* go where we like, on our own. It's impossible. There's no point even talking about it. You don't understand.'

'Hazel,' said Daisy, blinking at me in an absolutely maddening way. 'I am quite aware that I don't understand. And that is the point. *You* understand so well that you don't even want to try. *I* say that we *must* try, no matter how impossible it seems. And, in fact, I had a rather good idea just after dawn this morning. I shall consider it until I am more sure – but I have the inkling of a plan that might just manage to get us outside this compound without Ping, or Wo On, or any of the other grown-ups your father has surrounded us with.'

'He's just protecting us,' I said. It came out of my mouth automatically, from years and years of being told just such a thing. My father's decisions were wise, and for my own good. Even on the Orient Express, he hadn't been wrong, just misinformed. But now I knew that my father had thought of Teddy before me, and given him into Su Li's care even though she had not wanted it. Could I still believe in him the way I always had?

I must have looked stricken, for Daisy put out her hand and patted my arm.

Ping came in then, to dress us, and Daisy and I could say no more about her plan.

'I am going to Man Mo Temple today,' announced my father at breakfast. We were all surprised. This was my grandfather's temple, and the Tung Wah's – my father never liked going there.

'I have to meet Detective Leung,' said my father gruffly. His eyes were redder than ever this morning, and his lips were greyish. 'Appointment. Maxwell will watch the telephone while I am gone.'

'Can Daisy and I come too?' I asked at once. My father glared at me with bloodshot eyes.

'I— It meant so much to Ah Yeh,' I said. 'I want to see it again.'

My father made a cross face, but at last he said, 'All right, then. If you must. Be ready in half an hour.'

The cars let us out on Hollywood Road, so we could arrive on foot. People on the street turned to look at Daisy, at the flash of her gold hair, and she looked back at them haughtily – but, I saw, with a little twitch of nerves.

The trees above us curled their roots and vines down into the road, and the air was heavy with moisture. There were smells all around us of wood being cut and carved and varnished. The temple was ahead, with its white walls and slanting green tiled roofs, and red paper prayers fluttering.

We went inside the temple, darkness dropping over us like a cloak. All around was red and gold from hundreds of square lit lanterns, and the air was thick with incense. Daisy coughed, and I bowed. We walked towards the gold and red gods at the other end of the temple, the curling incense sticks above us dropping ash on our arms and hands and necks like hot kisses.

I love the Taoist temples in Hong Kong. The gods' altars are covered in shining, sweet-smelling gifts of fruit and flowers, and paper money in bright packages. Christian churches always seem so bare to me in comparison. I remember being taken by my father to St John's Cathedral when I was very little, and thinking that Jesus must be hungry, with only sour wine and bitter flat bread to eat. I am never quite sure if my grandfather's gods pay attention to me, but I thought there was no harm in trying. And, anyway, Man is a god of books and learning, and Mo is a god of war, so I thought that they would not object to being asked to help with a detective case. I closed my eyes and hoped that we would find Teddy safely, and avenge Su Li properly. I thought about Grandfather, who had believed in all this, even if I was not sure whether I did or not.

I understood like a heavy weight in my chest that, although we might get Teddy back, I would never come here with my grandfather or Su Li again, and whenever I did I would feel the space where they ought to be. That made me cry. I tried to pretend that it was only ash in my eye, but I don't think Daisy was tricked. My father looked red-eyed too, wiping his eyes on his silk handkerchief. My heart ached for him – but I was still angry with him as well.

Then Mr Wa Fan came through the doorway. Just behind him was Detective Leung. My father paused, and then bowed low to them, and Mr Wa Fan beckoned us over.

'Good morning, Vincent,' said Mr Wa Fan to my father. 'And good morning to you, Miss Wong and Miss Wells. It is good that Vincent has brought you here.' Mr Wa Fan spoke as if from a great height. This morning his gold-buttoned silk jacket was a deep purple. He reminded me, with an ache in my chest, so much of my grandfather, standing with his hands clasped before him. I saw that his rings were loose on his bony hands.

'Sir, good morning,' I said, in respectful Cantonese, bowing and nudging Daisy to remind her to bow too.

'Vincent, we are here to help you,' said Mr Wa Fan. 'Remember that.'

'I do remember that,' said my father stiffly. 'What news do you have?'

'I am tracking Wu Shing,' said Detective Leung, at Mr Wa Fan's nod. 'And Sai Yat's gang seem rattled. They are straying from their normal behaviour. I will keep watching them, and I believe I will be able to find the boy soon. Yesterday I cleared the maid – she was an innocent victim, nothing more.'

'This is not really much—' my father began, and then he caught Mr Wa Fan's eye, and stopped. I knew what he was going to say: that this was hardly worth getting us to drive to the temple for – but then I looked at Mr Wa Fan. He was smiling, and it ought to have been a kind expression, but somehow, on his thin face, it looked eerie. Mr Wa Fan had got my father to do something, even though he had not wanted to. I saw how much it meant to him.

I looked at him with my detective senses and saw an old man who was set in his beliefs, and who was as firm in his disapproval of certain things as my grandfather had been.

I suddenly thought of the relationship between my father and my grandfather, and I realized how much my grandfather had told my father what to do while he was at home. It was only when my father left the house that he could be the Mr Wong that the rest of the world saw. I understood that my grandfather's death had suddenly allowed my father to be much more of the person he wanted to be – but now Mr Wa Fan was trying to control my father all over again.

'How did you hear about what happened yesterday?' I asked Mr Wa Fan. 'The detective was with us so quickly, it was wonderful.'

'News travels,' said Mr Wa Fan, scowling at me. 'I was here, at Man Mo Temple, at the time, but my servants informed me on my arrival home.'

'Oh,' I said, trying to keep my face straight and calm. Mr Wa Fan had just lied to me. I knew from what Wo had told me that he had not been at the temple at all – he had been at the bank.

'Detective Leung will find him soon, you will see. He will solve the case,' said Mr Wa Fan, frowning through his beard.

He gestured for Detective Leung to follow him, but before he did the detective paused before us, bending forward to stare at me more closely. The little black speck at the corner of his eye flickered as he looked at me, and I leaned closer to Daisy nervously.

'Hazel Wong,' said Detective Leung very quietly. 'I have my eye on you.'

# 9

I returned to the Big House feeling shaken, but I had to come back to myself quickly. Almost as soon as we arrived, a steady stream of visitors started coming up the drive to see my father.

Mrs Fu arrived first, bowing very low as she stepped over the threshold. This morning she was wearing a sky-blue *cheongsam*.

'Mr Wong!' she said as she walked into the Library (Daisy and I positioned ourselves at the door, so that we could hear the conversation, and Rose came wandering up and sat down beside us, her doll in her lap). 'Is there any news?'

'Thank you for coming, Mrs Fu,' said my father, and his voice sounded cold. 'There have certainly been many developments in the case. We have had a ransom demand from the kidnappers, and we have been given a time and date for the handover of the money.'

'They've asked for a hundred thousand!' said Mrs Fu. 'Or so I have been told. Word spreads.'

'Does it indeed,' said my father, thunderous. 'And how did it spread to you?'

'I have my sources,' said Mrs Fu. 'Hong Kong is a small city.'

'If you have come to ask for money again, I can't give it to you,' snapped my father. 'I have other things on my mind.'

'As it happens, I haven't,' said Mrs Fu sniffily. 'Since we spoke last, I have had a change of circumstances. There are now other places I can get funds from. I have simply come by to ask after your son.'

My father said something that I will not write here, and a moment later Mrs Fu came hurrying back out of the Library. Daisy and I did our best to look as though we had not been listening in, but Rose stared at her in fascination.

'Rose!' I whispered, nudging her.

'Rude!' said Mrs Fu, glaring down at us.

I thought quickly. Mrs Fu was a very direct person – it seemed most sensible to ask her a direct question. 'Mrs Fu,' I said. 'Didn't we see you at the bank yesterday? I'm sure we did.'

Mrs Fu turned very pale. Her lips pursed and her collarbones stood out as her shoulders tensed.

'Don't you dare tell your father that!' she cried. 'It had nothing to do with what happened.'

She looked once more at me and Rose, a furious expression on her face, and then she rushed out of the house and down the front steps.

'What was that about?' hissed Daisy. 'What was she saying to you? Oh, listening to Chinese is like going through the Looking Glass.'

'When I told her we'd seen her at the bank, she got very upset,' I said. 'And, when she was talking to Father, she knew how much the ransom was, even before he told her. Then she said that she had money, and didn't need to borrow from him any more, and he told her to leave.'

'Interesting!' said Daisy. 'So you think—'

'What are you two doing?' Rose asked me curiously. Her English is so good now that she had understood almost everything we'd said. We both paused, and stared at her.

'None of your business!' I said. 'Stop listening!'

'*You* listen to everything,' said Rose.

'I'm older than you, I'm allowed to,' I told her, more sharply than I usually speak to her.

Rose's lip wobbled.

'I'm sorry, Ling Ling!' I said, putting my arm round her hastily. 'I'm just upset. Don't worry. It's going to be all right. Detective Leung is going to get Teddy back. We're just . . . watching to make sure he does.'

'I know,' said Rose. 'Father's going to pay the ransom. One hundred thousand dollars! I wish I was worth that much.'

'You do not!' I said to her. 'You don't want to be kidnapped!'

'But I want people to worry about me,' said Rose. 'Father notices you because you're clever, and he notices May because she's naughty. He never notices me. I want to go to English school so that I can run away like in the books.'

'Don't you dare run away!' I said, pulling her closer. Rose pouted and tried to twist away. 'You don't need to. We all notice you already.'

'You'd notice me more if I was a boy,' muttered Rose, and she pulled out of my grasp and ran upstairs.

I stared after her, feeling odd. It had not occurred to me that my sisters were upset about Teddy's arrival as well.

And then I thought about Mrs Fu. Where *was* she suddenly getting money from? Was it just a coincidence? Or . . . was it nothing of the kind?

# 10

I could tell that Daisy was feeling rather frustrated by her lack of understanding of Cantonese. She hates being behind, lagging, not having all possible knowledge sparking from her fingertips. So I was glad that, when Mr Svensson arrived, he spoke in English.

Mr Svensson brought Mrs Svensson with him, and Mrs Svensson brought her sunny smile and her soft purple scent.

'We've come to show our support,' said Mr Svensson, clapping my father on the arm. 'I'm fearfully sorry about all this. I had to stop Kendra bringing Roald. We have a maid who can look after him and I thought he might not be – well – a good reminder.'

'Probably not,' said my father shortly.

'Poor Vincent!' said Mrs Svensson sympathetically. 'How are you holding up? Is it too awful? I don't know what I would do – why, it would be the end of the world!'

'It is awful indeed,' said my father. 'Yesterday, we received demands from the kidnappers. I hope that we will be able to hand the money over successfully, and have Teddy back with us by the end of the week.'

'What good news!' cried Mrs Svensson. 'I hope you can find the money? I mean, of course you can, a man like you – and I'm sure too that you'll be able to make back the loss. I only wish we could help.'

'About that . . .' said Mr Svensson, nodding. 'Vincent, I know we've had disagreements in the past, but now – well – now this has happened, I want to put all that aside. I haven't much liquidity at the moment, but I want to draw on some of my reserve funds for this.'

I saw Mrs Svensson look worried. 'Are you sure, Sven?' she asked. 'I mean, poor Vincent, but—'

'At moments like this, one must be a man, Kendra,' said Mr Svensson magnificently, clapping her on the back. 'It'll come right, you'll see. I've asked Vincent for money enough times, after all!'

But my father shook his head. 'No, Sven,' he said. 'I thank you, but no. This is something I must do on my own. I can't ask this of you.'

'Oh, June!' said Mrs Svensson suddenly, looking past me. 'There you are! I didn't see you—'

We all turned and saw my mother standing next to the ornamental screen at the other end of the hall. Her face was impassive.

'Mrs Svensson,' she said, her voice icy. 'What a surprise.'

'June!' said my father. 'June, please take Kendra into the music room for tea. Hazel, Daisy, go with them. I must speak to Sven alone.'

It was so unfair, I thought. I might be growing up, but all the same, because I was a girl, I was still being left out of the truly important conversations.

Mrs Svensson smiled sympathetically at my mother, and my mother glared daggers back at her. As Daisy and I followed them, I looked back at Mr Svensson. He was still begging my father to reconsider, waving his hands animatedly, while my father frowned. Was the offer genuine? He did not have much money after all. But – Mr Svensson knew my father. He knew how proud he was. The more he offered, the less likely my father was to say yes. Was he counting on that?

Daisy nudged me. 'Don't be cross, Hazel,' she whispered. 'You know as well as I do that half of detecting is listening to idle chat. Mrs Svensson clearly adores gossip in all its forms, and so I am convinced that spending a few minutes in her company will give us at least six fascinating leads to follow.'

This was true, and quite sensible. But I was worried that Daisy might have another motive. She still thought of my mother as a suspect, and she wanted to watch her.

So, as I followed her into the music room, I felt strangely afraid.

# 11

My mother sat very upright on a cream silk sofa, glaring at Mrs Svensson as she wandered around the music room, tapping out a few notes on the piano, touching the ornaments on the sideboard and exclaiming at their prettiness. A maid came in and poured out the tea.

'Goodness, this is beautiful!' Mrs Svensson said, holding up a cloisonné bowl, goldfish chasing each other's frothy tails in a deep blue pond. 'You really do have the most lovely things, June.'

'Thank you, Mrs Svensson,' said my mother icily. 'It was very expensive. Do not drop it, if you please. Tea, Hazel?'

'Thank you, Mother,' I said, ducking my head, and the maid pressed a little cup into my hands, its heat streaming through my fingers, the steam from it curling sweetly around my nose.

I sipped awkwardly, sitting sideways on the sofa next to my mother. Coldness radiated from her, and even Mrs Svensson's cheerful glow was dimmed. It was up to Daisy to rescue the situation, and, of course, she did.

'I do so admire your dress, Kendra!' she cried, and Mrs Svensson beamed gratefully. Soon they were discussing fabric and cut, and somehow they moved on from there to jewellery. Daisy praised Mrs Svensson's engagement ring, with its flashing blue stone, and then turned to my mother. 'Your bangle is delightful,' she said, and my mother thawed an inch or two.

'It's jade,' she said. 'Jewellery is important to a woman. I wish I could make Hazel wear more.' She took my hand unexpectedly and twisted it around in hers, looping her fingers about my wrist and pinching my fingers. 'She would have pretty hands if they weren't so dirty.'

She meant, of course, the dust from my pencils. I write so much that my hands always seem to be covered in dark marks. I pulled my hands away from her in shame and alarm. My mother doesn't touch me much, and so, every time she does, it makes my heart jump.

'You ought to take more care of yourself,' said my mother, flicking my arm with her long, polished nails.

'I do my best to help Hazel, Mrs Wong,' said Daisy seriously. 'But she won't take time to consider important things like hats.'

I wanted very much to say that it's no good caring about clothes and hats when I can never look as well in them as other people do – but I saw Daisy narrow her left eye at me in the smallest of winks, and knew she did not mean it. I kept silent.

'I'm sure you must be planning outfits for your Season already, Daisy,' said Mrs Svensson. 'Oh, the fun of it! Mine was the happiest time of my life. No cares at all!'

'Oh yes. Being a grown-up sounds simply wonderful,' said Daisy blissfully.

'I remember when I thought just like you, dear,' Mrs Svensson went on. 'But in fact, now that I am one, I feel just like I did when I was a child, only with a dreadful lot of extra things for one to remember – and heaps of bills to pay.'

'Hah!' said my mother sharply. Mrs Svensson blushed and turned back to the mantelpiece.

'Oh, I shall *make* being a grown-up blissful,' said Daisy, seeming not to notice Mrs Svensson's embarrassment. 'I shall marry a lord.'

I grinned, and then covered my mouth with my hand, for I know that marrying a lord is the last thing Daisy would ever consider doing with her life.

'Of course you shall, dear,' said Mrs Svensson. 'And you, Hazel – June, you must have ideas for her.'

'Hazel will not marry,' said my mother coldly.

I looked at her, shocked. I have always known that my mother expected me to marry, and marry well, which makes me feel odd and uncomfortable. Why had she changed her mind now? Was it because of Teddy? Did I really not matter any more, to either of my parents? Or did she mean that she thought no man would ever *want* to marry me?

'Well,' said Mrs Svensson, clearing her throat. 'I— The world is changing, I suppose. Now, I wonder what our husbands are talking about?'

'Money,' said my mother. 'It's all they ever seem to discuss.'

'Dear Sven is quite set on the idea of helping Mr Wong,' said Mrs Svensson. 'I know I oughtn't to mention it but I really don't know where he'll get the money from. We are rather short at present, and there's Roald to consider. We must look after him, and ourselves!'

Daisy, despite herself, turned towards Mrs Svensson with interest on her face. My mother saw.

'Hazel, please take Miss Wells away,' she said to me sternly. 'This is not suitable conversation for you.'

'Yes, Mother,' I said. 'Come on, Daisy, let's go into the garden.'

# 12

I led Daisy not to the front of the house, where the men were still standing, but behind the folding screen, into the back hallway, with its wooden stairs reaching up to the first floor and its huge crystal chandelier. To our right was the side entrance, a narrower, darker doorway with two imposing metal pots like sentinels on either side of a tall set of steps.

Down these we ran, and out onto the gravel drive that surrounded the Big House. In front of us was the rise of the Peak, lush green trees and cool white buildings, and over to the right I could see Victoria Harbour, all its buildings and boats as small as toys. The rain had stopped, but everything was smoking with damp. All the plants around us were still covered in heavy drops that scattered across our shoulders.

I motioned for Daisy to follow me, and we tiptoed to the right, moving slowly and carefully until we were under the music-room window. It was open just a crack, and I could hear voices, so quiet that they sounded nothing more than ghosts.

'Ohhh!' whispered Daisy, patting me on the back. 'Good work, Watson!'

I beamed at her, and we both listened in.

'. . . unwise investments,' Mrs Svensson was saying. 'Poor Roald! It isn't fair on him.'

'I do not see why I should care, Mrs Svensson,' said my mother.

'Well,' she began. 'Imagine if it was Teddy. Or Hazel. Think of her future!'

'All I can say to that, Mrs Svensson, is that we are not friends,' said my mother, and I imagined her, straight-backed, glaring at her guest from her sofa. 'What you are saying has made that very clear. We are enemies.'

'Oh, how rude!' gasped Mrs Svensson, and at that moment a door opened and we heard Mr Svensson's big voice enter the room.

'Kendra, we must be going,' he said. 'Good morning, June.'

Then there was the bustle of Mrs Svensson getting up and wishing my mother goodbye – she did it very well, and I wouldn't have guessed that they had just been arguing bitterly if I had not heard them.

Daisy and I looked at each other. We crept away from the window, and then stood up and began strolling along the gravel path as though we had nothing to hide.

It is funny to think of the difference between our house's garden and Daisy's at Fallingford. Hers is all sweeping green grass, enormous old trees and a lake and a maze, everything frost-bitten in the morning. Wildness is tidied away, but it's never really gone. But, at the Big House, the Hong Kong jungle never comes within its gates. Our garden is set out in perfect gravelled tiers, with pretty painted steps and railings at each level; peach and star-fruit trees are trained to trail along the stone. Flowers for cutting (including my father's favourite roses) are tucked away behind a carefully built wall until they are blooming and perfect, and everything you see is in pots, even the fruit trees – pots so large you could hide behind them. So, as Daisy and I walked down the length of the house, towards the kitchens at the back, we dodged round pots spilling waxy pink and white camellias, rich red peonies and tall cannas like bolts of flame. Orange and cherry blossom bobbed above them all, and the warm air was heavy with their scent. My nose tickled, and I sneezed.

'Bless you, Hazel,' said Daisy. 'So. Mr Svensson's been making unwise investments, has he? Mrs Svensson's worried that he doesn't have enough money to look after Roald; upset enough to shout at your mother about it? But, if that's so, how can he offer money to Mr Wong?'

'Yes!' I cried. 'I know, Daisy. It's very odd.'

'It only makes sense if he's doing it because he knows your father would never take the money. That's right, isn't it?'

I nodded. 'That was exactly what I thought too. But then, what does that mean? Is it a clue?'

'It might be,' said Daisy. 'But it's only one example of false kindness that we've seen today. Mr Wa Fan, for example. Hiring Detective Leung for your father *seems* like a nice thing to do – but somehow I'm not convinced it is.'

'I agree!' I said. 'I think Mr Wa Fan is using Detective Leung like a bargaining chip, to make Father grateful. And it's working. Father wouldn't take money, but he will accept help. He'd even go back to the temple, for Teddy's sake. Mr Wa Fan knows him, just like Mr Svensson does.'

'That brings us to Mrs Fu. She's suddenly very independent, isn't she? From someone who was begging your father for money very recently, she now needs nothing at all.'

'And she knew exactly how much the ransom was!' I said.

We walked a few more steps along the path. I stared up at the house on our left, the high white walls, the wide windows and dark rooms.

'Hazel,' said Daisy. 'May I ask one more thing? It may be nothing – in fact, I'm sure it is. Does your mother usually wear a ring on the middle finger of her right hand?'

'Yes,' I said. 'Gold, with an emerald. Why?'

'I noticed her wearing it when we first arrived,' said Daisy. 'Very pretty. But now it's gone. I missed it today, when we were discussing jewellery.'

I looked at her sharply, and saw her staring back at me, her eyes very blue. 'She might have left it in her jewellery box, I suppose,' I said. 'She doesn't – she doesn't always wear it.'

'I see,' said Daisy. 'Yes, that could be it.'

'Stop it, Daisy!' I cried. 'I know what you're trying to do. Stop it!'

Daisy raised an eyebrow at me. 'What am I trying to do, Hazel?' she asked.

'Saying that Mother – that she's still a suspect,' I said. 'That she used the ring to pay for Wu Shing to kidnap Teddy, I suppose. Is that what you mean?'

'I hadn't got that far,' said Daisy, in a tone that infuriated me, because I knew it was her lying voice. 'But now that you point it out . . .'

'Stop it!' I hissed. 'You heard her just now! She's *worried* about Teddy, she said so. She was angry at Mrs Svensson. And, I told you, she liked Su Li.'

'She doesn't seem very sad about her dying,' said Daisy. 'She hasn't mentioned it once!'

'You don't know my mother!' I said. 'You don't understand her, or how things are done here. She *does* care about people, she simply isn't affectionate at all. Leave it, Daisy, please!'

Daisy stopped and turned. I thought she was ignoring me – until from the other side of the nearest plant pot stepped the boy we'd met the day before, the one with the shortened arm. He stood, staring at us.

Then he turned and ran.

# 13

I have got just a little faster since I first arrived at Deep-dean – though I suspect that has more to do with our five murder cases than our Games lessons. But running in Hong Kong air is heavy, and each breath you take is wet. I only got a few paces before I was wheezing awfully. The boy was nimble, and he darted away from me so quickly that I felt I was running in a dream, through treacle.

It's lucky that I had Daisy beside me. She leaped forward like a fox, like Atalanta in the myth, and in ten long strides she was upon him, her fingers pinching the back of his neck.

'OW!' he shouted in Cantonese. 'Get off me, girl!'

He also said much worse things than that, only I don't want to write them here.

'Tell him that I shall let go of him if he turns round and answers some questions, Hazel!' snapped Daisy. She twisted her fingers, and the boy yelped.

'Get her off me, she's horrible!' he shouted at me.

'Daisy, stop it! You're hurting him!' I cried.

'Of course I am,' said Daisy, looking puzzled. 'He ran away from us.'

'Let me talk to him!' I said to her. 'Daisy, leave off – you're only making things worse. Let me deal with it!'

Daisy's mouth fell open. 'But I always—' she began.

The boy was looking from Daisy to me and back again, as though he wanted very much to run away for a second time.

'Don't move,' I said to him in Cantonese. 'Don't even think about moving.'

In Cantonese I can be fiercer, not the polite Hazel that I am in English. English is full of phrases that mean nothing, like *If you wouldn't mind* and *Excuse me* and *Oh, I say*, but in Cantonese you can be sharp and to the point. Daisy has made me realize that it is difficult for a person who only speaks English to know when a person speaking Cantonese is upset and when they are not, because to their ears it is a hard, shouting language.

'What are you doing? Why did you run away?' I asked. 'And who are you?'

'I ran because you were chasing me,' said the boy, which I thought was both fair and sharp-witted. 'You can call me Ah Lan.'

'But why were you listening to us?' I asked. 'And you *were* listening just then, and before – I know you can understand English as well as Cantonese.'

'Yes, I can,' said Ah Lan, raising one dark eyebrow. 'Don't you know your father at all? He makes all his servants learn English.'

'Of course I know my father!' I cried, flustered. 'That wasn't what I asked you. We've seen your picture in Su Li's room. You knew her – do you have something to do with what happened to her and Teddy?'

'Yes,' said Ah Lan. 'But not in the way you think, all right? Su Li was my cousin. She got me the job here a few years ago. She was a good person, and now she's dead. And the person who killed her – Wu Shing – I knew him too. He got a job here at the same time I did, as a potboy. He was Su Li's boyfriend for a while, but last year she left him because he was being cruel to her. Your father fired him, so he had to get another job. He needed money, and I've heard someone paid him to commit the crime.

'I've been watching you too, because Detective Leung is wrong about where that pin came from. This has nothing to do with Sai Yat and his gang, or any gang at all. I heard you and Miss Wells talking, and I know it's yours. At first I thought that meant you were the one who ordered Su Li's murder. I was going to kill you. But then I realized that you don't know what happened at all. Someone else is behind it, some other rich person paid Wu Shing. And I thought that, if I followed you, you'd help me work out who that is.'

'What is he saying?' Daisy was hissing in my ear. 'What is it?'

'Su Li is – was – his cousin!' I told her. 'He wants to find out who killed her, Daisy. He's just like us.'

I turned back to Ah Lan. An uncomfortable thought had occurred to me. I remembered what Pik An had said: *It's not the* maids *in this house who are Triad* . . .

'How do you know that Sai Yat didn't do it?' I asked. 'How can you be sure?'

'How do you think?' Ah Lan's lips quirked up in a smile. 'I'm not like Ng. I haven't been initiated properly yet. I'm just a runner, a trainee. But I'm still one of Sai Yat's representatives in this house, so I defend his honour, all right? He swore to me he didn't do it, and that's important. I believe him. He wants his name cleared, and he wants the person who really did it punished.'

Part of me was terrified. We were talking to one of the criminals I had warned Daisy about! It's easy to say that Triads are nothing to be afraid of, until one of them is standing in front of you. But I knew I couldn't let myself be afraid. 'Then we're on your side!' I said. 'You're right – we're trying to find out what happened too. We want justice for Su Li, and we want to get Teddy back. We have to find out who planned the crime.'

'You're only pretending to be detectives,' said Ah Lan, smiling again in the same scornful way. 'This is a game for you.'

'Tell that boy that we *are* detectives, and we have solved FIVE MURDER CASES!' snarled Daisy. I looked at her, astonished – apparently, she can tell when the Detective Society is being demeaned in any language.

'Daisy is right,' I said. 'It's not a game for us. It's not just about Teddy, either. It – it matters to me, about Su Li. I loved her, just like you did. And we *are* detectives, proper ones, even though we don't look it.'

'And I'm the mountain master,' said Ah Lan, rolling his eyes. 'All right, all right! Don't glare at me like that. I believe you.'

'If you prove to us that Sai Yat didn't do it, then we'll help you find out who did,' I said. 'We can work together, all right?'

'Hazel!' said Daisy. 'What are you up to? Are you expanding the Detective Society *again*?'

Ah Lan brushed a strand of hair off his face, looking thoughtful. It was a little like one of Alexander's gestures, I thought, and my heart jumped just to think of him. But this boy, of course, wasn't like Alexander at all.

'I know where the gang meets,' he said. 'I can take you there, and show you a place to watch them from. There's a meeting tonight to talk about Teddy. You'll be able to hear for yourself that Sai Yat and his men have nothing to do with it.'

'But how can we get out of the compound?' I asked. 'There are people watching us all the time.'

'Hazel,' said Daisy. 'Hazel. HAZEL!'

'What?' I asked, whirling about to stare at her.

'Hazel, if you're talking about escaping, say to the boy—'

'Ah Lan,' I said.

'Say to Ah Lan: garden soil cart. That's all. Say it to him.'

I sighed. 'You heard her,' I told him.

I couldn't think why Daisy wanted me to say those words, which sounded rather dirty, and entirely beside the point. But Ah Lan's face lit up. 'Garden soil cart!' he cried. 'Of course!'

'Yes, he understands!' said Daisy, nodding. 'Listen, Hazel. This was the utterly brilliant idea I had this morning: the gardeners must get rid of dirt and leaves and things every evening. I suspect they put them in a compost heap that isn't in the grounds. So, now that we know we have Ah Lan's help, all he needs to do is—'

'I can hide you in the cart, under the dirt, and wheel you out this evening!' said Ah Lan to me in Cantonese. 'It'll be too smelly for the dogs to be able to catch your scent. All you need to do is make sure Ping falls asleep after dinner.'

'Hazel, we simply need to make sure that Ping goes to sleep after dinner,' said Daisy. 'Does your mother take sleeping pills?'

I sighed. I looked from Ah Lan to Daisy, and saw them beaming at each other, the same light of mischief in their eyes. I thought that, no matter how little Daisy understood Hong Kong, her brain was just as sharp and odd as ever.

'My mother does use something to make her sleep,' I said, giving in to the plan. 'And I know exactly where she hides it.'

# PART FOUR

# MISCHIEF AT MIDNIGHT

# 1

I pushed open the door to my mother's room. Daisy hovered behind me, watching the corridor for any passers-by. It's funny – I can count on the fingers of both hands the number of times I've been inside my mother's room in my life. It is a place where children do not go, where my mother goes to rest, away from us all. It hasn't changed in all the years I have known it. Even before I stepped inside, I knew what I would find.

My mother's room is as neat and clean as she is, pure white and gold. A high bed, hung with curtains and carved in dark latticed wood, a matching carved dressing table and chair with an oval mirror, perfumes and lotions lined up beneath it. Painted panels lick gold and silver across the walls, flowers and clouds surrounding great ladies in robes and elaborate hairdos.

'Ooh,' whispered Daisy, wide-eyed. 'Oooooh, *Hazel*! It's so chic! Just like your mother. Now I see why you're so odd about clothes and so on. You don't think you could ever match up to her.'

'My mother has nothing to do with it!' I protested, my face burning. As usual, though, I had the uncomfortable feeling that Daisy had hit the nail on the head. It's not just Daisy that I compare myself to whenever I look in the mirror in a new dress or coat. It's my mother. I used to stare at myself to understand how her features could have become mine, but all I could see was a rounder, softer version of my father's face.

'Of course she hasn't,' said Daisy, patting my arm. 'Just like she has nothing to do with the fact that you're such an excellent secretary. Your mother has an exceedingly tidy mind, just like you, Hazel. This room belongs to someone who makes lists, and plans everything out quite logically. Your father is clever, but he's far more hasty than you, you must see that. No, your *mother* is why you're such an excellent Watson.'

'But—' I said, and blinked. I have always simply known that because I am clever and bookish I take after my father. I said this to Daisy. She raised one perfect eyebrow.

'Hazel,' she said. 'That is you thinking like a daughter, not a detective. Have I taught you nothing? Now, where is this sleeping draught that your mother has?'

'It's a remedy,' I said. 'My mother uses Chinese medicine, not Western. She's always been cross that my father sends us to a Western doctor. This tea was mixed specially for her. It helps her fall asleep when she's upset.'

My mother keeps her remedy hidden in one of her magic boxes. My father used to give them to her when they were first married, before I was old enough to be shown how to use them, and she still has them.

I stepped across the room, my feet soft on the carpeted floor, to my mother's glossy wooden chest of drawers. Each of its handles was two silver birds, their wings touching, soaring upwards. On the top three carved wooden boxes were arranged next to my mother's lacquered jewellery case. I picked up the smallest, and weighed it in my hand.

Opening magic boxes is a trick that I have used once before in our adventures. It's all about pressure, knowing where to twist and where the give will be. I love the puzzle of it, how contained each problem is. The rest of the world melts away as I work on one, and the moment when the lid clicks open gives me the same rush of excitement as I get when we solve one of our detective cases.

This box was quite easy, and in less than thirty seconds I had it open. Daisy peered over my shoulder at what was revealed inside it – plump, strong-smelling little twists of paper from my mother's favourite medicine shop.

'They smell like penny chews!' said Daisy, sniffing and then jerking back her head in surprise.

'That's the liquorice,' I said.

'Well, you'll have to make sure that Ping doesn't smell it before she can drink the tea,' said Daisy, drifting away. She wandered around the room to my mother's dressing table, breathing deeply to take in the smell of her scents – sweet flowers with a bitter after-note.

'Come on, Daisy,' I said, pocketing three of the little packets before clicking the puzzle box shut again and carefully putting it back in place. 'Let's get out before someone catches us.'

# 2

I had been afraid that our ruse wouldn't work, but in the end it was surprisingly easy. We asked Ping to bring us some tea after dinner, and while her back was turned I tipped the contents of the packets into the pot.

'Ping, I'm sorry, but we don't want this any more,' I said. 'You can have it if you like.'

Ping drank it down – and ten minutes later she was yawning and rubbing her eyes. 'I'm so tired, miss,' she said apologetically. 'Please excuse me.'

I had a stab of guilt at that. It didn't seem fair to trick someone so trusting. But it had to be done. I knew that. Ping staggered out of the room, and we were alone.

I went to the window and peered out. Dark had dropped, the sky was velvety and the lights of Hong Kong prickled across the mountain down to the bay. I could hear low voices as the house settled for the night, and soft pattering feet as the dogs, let out of their kennels at the back of the house, nosed about. Ah Lan would be in the garden, wheeling the cart towards us. All we had to do was meet him at the side door and slip under a dirty old sack in the cart – and then hope that the dogs didn't smell us.

I told myself what I knew: that the dogs weren't *so* fierce, that the real night watchers were the gardeners and house servants, and the men in their little huts near the gates.

But my heart was still thumping as I turned away from the window and nodded to Daisy.

I had changed into a dark tunic and trousers which were perfect for our adventure, and dressed Daisy in a matching set, tied tight with a bit of string. A dark scarf was wrapped around her head to hide her gold hair. She ought to have looked ridiculous, too thin and too tall, but of course she somehow managed to look utterly dashing, like May's pirate queen.

'You look marvellous,' said Daisy to me. 'Hazel, Hong Kong suits you.'

'That's not true! It's you who look marvellous!' I protested, blushing.

'Hazel, I look as though I've borrowed your clothes,' said Daisy. 'I do not belong here in the slightest, but you do. Here you are more . . . Oh, I don't know. More *Hazel*. But I must say, even though I do not belong, I *like* it here very much. And I like that we are about to go on one of our most exciting adventures to date. Creeping out of your house in the middle of the night to go to a robber meeting!'

'It isn't a—' I began, but stopped myself.

'Detective Society handshake before we begin?' asked Daisy.

We shook, smiling at each other, and then, hand in hand, we crept out of our bedroom and down the dark stairs.

Ah Lan was waiting for us, exactly as he had promised. Seeing him, I got an anxious fear in my stomach. We thought we could trust him – but were we right? What if he had lied about being Su Li's cousin, to lead us into danger? He had admitted to being part of Sai Yat's Triad gang. What if he was about to simply turn us over to them? What if they had taken Teddy, and Daisy and I were to be their next victims? A lord's daughter would be an excellent prize.

But I swallowed down my fears. I let Ah Lan tuck us into the cart, pushing a scratchy, smelly bag around us with his right arm and covering us up with clods of earth and rotting leaves. I breathed carefully and slowly, hearing Daisy breathing next to me, my eyes closed so that I could not see the rough weave of the bag in front of them.

The cart was lifted, and moved. Ah Lan groaned. 'You're heavy,' he whispered in English.

'We are exactly the right weight!' hissed Daisy.

The cart jolted over the gravel of the path, then over earth, bumping and bucking so much that I was afraid we would be shaken off. I was embarrassed to think it now, but I had not been sure how Ah Lan would manage lifting the cart with his short left arm, but I saw now that I need not have worried. He manoeuvred it with ease, tucking his left arm under the handle expertly and pushing it forward. I could smell greenery, and hear cicadas screaming in the trees. My hands were fists at my sides. I heard the noise of feet pattering towards us, and panting.

'Hello, Bark,' said Ah Lan. 'Good boy.'

Bark huffed, and I heard him snuffling around the cart. Then he sighed, and padded away. 'Stay still,' Ah Lan whispered to us. 'Gate coming up.'

The cart paused and dropped, and I heard Ah Lan walking away. There was a clank, a click, and then we were moving again.

'Night, Ah Lan,' called the guard on duty at the back gate – and then we were out of the compound. We had done it. We were free, in Hong Kong, at night – and we were going on a real adventure.

# 3

Down the little side road we went, the trees low above us, dangling vines in our path. Once Ah Lan ducked, and I said, 'What?'

'Spider,' said Ah Lan briefly in Cantonese, and I moved the sacking aside and squinted up to see a heavy round body and long thick legs, darker against the dark sky. It was so close that I could have reached up and touched its thick web. I shuddered. Spiders in England, as little and scuttling as flies, have never frightened me, for *this* is what a spider is in my mind – something teacup-large, a horrid weight on your hand or on your shoulder, shiny and brightly coloured in the daytime. Hong Kong spiders are worth being afraid of.

'What was it?' Daisy asked.

'Just a low branch,' I said reassuringly. 'Don't sit up for a while, all right?'

Then, in one of the strange jumps that Hong Kong is

full of, we jolted out of the jungle and turned left onto the main road. Suddenly we were among other carts, smooth black cars, rickshaws and street hawkers. The air was full of sound, and Daisy and I had to duck under our covering so as not to be seen.

Ah Lan wheeled us down the road, going west, the cart dodging and bouncing on the tarmac, and then sent us shooting down a side street. There was a plunge, and teeth-rattling jolts. Daisy let out a small shriek, and I bit my tongue. We were going down a ladder street – stone steps that cut down the hill between the long parallel streets of Hong Kong.

We spun, we bounced, Daisy yelped again, and then we were running along a flat main street in Western District. There were neon lights burning above our heads, from pawnshops and medicine shops and jewellery stores and laundries. I peeked out from under our covering and saw them spinning by like a rainbow above my head, flashy and gorgeous. I could smell hot, steamy cooking, see billows of smoke from street vendors' stalls, and in the tenement flats above the shops people leaned out, lit from below by the neon signs, smoking or talking or just staring down at the street.

I ducked back under cover, and when I peered out again we were in a darker side street, rushing past high warehouses, Ah Lan's steps echoing against their walls. I shivered, just a little. And then the cart stopped.

'Get out,' said Ah Lan. He said it in English, for Daisy. I sat up, and Daisy did too, and for a moment we stared at each other. The whites of her eyes were pale in the dark, but her hair was still hidden under its wrap.

'Where do we go?' I whispered to Ah Lan. We had come to a stop next to a high stone wall, with a tree cutting down the middle of it, its roots wriggling into the stones.

'Up,' said Ah Lan briefly, gesturing. 'Over the wall is the house we are going to. We need to get up high, and look through the window. I will show you. It's always kept a little open, and through it you can hear every-thing. All right?'

My heart sank, but Daisy said, 'Oh good! Climbing!'

'Why *is* it always climbing?' I said. 'Wherever we go!'

'Stop complaining, Hazel, or you'll have no breath left to climb,' said Daisy with a wink – and she seized hold of the lowest root and began to scamper up the wall, as balanced and sure-footed as a monkey.

'She's done this before,' said Ah Lan approvingly. 'Go on.'

I winced, for I knew that I was about to disappoint him very much. I put my hand on the same root Daisy had, its bark scratching my palm, and began to haul myself up. My heart pounded, and I tried not to look down. Daisy, perched high above me, whispered cheerful encouragement (mixed in with criticisms about my choice of branches that I could have done without).

Sweating, I finally pulled myself up beside her at the top of the wall, and looked down the dizzying perspective below us to see Ah Lan swinging himself towards us, kicking off with his legs, seizing branches with his right arm and using his left to steady himself.

'Honestly, Hazel, he's far better at it than you,' Daisy muttered in my ear. 'You must apply yourself if you want to get ahead!'

'Shush,' I said to her, as rudely as I dared. 'Or someone will hear.'

In another minute, Ah Lan was up beside us. The three of us teetered at the top of the wall (I breathed out, trying to calm my nerves, and stop the spinning in my head – I really am still not good with heights, despite all of Daisy's attempts to cure me), and Ah Lan pointed down below.

There was a courtyard leading to a tall warehouse that looked quite old and uninhabited. In fact, I was almost wondering whether Ah Lan had brought us to the wrong place when I saw two figures appearing from the shadows at the other side of the courtyard and walking silently up to the building's main door.

The first figure knocked, a pattern of five long and short raps. There was a pause. Then a bolt was drawn back. The three of us, listening, all heard it, and Daisy nudged me so hard that I almost fell off the wall.

'I was born poor,' said the first figure below us.

'But at least I still have the five fingers of my hand,' said the other.

There was another pause, and I could tell that someone inside was speaking.

'I died once,' said the first figure.

'Stabbed five times by a jade pin,' agreed the second.

I gasped. 'What is it?' hissed Daisy. 'What are they saying? Oh, this is infuriating!'

'They're talking about a jade pin,' I told her.

'It's just the password!' hissed Ah Lan. 'It doesn't mean anything! This is the House of Five Jade Figures.'

But, in the dark, in a place that I did not know, on a mission that (I was beginning to see) was not only more illegal but also more dangerous than any we had been on before, I was not so sure.

With a clank, the door below opened, and the two figures disappeared inside.

'Come on,' whispered Ah Lan. 'Nothing more to see here. We have to go to the window.'

He stood up in a half-crouch, and led us along the wall, and then up a gable and onto the building's roof. We stepped across tiles, using hands and feet to steady ourselves, and at last (it seemed like an eternity) came to a little skylight, a window that was slightly open. I peered down into it, and this is what I saw.

# 4

Below us was a room, bare-floored but hung with flags in red and black. On each side were dark stone tablets, and at the opposite end of the room to us was a large metal pot, half full of what looked like sand. Sticking out of it was a terrifying array of swords and warlike poles with yet more flags hanging from them. But I saw that joss sticks were in the sand too, smoking as though they had been recently lit, and there was a dark object behind the pot that looked very like an altar in a temple, but bare of fruits and flowers.

A group of people were gathering in the centre of the room. They were all men (I looked carefully), and they were all wearing red and black robes, with knotted handkerchiefs on their heads. It ought to have looked silly, but in fact it was rather menacing.

They were all talking in low voices, and I was somehow reminded of one of my father's drinks parties.

These men might look strange (especially to Daisy's eyes – I glanced at her and saw her open-mouthed in amazement), but all the same I thought that they behaved as though they were there to do business. Business with something dangerous and also sacred to it (I looked at the altar and the joss sticks), but business all the same.

Then one more man came into the room. He was short, and skinny, with a hungry-looking face – like a Hong Kong street boy grown up – but he drew everyone's eyes. He looked sure of himself, powerful. He stood beside the altar and raised his hands, and all the chatter fell silent. The men arranged themselves in two lines, to his left and his right, and bowed.

I knew that this was the leader, Sai Yat, and the meeting was about to begin.

'Greetings, Jade Figures,' said Sai Yat. Then he turned towards the altar and bowed solemnly. All the other men bowed again.

Then there was a ceremony. I won't say much about it (for politeness's sake, as well as safety's – it's not wise to get on the wrong side of the Triads). It was a little like one of the ceremonies at a temple, but more warlike and dangerous, and as though I was seeing it through thick glass, everything half ordinary and half strange. I knew that Daisy didn't understand it at all, and it made me feel terribly odd that *I* did. I was reminded, all over again, how different my life had been to hers before we arrived at Deepdean.

'And now to business,' said Sai Yat, clapping his hands. The men around him all stood up straighter and began to murmur among themselves.

'We are being watched,' said Sai Yat. I flinched. He was so fierce, I could almost believe that his eyes saw all the way up to the little skylight where the three of us crouched, looking in. 'Detective Leung is watching us.'

I breathed again.

'We all know what the detective wants: to find the Wong boy. He thinks we have him. He thinks we paid the lift man Shing to kill the maid and take the baby. Now, you are in a sacred space. You are under oath to speak truthfully. Do any of you have Edward Wong, or did you have anything to do with his kidnapping?'

'No,' said the man to his left.

'No,' said the man next to him – and on, down the row and back up again.

'No.'

'No.'

'No.'

Sai Yat nodded. 'Good,' he said. 'That is the truth. None of us here have Edward Wong, and we had nothing to do with his kidnapping. There was a pin found in the dead maid, but it was not one of our pins. It was a trick, to throw suspicion on us. Truthfully, I say that we are innocent of this crime. Miss Wong, is that good enough for you?'

I jumped. I almost fell through the skylight. Because Sai Yat had raised his head, and he was looking – I could not deny it – directly at me.

Ah Lan put his right hand on my arm. 'I have to take you downstairs now,' he said.

'What is it?' asked Daisy. 'What's happened? Why are they— Hazel, why are they all looking at us?'

'They know we're up here,' I whispered. 'Ah Lan told them. Daisy, they knew we were coming!'

'I thought it was too easy!' cried Daisy. 'That wall, and this window – I wondered why a criminal gang wouldn't guard it. Oh, bother it. We should never have trusted Ah Lan!'

My heart shrank and faltered in my chest. As Ah Lan guided us back down the way we had come, I wondered exactly what we had walked into, and how on earth we would get out of it again.

# 5

Ah Lan led us down and into the courtyard. We came through the door that we had heard being unbolted before. It clanked forbiddingly, and before us was another door, and another and another, all smelling of rusting metal, a little like blood.

And then the hall was in front of us, and we were facing two rows of expressions that made me quail. These men were fierce, warlike, criminal. This was the Hong Kong of maids' stories – the bogeymen who would come and eat us up if we were not good little girls. Well, Daisy and I had not been good little girls at all, and here were the bogeymen.

Sai Yat moved down the middle of the hall towards us, his slippered feet making no sound on the dirt floor. Tigers are sometimes still found in the New Territories, slinking from house to house in the villages and making away with chickens and dogs and babies. I thought they were made-up stories until one day I saw a picture in my father's *South China Morning Post*, of a group of moustached and turbaned policemen standing over the sleek striped body of a tiger that was as long as they were tall. I thought now that, if Sai Yat had been that tiger, he would never have allowed himself to be caught. He was more muscular than anyone I had ever seen, every inch of him purposeful. He was almost as short as I was, but the look on his face told me that he was used to being obeyed absolutely.

'Good evening, Miss Wong,' said Sai Yat, and he bowed his head very slightly.

I bowed as deeply as I could, almost down to the floor. This was a moment to forget that I was Mr Wong's eldest daughter, with a maid and a chauffeur of my own.

'Bow, Daisy,' I said out of the corner of my mouth.

'But I—' she began.

'BOW,' I said, as firm as I have ever been with her. And Daisy bowed.

She did it awkwardly, but she did it, tipping over almost as low as I had, her hair glinting gold in the light from the hall's torches as it slipped out of her headscarf.

'Hazel,' said Daisy, her nose still nearly touching her knees, 'are they going to kill us?'

'I don't know,' I said, trying to keep my face calm.

'We are not going to kill either of you,' said Sai Yat, also in English. 'Don't look so surprised. English isn't a sacred language. I did not ask Ah Lan to bring you here so we could kill you or kidnap you. I asked him to bring you here because I have heard of you, Miss Wong. I have heard the stories about what you have done in England.'

For a moment I couldn't imagine what he meant. Stories? But then—

'You keep coming across dead bodies, and then somehow the crime is solved,' said Sai Yat. 'The maids all talk about you at the Big House. Ah Lan and Ng told me so. Your father thinks you have bad luck, but I think you have a talent.'

My head jerked up. I couldn't stop staring at him. I couldn't quite feel the tips of my fingers either. My tongue tingled.

'*Excuse* me!' said Daisy. '*We* have talent. *We* are detectives. Hazel and I have solved five murder cases, but we have done it together, so don't you go about saying it's all Hazel!'

The hall went very silent. I heard a fly buzz into one of the lamps and fizz out into soot.

Sai Yat smiled. 'Miss Wong's friend,' he said. 'You are her *sidekick* – is that the word?'

'I am not—' Daisy spluttered.

Sai Yat held up his hand, and Daisy shut up her mouth like a fish.

'So, here is what you must do for me, in exchange for not killing you, or kidnapping you, or any of the things that I *could* do – because, as you see, I am a dangerous criminal, and the head of a very large gang, and you are two little girls who are away from home in the middle of the night. I need you to hear me say that my men and I had nothing to do with the kidnapping of your little brother, or the murder of his maid. We do many things, but we did not do this. We have no reason to – we make our money in other ways. When I speak in this sacred hall, I speak the truth, so you must believe me. And you know the truth of the pin, don't you, Miss Wong? It is not ours. It is yours. Ah Lan has told me that also.'

I swallowed. My mouth had gone very dry.

'I need you to hear me say that I am gravely offended that the real culprit used the jade pin symbol in their crime. They have demeaned us, and I think you too. We must work together to make them pay.'

'How?' I asked, swallowing again with difficulty.

'First, you must admit that the pin is yours.'

'But what if my father blames me?' I whispered.

'Partly I would say that it is none of my concern,' said Sai Yat. 'Because it is not. But partly I would say that you are more than able to handle this problem. Fight back with the truth. You know as well as I do that this is not an ordinary kidnapping. It is only pretending to be. It was done not by one of us, but by one of the people your father knows and trusts. You have suspects, do you not?'

'Yes,' I said. 'Mr Wa Fan, Mrs Fu and Mr Svensson. We don't think Wu Shing was working on his own. We think one of them paid him to take Teddy.'

'Very good,' said Sai Yat. 'You are the detective. You will discover who has your brother. I will help you – my men are already looking for Wu Shing, and I will have them watch those three too. Ah Lan will give you any information we uncover, and you will use it to unmask the culprit. Yes?'

It was hardly a question.

'Yes,' I said.

'Yes,' said Daisy, after I nudged her hard in the ribs. I could tell she was sulking because Sai Yat was speaking directly to me. She was in the room, but not the centre of attention, and that, for the Honourable Daisy Wells, was very strange indeed.

'Excellent!' said Sai Yat. 'As a result, I will not kill you.' He winked at us, but I had a wobbly feeling that perhaps the joke was not quite as funny as he was making it seem.

'Good luck, Miss Wong,' he said to me, inclining his head just a little. I bowed back. 'And good luck, Miss Wells,' he said, and he reached out and patted Daisy on the head. She jerked back, affronted.

'Gold hair,' said Sai Yat, grinning. 'It's lucky here. Hasn't anyone told you?'

'There are plenty of things I was not told about Hong Kong,' said Daisy, narrowing her eyes at me. 'But I suppose being lucky is one of the better ones.'

The doors at the back of the hall banged open, and a man came hurrying in.

'Sai Yat,' he said, bowing deeply. 'We have found Wu Shing!'

'Yes? Bring him here!' snapped Sai Yat.

'He is in Peking Mansions, in Wan Chai,' said the man. 'He took Room 440 there for a week. He has been boasting to anyone who will listen that he is coming into a fortune and will not need to be there for long. He told them that he has a rich benefactor who will be very generous with money and jewels. We have men who can pick him up now.'

'No,' said Sai Yat. 'Tell them to stay where they are for the moment. Let these three go.' And he nodded at Daisy, Ah Lan and me.

'Where are we going?' asked Daisy. 'Is it another adventure?'

'Peking Mansions,' I said. 'It's where Wu Shing has a room – 440.'

'Mansions?' said Daisy. 'Are lift operators rich here?'

'They aren't the English sort of mansions,' I said, gulping rather. How could I explain to Daisy the difference between what was in her head and the reality?

Peking Mansions is a place I had never been. It is where you go when you don't have the money to go anywhere else – a place that I had been told was dirty, and dark, and full of illness and sorrow. I did not want to go there at all. But I looked at Sai Yat, and I knew that we could not say no to him. He had asked us to work for him, and we had to do what he said.

I bowed my agreement, and Sai Yat nodded at me sternly. Ah Lan touched us both on the shoulder. We turned and followed him back out of the hall. Just as we were about to step through the doors, I looked back once more and saw Sai Yat standing in the middle of his hall. He was watching us, head thrown back and arms crossed. I could feel his confidence like a hand on my back, and I knew very clearly that this was a man whom we must not fail.

We had ruled out a very important suspect, and were on the way to speak to another. And the crime seemed one hundred times more dangerous than it had before.

# 6

We piled back onto the cart, and off we went again. We
rattled through the streets – darker now, lights dimmed,
shouts in the distance. I felt very wide awake, and also
rather like I was dreaming. I did not know what time it
was – I had left my wristwatch at home – but I knew we
were travelling for a long time. From Western, Wan
Chai is a long way to go in a cart.

Ah Lan shoved us along, but I was worried that he
was tiring.

'Let us push,' I said at last, sitting up.

'No,' said Ah Lan. 'Your hands – you'll hurt them,
and people will notice. But you can get out and run
next to me, *if* you can keep up.'

I heard the hint of a mocking smile in his voice
again, and felt myself blush.

'Of course we can keep up!' said Daisy scornfully.
'I'm faster than you are – or have you already forgotten?'

We climbed out of the cart (I wobbled, and Daisy had to catch me) and then we were standing on the tarmacked street. Ah Lan took off lightly, the cart bouncing in front of him, and Daisy bounded after him. Wishing most desperately that detecting didn't have to be so athletic, I followed. I was terrified that I would run into something hard, and even more afraid I would run into something soft.

At last Ah Lan slowed in a dirty, rubbish-filled street, in front of an ugly building that rose up before us hugely, speckled with lighted windows and humming with activity. Heat and noise seemed to pour out from it like steam from a pot. I saw Daisy, half in shadow, wrinkle her nose, and heard her say, 'Ugh! Gosh!'

'Peking Mansions,' said Ah Lan, bowing ironically. 'Let me hide the cart, and we will go in.' I saw him nod his head to someone beyond us, and turned to see a man in dark clothes slipping into the shadows on the other side of the street. Sai Yat's men were here, on guard, and that meant Wu Shing must be inside.

My heart sped up at the thought of going in – and not just because we were about to face a suspect. I could smell the building already, thick and heavy with a urine-sharp edge. But I took a deep and careful breath, and held out my hand to Daisy, who had gone rather pale. 'Detective Society handshake!' I whispered. 'Buck up!'

'You don't need to tell me that!' hissed Daisy. 'I am always perfectly bucked!'

But as she shook my hand she smiled at me properly for the first time since we had entered Sai Yat's hall.

'Thank you, Watson,' she whispered, very quietly.

Following Ah Lan, we stepped inside Peking Mansions and climbed the stairs, which were dirty and echoing. We passed people lying slumped across them – I was afraid they were dead, and clutched at Daisy's arm, but she whispered, 'Don't be a chump, Hazel, they're just tired. Look, they're breathing.'

Wu Shing's room was 440. The number four, unlucky in Hong Kong, gave me a nervous prickling feeling, but I could not explain that to Daisy. When we reached it, we found the room's door hanging slightly ajar. Inside it was dark.

My heart began to pound. What if Teddy was here? What if this was the end of our adventure?

'Torches,' said Daisy. I pulled my torch out of my pocket, and she took out hers. Ah Lan looked at us, and raised his eyebrows.

'You came prepared,' he said. 'Good.'

Together we went forward, and pushed open the door.

Inside, our torches played about on what seemed to be an empty room. It was square, windowless, with a pile of dirty blankets in one corner. It smelled – of dirt and pennies and something sweet. There was a basin half full of dark water, and on the floor . . . was blood.

I walked forward with trembling legs and a hand that shook rather, so that my torchlight bobbed like a living thing on rusty specks and smears that looked days old. I had a terrified moment in case we found— I do not even want to write it. But we quickly saw that there were no signs of a baby in the room, and no sign that one had ever been here. And this couldn't be where the ransom call had been made from, either. There was no telephone, and I had seen none in the hallway. Teddy was not here, and I did not think he ever had been.

Then Daisy exclaimed. She and Ah Lan had started forward towards the blankets, and I saw suddenly that the specks of blood led to them. I clutched my fingers around my torch.

Daisy bent down over the blankets and twitched them aside. And, just like that, the pieces of the case flew up into the air and came back down in a different pattern.

# 7

There was a body lying under the blankets. It was wearing a plain jacket and trousers, and a red uniform with gold trim and a small, smart cap was folded and shoved next to it. I knew, although I had only seen him once in person and once in a picture, that this was Wu Shing.

He was crumpled in a heap, just like Su Li had been, and he looked so undignified that I had a moment of feeling sorry for him, until I noticed his hands. They were scratched and cut, and I remembered the scratches on Su Li's hands. It seemed certain that her murderer had been Wu Shing.

I could not see what had killed him, for he had no marks on his front – until Daisy nudged the body with her foot, and it rolled over. Then we saw the dark mark on his back, and the blood streaming down his jacket. Wu Shing had been shot, and the wound told us it had happened while he was facing away from his attacker.

This was a horrid place, where horrid things clearly happened, but all the same, the coincidence was too great. Someone had murdered him, and it seemed logical to assume that it was the person he had been boasting about, his rich benefactor. Someone had paid him to kill Su Li and take Teddy, and if Teddy wasn't here, it seemed likely that he was with that person now.

The thing that still shocks me, after all our cases, is how easy murder is when you get down to it. People are so unbearably breakable. It's nice to be able to believe, as I used to, in good people and bad. But now I have seen for myself over and over again how small the step is, how you only have to put out one hand at the wrong moment, how all your plans and all your good intentions can vanish in a breath.

Although, I reminded myself, *this* person's intentions had not been good at all, even before they killed Wu Shing. They had planned Teddy's kidnap – and Su Li's murder.

'Cover him up, Daisy,' I said, hand over my mouth.

I had a sudden odd feeling, as though I was hovering high over my own right shoulder, looking down on myself, watching Daisy and Ah Lan look at Wu Shing. The smells in the room – of blood and a strange, soft sweetness that reminded me ridiculously of garden parties – had got into my nose and made me dizzy.

'Sai Yat was right. We really do have a talent for finding dead bodies,' said Daisy cheerfully to Ah Lan. 'Here, help me examine him. He may have a useful clue on him.'

'He's been dead for more than a day,' said Ah Lan. 'See, he's going . . . floppy. That happens about a day after someone dies here.'

'Ugh!' I said, horrified.

'But he didn't die as soon as he got back from the bank,' said Daisy. 'We know that because he had time to change out of his uniform. So he came back here, changed and then died . . . some time later?'

'Look!' said Ah Lan suddenly. 'Here!' He held something up that he had taken out of Wu Shing's hand. It was a torn bit of paper – a piece of a Hong Kong banknote. 'Someone's gone through his pockets too. Some of the stitches have been torn out.'

'I think I see what happened!' Daisy exclaimed. 'Wu Shing killed Su Li, took Teddy and gave him to his employer. That person went off and made the ransom call. A few hours later, they came back to meet Wu Shing here because . . . Oh, because they'd heard he'd been talking about being paid, and wanted to shut him up. Perhaps they pretended to offer him more money? Anyway, they waited until his back was turned, then shot him, took the money back, shoved him under the blankets and left. Does that make sense?'

'It does,' I said, nodding. 'It's – it's awful, Daisy. He

was a terrible person, if he was willing to kill someone he used to love, but still, no one deserves this.'

Daisy wasn't listening to me. She was pulling back another corner of the blanket, exclaiming in excitement. 'Look here! Another clue! More paper, is it? I can't read it!'

I shone my torch at her. She was holding thin strips of paper covered in Chinese characters and numbers.

'Hey, I know what those are!' said Ah Lan. 'Betting cards. And those races – they're from Happy Valley racecourse. So Wu Shing was a gambler! Maybe that's another reason why he took this job, to pay for his habit. I can have Sai Yat's men look into this.'

'Yes,' I said, nodding. 'And we need to know exactly what Wu Shing did on Monday afternoon. *When* did he come back here?'

'Very true, Watson,' said Daisy. 'And now I think we should go home before we're discovered.'

I took a deep breath in – which was a mistake: I coughed and shuddered at my coughing – and gritted my teeth. We had ruled out both Sai Yat and (because of his death) Wu Shing. We suspected that Teddy was now being held by someone else, the person who was trying to frame me. Who was it? Mr Svensson? Mrs Fu? Mr Wa Fan?

We were getting closer. But I knew that the case was more dangerous than ever. As part of our bargain, I had to confess the truth about the jade pin to my father.

# 8

Our cart wheeled out again into Hong Kong night-time streets that were cooler and quite dark, the laughter and shouts of earlier faded and all the lights flickered out.

We ran up passages and along streets, and Daisy, next to me, kept up an urgent monologue in my ear.

'We found another *body*, Hazel! How exciting! And – golly. We're working with *criminals*!'

'She does know that I can hear her?' Ah Lan said to me in Cantonese, shoving the cart up a set of steps in ten heavy jolts.

'Of course,' I said, panting along beside him. 'Daisy,' I said in English. 'Don't be silly. You know we have to trust Sai Yat. He promised in the hall, and that place is holy to him.'

'That reminds me!' said Daisy. 'Why are *you* the famous one here, Hazel? That's hardly fair. I'm the President of the Detective Society, and I am the one who invented it. It ought to be me who's talked about.'

'It's my father's servants doing the talking,' I reminded her. 'They'd hardly be talking about you.'

'Well, they *should*!' cried Daisy, furious. 'It's – it's – oh, Hazel, everything is upside down in Hong Kong! I don't entirely like it.'

'Nearly home,' said Ah Lan at last, in English. 'Just up the hill. Be very quiet – you'll need to get back into the cart in a moment.'

We were in the jungle again, rolling through the heavy leaves on the path. The cart pushed aside branches, sending wafts of green, juicy scent into the air. Under the canopy it was still dark, but I could begin to make out the ghostly edges of the trees. In this grey half-world, anything could be a person waiting to jump out at us. And what if our absence had been discovered? What if there was already a search underway? My breath caught.

Daisy and I climbed back into the cart and I saw the gate ahead of us. The same guard was still in his hut, his turbaned head nodding, his hand barely on his knife. When he saw Ah Lan wheeling the cart towards him, he blinked and stood upright.

'Morning,' he said. 'You're early.'

'Work to do,' said Ah Lan, nodding vaguely. I was impressed – he seemed quite calm and ordinary. Only his right hand, clutching the handle of the cart so tightly its knuckles were white, gave him away.

But the guard didn't look at Ah Lan's knuckles. He simply nodded him through, and went back to staring blankly out into the jungle.

Ah Lan pushed the cart more and more slowly as we moved further into the garden. At last it rattled to a stop next to the fish pond, its Monkey King statue coming into focus as the light around us grew.

'Get out here,' said Ah Lan. 'You can go the rest of the way on your own. If anyone sees you, lie. Say that you went out for a walk before breakfast.'

'All right,' I said. 'Thank you for your help.'

Ah Lan shrugged, and wiped his hair back off his sweating forehead. He was tired and dirty, and he looked at me as though I was both of those things too.

'I'm glad you're on the case,' he said. 'I'm sorry I had to lie to get you to the meeting. You really are fearless.'

'Daisy's fearless,' I said automatically. 'Not me.'

'Oh?' said Ah Lan, raising an eyebrow. 'If you say so. When I have information, I'll put on my hat and stand by the fish pond. If you want to update me, sit by the pond and I'll come by. All right?'

I nodded. I turned away, towards the white wedding-cake shape of our Big House. Its windows were empty and closed. It was still asleep. We had succeeded.

Except that on the first floor a curtain in my mother's room twitched, once, and fell still. It was so quick, I might have imagined it. But I didn't think I had.

# 9

We crept back into the house. The side door was still slightly open, just as we had left it. The funny thing about security in the Big House is that there really isn't any, not in an English way. The wide front doors are kept folded back at night to let the breeze through, because there are dogs and servants ready to attack any intruder before they ever reach them.

My nerves were jangling and my head felt thin, stretched out by lack of sleep.

Up the stairs we crept, into our hallway, and I began to breathe more steadily again.

I thought about what Ah Lan had said at the pond, that I was fearless, and a feeling flowed through me that was both shameful and strangely warming. In England I was always in Daisy's shadow. But here *I* was the famous one. Sai Yat had heard of me. Not simply us, the Detective Society, but *me*. I knew that I could not be a detective without Daisy – we worked together, always, and that was our strength. But I felt proud, and very strange, to know that my name was known, not just as Daisy's friend, but as myself.

Into our bedroom we went. And there was someone already in it.

For one horrid moment I thought it was my mother. But it was Ping. When we came in, she let out a little gasp and a shriek. 'Miss Hazel! Miss Daisy! Where have you been?' she cried. 'I woke up an hour ago and felt – I can't explain it. I knew I had to see how you were, but you were *gone*! And now you're so dirty!'

I looked down at my clothes, and saw that they were sooty, my hands filthy with dust and grime. Daisy's face was dirty too, her headscarf disarranged and her gold hair almost brown.

I swallowed. 'We were . . . out,' I said. 'Ping, listen to me.'

'Tell her we shall torture her if she rats on us!' cried Daisy.

'No we *won't*!' I said, nudging her. 'Shh!'

'Miss!' said Ping. 'It isn't – it isn't to do with Teddy? You haven't . . . done something silly?'

'No!' I said, horrified by her worried expression. 'I promise, truly, I didn't have anything to do with him being taken. That's why we *had* to go out. You see, Daisy and I are trying to find out where he is, to prove that the pin was just a mistake. You helped me once before. Please, help me again. Don't tell anyone about this.'

Ping paused. 'All right, miss,' she said at last. 'Only – you aren't doing anything dangerous, are you?'

I thought about Wu Shing's body, about the Triad meeting, about running through the streets of Hong Kong at night.

'No,' I said.

'Thank you, miss,' said Ping. 'That's important.'

She took my hand in her warm little callused one and smiled at me, and with a jump I realized that Ping and I had become – not exactly what Su Li and I had been, but still somehow – allies.

'Now, come and clean yourselves up,' she said, 'or your parents will be furious.'

Ping filled the wooden tub in our bathroom, and we washed until we were pink and clean and the water was an alarming brown colour. Just like that, the adventure was cleaned off us. Only our memories of it remained.

'Thank you, Ping,' I said, once we had dressed again. 'You can go back to your room. Daisy and I need to talk.'

# 10

Ping bowed, and backed out of the room. I turned to see Daisy regarding me. 'You are getting quite queenly, Hazel Wong,' she said. 'I don't need to understand what you said to know how you said it. I'm impressed.'

I blushed, feeling very un-queen-like. 'I like Ping, but she can't be here for a proper Detective Society meeting!' I said.

'You are quite right,' said Daisy. 'I was just about to suggest the same thing myself. Get out your casebook, and let's sit down. Now – all right – there have been *many* exciting new developments in the case! First, our suspect Sai Yat has ruled himself out. Hazel, are you really sure we can trust what he said?'

I nodded. 'Yes. He swore an oath, and so did the rest of the gang. And, when we found Wu Shing's body, I saw that Ah Lan was as surprised as we were. Surely he'd have known if his gang had been behind it? Sai

Yat was sure that the pin was a blind, and I agree with him.'

'Our hypothesis that this crime is personal is looking more and more likely,' agreed Daisy. 'The person who's behind it hates your father, and hates *you*. And we also now know for certain that, although Wu Shing was the murderer, he did not plan and carry out the crime on his own. He was talking about someone hiring him, and we know that he needed money to pay for his gambling habit. His room was dreadful! He clearly needed funds. And since he couldn't have shot *himself* in the back, his death, and the piece of banknote we found in his hand, prove that he was paid off and then silenced!'

'It's so horrid!' I said. 'I do almost feel sorry for him, Daisy. He was tricked!'

'Don't be a chump. He's a dreadful man who killed Su Li!' cried Daisy. 'But yes, the way he was murdered is quite foul. At close range, and from *behind*. It's got a sort of mean, creeping feeling to it. As though – well, as though the murderer was an old man, or a woman, or a businessman who isn't used to killing people. Not a gang member at all.'

I shuddered. 'Wu Shing's death changes things,' I said. 'It shows how ruthless the person behind all this is. From what Ah Lan said we know that he's been dead since Monday. His clothes told us that he came back to

Peking Mansions and changed before he was killed. But, since the room didn't have a telephone and I didn't see a telephone in the hallway, he couldn't have made the ransom call from there. And since there weren't any baby things lying about, nappies or bottles, I don't think Teddy was ever taken there.'

'Yes. All the signs point to the fact that there *is* a co-conspirator, and that this person has Teddy somewhere else,' said Daisy, nodding. 'The place they made the call from, most likely.'

'We still don't know exactly when Teddy was handed over to that person – but I think, from what we have discovered tonight, that we can make an educated guess. It either happened just after the crime, at the bank itself, or very soon after that, in the early afternoon. So – the person who has Teddy and planned this crime must have been out at that time for long enough to take Teddy and kill Wu Shing.'

I turned back to our suspect list. I had already crossed out Sai Yat's and Wu Shing's names. Now I saw something else. If Wu Shing had been killed in Peking Mansions on Monday afternoon, my mother couldn't have done it. She hadn't left the house that day, for my father had forbidden it. I breathed out a sigh that I didn't know I had been holding in.

'It can't be Mother!' I said. 'Think, Daisy!'

Daisy wrinkled her nose, and then her brow cleared. 'Correct,' she said. 'What a relief, Hazel. I admit I didn't like the idea of your mother being a murderer.'

I crossed out her name, pressing hard into the paper with my pencil. I felt ten times lighter.

We had three suspects left. Mrs Fu, Mr Wa Fan and Mr Svensson.

'We ought to make notes on their movements on Monday!' I said. 'It might help. Everything rests on who was on the eighth floor at the right time, doesn't it?'

'Hmm,' said Daisy. 'Yes. Mrs Fu first – we saw her beside Wu Shing's lift at eleven fifty-five, and then again in the main bank hall at ten past twelve. We don't know where she went after that. Mr Wa Fan – we only know from Wo On that he came out of the building at about twelve fifteen. And Mr Svensson – he was in the main bank hall at ten past twelve, and then we saw him leaving the building at twenty past. All of them are highly suspicious!'

I nodded, and scribbled all that down. Then I thought again about the ransom call and I had another idea.

'Remember what my father said about the ransom call?' I asked. 'He heard—'

'Rattling!' said Daisy. 'Yes?'

'So what rattles?' I asked her.

Daisy shrugged elegantly. 'Pipes?' she asked. 'They rattle. Or – cars rattle when they start, but then your father would have called it a car noise. The bother is that we don't know what he meant. But we *can* be alert for any suspicious rattling noises in the places our suspects frequent.'

'Exactly!' I said. 'I know something that rattles – dishes, and chopsticks against plates! What if *Mrs Fu* has Teddy, and she's keeping him in her teahouse?'

'HAZEL!' cried Daisy, sitting upright on the bed with a bounce. 'That's very clever! And I think I have just had another of my brilliant ideas. I know how we can tell your father, investigate Mrs Fu's tcahouse, and go back to the scene of the crime.'

'How?' I asked.

'Well,' said Daisy. 'What was that thing you were telling me about – that food that sounds like ... addition?'

'*Dim sum?*' I asked, stifling a giggle.

'Yes,' said Daisy. 'That's the sort of thing that Mrs Fu's restaurant makes, isn't it? Now, what if you asked your father to take us there as a special treat? You can use that time to tell him about the pin. He can't be *too* angry at you when there are other people about. And what if I ate something there that disagreed with me, making everyone hurry to my side? You'd have time to look about to see if there are any babies stashed away at the teahouse, and then we'd quite probably have to rush me to Dr Aurelius's.'

It was a typical Daisy plan – quite mad, and utterly daring. But, I thought, it was far better than anything I had yet come up with.

'All right,' I said after a moment. 'Let's try it.'

'Excellent!' said Daisy. 'And now you can do some secretarying and write all this out while we rest before breakfast time.'

## SUSPECT LIST

1. The lift operator (find out his name!) Wu Shing. ~~The simplest explanation is that he committed the crime. But why? We think he and Su Li knew each other, and she was afraid of him, but we must find evidence to back this up. So was this his motive, and he kidnapped Teddy almost as an afterthought, or was he simply interested in making money by kidnapping Teddy, and Su Li got in the way? Was he working on his own, or did he carry out the crime for someone else? (The pin makes it very likely that he was working with another criminal.) If so, who hired him, and why?~~ NOTES: We know from the photograph that he knew Su Li! He was her ex-boyfriend. So was he paid to kill her, or did he kill her because he didn't like her? RULED OUT.

Although he may have agreed to kill Su Li because they were once in a relationship, he did not plan the crime on his own — he talked about this to his neighbours in Peking Mansions. He has now become the second victim! Someone killed him in the room he rented on the day of the kidnapping, after he had arrived back and changed out of his uniform. They gave him money, and then took it back off his body. We do not believe Teddy was ever at Peking Mansions — Wu Shing must have handed him over to the person who hired him after Su Li's murder.

2. *Sai Yat's Triad gang.* ~~MOTIVE TO KIDNAP TEDDY~~y: ~~Money, plain and simple! The pin stabbed into Su Li's throat is the calling card of a Triad gang (we heard someone say this, and Hazel confirms it) — but it is odd that they chose to use Hazel's pin. Were they trying to frame her? Was it just a mistake? NOTES: We heard from Pik An that she believes some of the servants are indeed Triad. Could this be Ng? But he says that Sai Yat had nothing to do with this — is that just a blind?~~ *RULED OUT.* We have Sai Yat's word that he did not take Teddy or kill Su Li. He swore it in a sacred place, so we believe him.

Also, Wu Shing's murder was carried out in a way that does not fit with Sai Yat's gang method.

3. *Mr Svensson.* MOTIVE TO KIDNAP TEDDY: He needs money, and Mr Wong will not give him any. He is also angry with Mr Wong — might this give him a motive to frame Hazel for the crime? NOTES: He was seen at the bank at the time of the crime in a strange mood, and there are ten minutes where his movements cannot be accounted for. He was also at the party the night before, so could have picked up Hazel's pin and given it to the lift operator! He knew that Teddy was due to be at the doctor's the next day, because he heard Mr Wong mention this. Ng confirms that Mr Svensson is in need of money! He has offered to help pay Teddy's ransom, but we have heard from Mrs Svensson that he is in fact having money troubles and cannot afford to pay. Is his offer a ruse — and does his lack of money give him a motive? He is the least likely to have killed Wu Shing, as he is big and strong, and would not have had to worry about Wu Shing overpowering him. TIMINGS: He left the

bank at 12:10 but did not leave the building until
12:20. Highly suspicious!

4. **Mrs Fu. MOTIVE TO KIDNAP**
   TEDDY: She also seems to need money — and she
   was talking angrily with Mr Wong at the party.
   NOTES: She was seen at the bank at the time of
   the crime by Hazel Wong and Daisy Wells, so could
   have given the pin to the lift operator. She was also at
   the party the night before, so could have picked up
   Hazel's pin and overheard about Teddy's
   appointment! We have found a letter from her to
   Mr Wong asking him for money to save her
   teahouse! Daisy and Hazel overheard her saying
   that she was about to come into money — could this be
   Teddy's ransom payment? And could her restaurant
   be the source of the rattling sound Mr Wong heard?
   Wu Shing was shot in the back — this method fits
   someone who is weaker than he was, like Mrs Fu.
   TIMINGS: She was by the lifts at 11:55, and
   then in the bank at 12:10.

5. **Mr Wa Fan. MOTIVE TO KIDNAP**
   TEDDY: He is angry with Mr Wong because he

thinks he is not being dutiful. But is this a good motive for kidnap? He was at the party, so could have taken the pin and heard about the appointment. ~~But he was not seen at the bank, and we do not know if he is a patient of Dr Aurelius.~~

NOTES: Wo On the chauffeur says that he saw Mr Wa Fan leaving the bank with a bottle of medicine just before the murder was discovered. He was on the scene, and in a hurry! He has paid the detective, Mr Leung, to help find Teddy. But is this a kind gesture — or a controlling one? Wu Shing was shot in the back — this method fits someone who is weaker than he was, like Mr Wa Fan.

TIMINGS: He left the bank building at approximately 12:15.

6. *June Wong.* ~~MOTIVE TO HAVE TEDDY KIDNAPPED: She does not like him, because he is the son of her husband's other wife. But, if she had arranged to have him taken, she must know that when he was recovered he would be more adored than ever. Hazel remembers her being friendly with Su Li — why would she arrange to have her killed?~~

NOTES: She was not at the bank on the day of the crime — she had a headache. And the pin implicates Hazel, her own daughter — why would she arrange a crime that did such a thing? Her bound feet would slow her down, though they do not rule her out. RULED OUT. She did not leave the house during the afternoon after Teddy's kidnapping — she could not have killed Wu Shing, or taken Teddy from him.

## PLAN OF ACTION

1. Eliminate Wo On and Ping from our list of suspects.

2. Find out more about the lift operator Wu Shing — who was he, and why did he become a murderer and a kidnapper? Was he paid to do it, or was it a personal motive?

3. Find out more about the Triad gang who use pins as their calling cards.

4. Look into all the motives of our suspects further.

5.  Find out more about Dr Aurelius's office to understand how the crime was not discovered, and how Teddy was taken out of the building.

6.  ~~Find a way to investigate Sai Yat.~~

7.  ~~Begin to rule out suspects.~~ Continue to rule out suspects — discover where they were during Monday afternoon.

8.  Consider where Teddy may be hidden at the moment. Visit Mrs Fu's teahouse and see if it is the source of the rattling sound.

9.  Tell Mr Wong about Hazel's pin.

# PART FIVE

# DEATH COMES HOME

# 1

Our plan was made – now I was the one who needed to set it all in motion. At breakfast I steeled myself and turned to my father.

'What, Hazel?' he asked, looking up from his *daau jeung* and pushing his glasses up his nose in a rather threatening way.

'I wanted to ask you something,' I said, failing to suppress a gulp of nervousness.

'What?' asked my father shortly. 'Today is busy, Hazel. It is the last day before—'

He did not need to say, *before the ransom.*

'I – I was wondering if you would take me and Daisy for *yum cha*,' I said, and I felt a blush spread across my face. I was worried I sounded false, and even more worried that I sounded eager.

'I want to go too!' shouted May. Rose pinched her.

'No, Hazel,' said my mother. 'You shouldn't leave the house.'

I jumped. Was this a coded way of saying that she had seen us coming home?

'Hazel, I do not have time for this,' said my father. 'Go with Ping, if you must.'

I opened my mouth to agree, to apologize for not thinking. But somehow what came out was, '*I'm* not the one who's been kidnapped.'

'Do not joke about this,' said my father, so quietly it was almost a whisper.

'I mean—' I was stumbling over the words. 'Teddy is gone, but I'm still here, and so are Rose and May. You have four children, not one.'

I thought my father was about to hit me. He raised his hands – and then he covered his face with them. Next to me Daisy's eyes were wide. My mother sat frozen.

'Take them, Vincent,' said Jie Jie suddenly. 'Nothing will happen. I'll be here; Maxwell will be here. Hazel is right.'

'You should go, sir,' said Maxwell in his starchy voice, from where he was standing at the edge of the room.

My father took off his glasses and polished the lenses.

'Eleven o'clock,' he said, without quite looking at me. 'Maxwell, tell Wo to bring the car round.'

May cheered.

As I got up from the table and went out into the corridor, my mother followed me, putting her soft hand with its painted nails on my arm and pulling me away from Daisy. I turned to her nervously, and I saw that she was wearing her shining gold ring again. I breathed out. She *had* simply not put it on the day before. Daisy had been wrong, and my mother was ruled out even more clearly.

'Ying Ying,' she said in a low voice. 'I saw you last night. And I know about your pin. I know where it was found. Whatever you are doing, you must stop it. You don't understand what might happen if you don't. But, if you keep quiet, it will go away. I swear it. Do you hear me? I . . . You are my daughter, do you understand?'

I wanted to tell her that she had misunderstood, but something in her eyes alarmed me. She looked not just angry, but frightened. 'Yes, Ah Mah,' I whispered.

I realized that my mother had put the pin together with what she had seen this morning and come to the wrong conclusion. But did that mean she thought that I *was* the person who had planned Teddy's kidnap? And, if so, was this her way of saying that she would try to protect me?

# 2

Daisy and I made our way out into the gardens. The sun was low still, the air chilly, but the trees buzzed and clicked with morning insects.

We sat at the edge of the pond. Its stone lip was cold through the cotton of my trousers, and I shivered a little and shifted closer to Daisy. She was bending over the surface of the pond, dangling her fingers above the red and yellow and black koi who drifted, making the water flick and clop as they shoved against each other with their heavy bodies.

We knew that Ah Lan would be watching and, sure enough in another minute he appeared on the other side of the pond, around the side of the Monkey King statue, a basket tucked under his short left arm, and began to toss handfuls of pellets into the water. It churned silver as the koi leaped up, mouths open, to eat. Ah Lan was wearing his conical hat up on his head, which put his face in shadow.

'I wonder,' said Daisy idly, 'whether that food tastes as nice to them as cake tastes to us?'

'I used to give them cake sometimes,' I admitted. 'I think they prefer it. Only it was Chinese cake, not English. I don't know if they'd like chocolate.'

As Ah Lan came closer, throwing pellets in regular, long arcs with his right hand, I raised my voice.

'We're going to Mrs Fu's teahouse this morning,' I said, carefully keeping my eyes on Daisy. 'We think it's possible she might have Teddy there with her. Then we're going to try to go back to the doctor's office. We need to look at the scene of the crime. I wonder if there's any news on our three suspects?'

'I have heard something,' said Ah Lan, nodding under his hat at the fish. 'Mrs Fu withdrew all the remaining money in her bank account just after twelve on Monday. Mr Svensson arrived at the bank at twelve, and did not return to his car until twenty-five past. His chauffeur said that, when he did, he seemed alarmed and upset. He went home, but went out again that afternoon, and was not back until almost six. And Mr Wa Fan paid *his* chauffeur to tell everyone he spoke to that they had visited the temple that day, not the bank.'

'If he paid him, how do you know?' Daisy asked me loudly.

'We paid him more,' said Ah Lan, a smile on his face. 'We paid many people. Mr Svensson's chauffeur was especially grateful. He hasn't seen much money lately.'

'What about Wu Shing's betting stubs?' I asked. 'Um – could you – could you read them?'

This would have seemed like a rather silly question to Daisy, but it wasn't. You see, reading in Chinese is not the same as in English, where once you know your twenty-six letters you have the key to everything. Each character in Chinese is not a letter, but an idea, and so there are thousands and thousands of them. Reading or writing in Chinese is as far from reading or writing English as baking a mooncake is from making shortbread.

'I can read well enough,' Ah Lan said to the fish, which were thrashing wildly, mouths open so hopefully wide that their jaws seemed ready to dislocate. 'The stubs are from a number of different races. My contacts will get more information. Meet back here at six this evening, just before dinner, and I'll tell you. But remember – you have to hold up your side of the bargain. You must tell your father about the pin today, all right?'

'I will,' I said, and Ah Lan threw his last handful.

Daisy stood up and offered me her arm and, as Ping came hurrying out from the door of the house to find

250

us, we waved lazily at her, as though we had all the time in the world.

'Do you know, Hazel,' said Daisy as Ah Lan walked away. 'He may be a criminal, but he's quite helpful, for a boy.'

To Daisy, I know, everyone in the world who is not me or Bertie or Uncle Felix (and perhaps now George) is slightly less than real, to be used as she sees fit. The more I know of life, the more I wish that this was not so – and the more I understand that I can never change it. It is what makes Daisy Daisy, the key to the marvellous pull of her. She simply does not care.

So I made up my mind to be simply glad that Daisy had decided to let Ah Lan into the investigation, and not to let myself think quite yet of what might happen when I told my father about the pin.

# 3

When we came out of the house again at eleven, Wo On was waiting in his freshly pressed uniform, holding open the shiny door of the car for us.

My father was punctual to the minute, as he always is, but he did not look as fresh as Wo. In the sunshine, I could see that his suit was the one he had worn the day before, hanging limp and dirty, and his glasses were sitting rather crookedly on his nose. He looked at Daisy and me as though he rather wished we would go away, and my heart sank. May and Rose came scampering out after him, and I felt more nervous than ever. They would be there. They would hear what I had to say.

When the car pulled up outside the Luk Man Teahouse in Central, I saw that its sign, which I remembered as so bright and lovely, was fading rather, its gold and red needing paint. The very walls of the building were cracking too. It was on four floors, on one side of a busy, rather dark street, the entrance guarded by two stone Chinese lions, much smaller than Stephen and Stitt at the bank, and wearing themselves away to grey lumps.

Mrs Fu herself came out to greet us, bowing profusely (and not looking particularly guilty – though perhaps that was a just a blind), and then guided us up two steep flights of wooden stairs, hung with screen paintings of flowers and birds, to the most ornate room of the teahouse. It was softly lit by square lamps, the walls covered with beautiful calligraphic pictures. We were seated at a small round table on hard dark chairs, and an old waiter came stomping up with our tea.

Rose poured (May not being trusted) for my father, and then for Daisy and me and May, and I noticed again the little things that are the true differences between England and Hong Kong. The way a face is expected to look, the way a person is expected to dress, those are unlike enough, but somehow not as starkly different as the smell a pot of tea has as it is being poured, the drum of fingers on a table in thanks for the cup, the particular light from the lamps – that is how I know I am in Hong Kong, not in England. I truly feel it in my bones.

The old waiter shuffled over and my father ordered imperiously, without glancing at the menu. The waiter limped away again, and there was a long, awkward silence. Rose fiddled with her chopsticks. May hugged the stick she had brought with her.

'So, girls,' said my father. 'How are you?'

'All right,' I said. I couldn't find the words, again, to say what I really wanted to. I was suddenly desperate to ask Father about Su Li. Did he think about what he had done to her with his order? Did he feel sorry that his choice had put her in that lift? Did he mind that she was dead?

'I'm a pirate, and I'm going to find Teddy!' said May loudly, and the table went very silent. I couldn't look at Daisy.

The waiter limped back over to us and thumped a stack of bamboo *dim sum* platters down onto the clean white tablecloth. He lifted up each one in turn and pointed to it. '*Siu lung bau. Har gau. Fung tsao. Lo bak go. Tsaa leung. Char siu bao,*' barked the waiter, glaring at Daisy as if threatening her to protest. Daisy gave him her best beaming smile, but it faltered under his withering gaze.

'Is it a clue that the waiter's being terribly rude?' she whispered to me.

'They're always like that,' I whispered back, looking over at the other waiter, who was glaring at us, lip curled, from across the room. 'But you could be right . . .'

I took a nervous bite of turnip cake and swallowed it in a heavy, gluey gulp. How was I going to manage this?

Daisy was peering at the dishes in front of her, while May giggled and Rose tried to hide her smiles behind

254

her hand. 'Oh!' said Daisy as she saw the plate of orange chicken feet, their claws curled together as though they were in agony. I think chicken feet are delicious, fatty and meltingly soft, but it is not polite in England to show that the meat you are eating once came from an animal, and so beaks, eyes and feet are removed before the dish ever reaches the table. In Hong Kong, many people love those bits best, and it is quite normal to enjoy them.

'It's perfectly all right!' I said, grinning at her.

'I shall try it,' said Daisy, recovering herself bravely. 'How does – how does one eat it?'

'The trick is to start with the toes,' I said helpfully.

'Ugh!' said Daisy. 'On second thoughts, what about some dumplings?'

The waiters were watching, glaring, and behind them I saw Mrs Fu. She was wearing a green brocade *cheongsam*, peeping out from a half-curtained doorway, her eyes narrowed. She was watching us too. My heart beat faster.

'Um,' I said. 'Ah. Um. Father. I wanted to say that – I'm sorry about Teddy.'

My father took a deep breath. Then he reached out and touched my hand.

'That is good of you,' he said.

'There's something I've been meaning to tell you,' I said. 'It's – well, I thought it wasn't important, but—'

'What is it?' asked my father, frowning.

'The pin,' I said. 'The one they found in—'

'STUCK IN THE BODY,' said May loudly.

'MEI LI!' said my father.

'That one,' I said, my stomach swooping and plunging. 'It was – it was the one Grandfather gave me. I lost it the night before, at the Svenssons' party. I don't know how it got there. In the lift. I didn't put it there. I didn't have anything to do with it, I promise!'

I was babbling, I could feel it. My face heated and my hands shook. I put down my chopsticks on my bowl.

'Why did you not tell me this before?' asked my father. May and Rose were both staring at me, their mouths identical Os.

'I thought you might think I did it,' I whispered. 'I thought Detective Leung would suspect me.'

'You lied to me,' said my father quietly.

'No!' I said. 'I just – I didn't tell you because—'

'Because you care more about yourself than your brother.'

My eyes watered at the shock of his words. 'That isn't true!' I said. 'I *do* care about Teddy. I want to get him back. I've been—' But of course I could not say what Daisy and I had been doing. I had to keep on, I told myself. I had to say what Sai Yat had asked me to. 'Father, what I mean to say is – don't you see, the pin isn't just any pin? The person who took it has to have been at that party too! It's not Sai Yat who took Teddy at all, it can't be. And it's not just Teddy, it's Su Li. She's dead, and that matters. Why don't you understand?'

Last summer my father had listened to what I told him about a case. But this was not last summer. I saw his face close up, his jaw harden. And I knew that he would not hear me this time.

'GOODNESS ME!' said Daisy very loudly beside me. 'IS THERE PRAWN IN THIS DUMPLING?'

# 4

She had her hands to her mouth, and the *har gau* she had been served was gone. Her cheeks did indeed look flushed, her blue eyes bulging in most excellently manufactured panic and her lips puffy. I was impressed. As usual, Daisy did not do anything by halves. She must have used the chilli oil on the table, I thought. It was very inventive of her.

'She's allergic!' I cried. 'Quick, she needs help!'

My father glared at me. I knew our conversation wasn't over, but now he leaped into action. He barked out a command to the waiters, and they came rushing rather unsteadily over to help him. Even Mrs Fu burst out of her hiding place and ran for the telephone, which was set up in a little alcove at the top of the stairs.

I looked at that telephone. It was secluded enough for the kidnapper to make the call, close enough to the kitchen and dining room to make the noises my father had heard. Our theory could work.

'Telephone Dr Aurelius,' my father called out to her.

I looked at the scene. Mrs Fu was occupied. This was my chance. Daisy wheezed and coughed, and I went rushing towards Mrs Fu's alcove, which I knew led to her rooms above the restaurant.

'I'll go and get towels!' I gasped out, for in books towels are always used in medical situations for purposes that are left mainly mysterious by the books' writers. However, they are always there, and so I thought that this would be a good enough excuse.

The stairs were dark and narrow, their walls grimy with years of wok smoke. I scrabbled my way up them, hearing my own heavy breathing, fearing terribly that at any moment someone might come upon me and stop me before I could carry out my search.

There ahead of me was a curtained doorway. I pushed my way through it – and out into a room that was not at all what I had been expecting.

It was clean, its plain walls and wooden floor scrubbed. It had once been a rather pretty room, but I could see lighter patches where paintings had hung, and dents on the floor where tables and chest of drawers had stood before they were pawned. This was a room whose owner could hardly afford it any more.

Mrs Fu's money worries really were serious. She must be desperate. Her business was failing. She had every reason to kidnap Teddy for the ransom. But, if she had, where was he? Not here, certainly. There was nowhere to hide him, not even a cupboard set into the wall.

But, on a small, low table, I found a little pile of betting stubs, with the words HAPPY VALLEY RACECOURSE printed across the top of each one. My scalp prickled. They looked just like the ones we had found in Wu Shing's room. Mrs Fu had been seen in Wu Shing's lift on the morning of the murder. Was this the clue we needed to prove the connection between them? Teddy wasn't here, but had we just discovered once and for all who had taken him?

There was a roar from below. 'HAZEL!' bellowed my father. 'WHERE ARE YOU?'

I had to go. I picked up a towel – only slightly used – from a pile as my cover, and ran back downstairs.

# 5

I was not at all prepared for what I saw when I came rushing back out through the alcove door, the towel still clutched in my hands.

Daisy was not, as I had expected, sitting up and sipping prettily from a glass of water, waiting to go to the doctor. She was lying flat on the floor, making a strange gasping noise, while everyone crowded around her.

'Where have you been?' my father shouted at me. 'We are taking Miss Wells to Dr Aurelius. Hurry, Hazel!'

'Daisy!' I said. 'Daisy?'

Daisy did not stir. And I suddenly wondered – even though I knew we had agreed on this plan – how had Daisy known that it was the *har gau* that had prawns in it? I had never told her, and I know that, to European eyes, all dumplings look the same. What if . . . What if she really *was* allergic?

'Come along!' said my father. 'You, boy, lift her. Wo is waiting in the car.'

One of the cooks picked up Daisy. Her arms and legs hung down on either side of his body, and her head lolled.

'Daisy!' I cried. I had never in all my life seen her like this, so pale and still. What if Daisy did not get better? What if . . . What if she died?

My breath felt short. The stairs, as I ran down them behind Daisy, seemed to rise up to meet me, undulating most alarmingly. I had thought we were playing a detective game, but suddenly this did not feel like a game at all.

Out we ran into the street, the hot noonday sun striking down on us. Wo was holding open the door of the car, his face drawn and worried. Ping was crouched on the seats inside, a makeshift bed of towels and scarves ready for Daisy. I thought, nonsensically, that I knew at last what the towels were for.

As soon as my father had closed the door behind us, Wo pressed down on the pedal and the car leaped forward, scattering dogs and cats and pedestrians, who shouted at us and waved their arms.

'Will she be all right?' I asked my father. 'Will she?'

His face was set and his jaw was tensed, and he didn't answer me.

*

We screeched up to the entrance of the bank, the lions Stephen and Stitt gleaming in the sun, and my father and Wo pulled Daisy out of the back seat and rushed her inside, Ping and I following with May and Rose. We all paused instinctively at the sight of the lifts.

The middle lift was open, and the lift operator in it was new. He was shorter and plumper than Wu Shing had been, cheeks pink and shining. He bowed to us and motioned us in.

Rose made a whimpering noise, and I stepped backwards, but my father glared down at us. 'Get inside,' he snapped, and in we went.

The lift moved upwards and I stared around, my stomach feeling as though it was a floor below my feet not simply because we were rising. The carpet had been replaced, clean and soft and red, and the shining gold walls had been cleaned, but there was still a dent on the inside metal grille that my eye was drawn to again and again. Su Li must have kicked out as she fought Wu Shing. I was horrified all over again. Daisy and I had investigated many terrible crimes, but I thought this must be one of the saddest and the worst.

I saw how very isolated the lift was – and how closely controlled it was by the lift operator. The new one had his gloved fingers on the controls, which could start the lift with only a touch, or pause its ascent. Wu Shing could have held it just below the eighth floor while he did the deed, and then climbed up and out onto the eighth floor with Teddy, shutting the doors behind him afterwards. That made sense – but how had he known he could get away without being seen?

It was hard to force myself to be a detective when all I wanted to do was watch Daisy though. She was lying on the low bank of seats at the back of the lift, with Ping hovering over her. Although her gasps had stopped, her breathing was shallow and her face was very pale. She lay with her eyelashes fluttering, her lips slightly open. Her arms were draped across her body, hands open, fingers spread.

There was something in that pose. It was so like an angel on a tomb, like the illustration in my copy of *Little Dorrit* (Daisy's Uncle Felix got a set of Dickens for me for Christmas, and it was the second one I read). It was so like something from a story.

And then I knew.

My breathing slowed. My heart unclenched. I let out a choking sob and put my hand on top of Daisy's.

'Will we be in time to save her?' I asked, as affectingly as I could, and very slowly I pinched the delicate web of skin between Daisy's left thumb and forefinger.

And Daisy scratched the inside of my palm with her index finger.

'What if she dies!' I cried, my pulse leaping, ready to laugh with joy and annoyance and embarrassment all at once. I should have *known* after more than two years of friendship if Daisy was allergic to prawns – but, all the same, I had been afraid.

'Dr Aurelius will save her,' said my father. 'Be quiet, Hazel.'

He was still angry with me. I knew I was still facing terrible punishment once this was over.

Then the lift stopped on the eighth floor, and the lift operator opened its doors onto the white corridor and the gentle scent of antiseptic. The air up here was cool, if a little stale, and wafted about by an electric fan away to our left. As Daisy was lifted up, I bent over her.

'Say you need the loo,' she breathed into my ear. 'Go exploring. I shall be making a miraculous recovery in approximately ten minutes. I need your eyes, Watson.'

I had my mission. Daisy was carried away from me to Dr Aurelius, and I was left to investigate the scene of the crime.

# 6

I was in the quiet marble hallway, with doctors' doors stretching away from me in three directions. The lift doors were all closed behind me, but feeling them there made my skin prickle. How *had* Wu Shing got out of the building? He couldn't go down in his own lift, as it had been stuck on purpose with Su Li's body in it. He couldn't have gone down in one of the other lifts, because with his scratched hands he would have been noticeable. So he must have left by a quiet side exit.

I looked around, and saw a door at the end of that corridor that did not have a gold doctor's plaque on it. I padded towards it, on tiptoe, past three doors on my right, noticing as I did so that one of the doors' plaques was blank. I pushed the door open, just a little way, and saw a waiting room, its desk covered by a dust sheet. This building was still new, of course – not all its offices were occupied. There on the floor I saw a tiny speckle of blood, and then I knew. This was where Wu Shing had gone after he left the lift. Could this even be where he had given Teddy to his employer?

I closed the door and moved forward again to the end of the corridor. I pushed that door open, and this time I found a set of plain stone stairs leading up and down. This was the other way out, apart from the lifts. I hung over the railing and looked down, down, down – all the way to the ground floor of the building. I thought about simply going back to find Daisy and telling her that I knew what had happened. But, as soon as I thought it, I knew with a rather cross sinking feeling that it would not do at all. I had to be a proper detective, and prove what I had guessed.

I set off, at a gallop. Down the stairs I went, down and down, until I was dizzy and my eyes spun and my legs wobbled. I clutched the banister and felt my breath hitch and my brain swirl.

And then, at last, just as I thought I would be trapped on the staircase for ever, the steps beneath my feet turned flat, and I was on solid ground. There was a door in front of me, and I pushed it open – out onto the dazzling pavement, Hong Kong sun beating down on me. People's faces turned towards me, and I knew I must look a sight, flushed and gasping, a girl alone without her maid. I thought back to Wu Shing. I imagined how people would stare to see a dishevelled lift operator without his lift suddenly emerge from the side door. If he'd had a baby with him, one that might even be screaming – why, someone would have stopped him, or mentioned something to Detective Leung. I got a funny creeping feeling. Had I just proved what I had guessed: that Wu Shing must have handed Teddy to his kidnapper in the empty office, *before* he left the eighth floor?

A fruit stall had been set up near the door. Its seller, a short, broad-faced woman, was watching me curiously. 'Excuse me,' I said. 'Were you here on Monday?'

The woman nodded at me. 'I'm always here,' she said.

'Did you see . . . a man in a lift operator's uniform come out of this door?' I asked.

'I did,' said the woman. 'Thought he looked lost.'

'He didn't have a baby with him, did he?' I asked.

'Why would he have a baby with him?' she said, looking confused. 'What are you talking about? Who are you?'

'Never mind!' I gabbled. 'Thank you! Goodbye!'

I scuttled as quickly as I could round to the main lion entrance, and darted towards the bank of lifts. The lift on the left was waiting for me, and I saw that the operator was the same old man whose lift we had gone up in on Monday.

'Eighth floor, please,' I said to him, wheezing a little, and the lift clanked to life. I looked sideways at the old operator, and saw him staring back at me, his face wrinkled up with curiosity.

'Miss Wong?' he asked at last.

I nodded. 'You were here on Monday,' I said.

The old man bowed.

'Yes, miss,' he said. 'I saw nothing, I am sorry. The murderer Shing never came down in my lift, or the other. If he had, we would have stopped him and saved your brother, I promise.'

I decided to be bold, like Daisy. 'Mr Svensson did, though, didn't he?' I asked.

'No, miss,' said the operator, puzzled. 'In my lift he only came up, to look for his wife. Mr Wa Fan came down just after him, and then you – you came back up with your friend and the chauffeur, and we discovered what had happened.'

My heart beat fast. 'Did Mr Wa Fan—' I struggled to find the words. 'How was he?'

'Sad, miss,' said the lift operator. 'I think he had been given bad news. He struggled to carry even his medicine and his small bag, and I had to take them for him.'

The lift juddered to a stop, and the operator pulled open the grille and opened the doors. 'Here you are, miss,' he said, bowing, and, although I was desperate to hear more, I had to step out into the white doctors' hallway.

I padded back along it, down the middle corridor, doors to my left and to my right. Dr Aurelius was the last on the left. I paused to stare out on the harbour as I passed the windows at the end, at the muscular, churned-up look of the water in the bay as the junks and the ferries passed across it. There was the Star Ferry, white and green, halfway across to Kowloon, a red-sailed junk dipping in its thick white wake. I pushed open the door and went in.

# 7

There was the receptionist again, looking up from behind her desk – and there were my father and Daisy, with old Dr Aurelius between them.

'Wong Fung Ying, where have you been?' snapped my father.

'I had to powder my nose,' I said, feeling the heat rising from my face.

'Dr Aurelius is miraculous,' said Daisy, beaming at me. 'I'm quite recovered!'

I saw my father frown at her.

'Daisy is awfully resilient,' I said quickly.

'So you have told me before,' he said, still glaring.

'A wonderfully healthy girl,' said Dr Aurelius, who had the same fat nose and shock of silver hair I remembered from old appointments. 'An excellent patient to treat. Her heart rate returned to normal almost immediately!'

He seemed to have no suspicions at all, but I could see that my father did.

'Come,' he said, and he ushered us out of the office, Ping bustling behind with Rose and May.

The lift operator had waited for us, and we travelled back down in terrifying silence. I couldn't bear to look at my father. I could sense that he was confused about Daisy's recovery, and still upset about my revelation.

He didn't speak until we were in the car, Wo On pulling away from the bank entrance. And suddenly I couldn't bear it any more.

'Father!' I said. 'I'm sorry! Please believe me – I should have said something before, about the pin. I was stupid. All I want to do is help find Teddy. I would *never* have hurt him, never, and I want to get him back, and I'm sorry! Please believe me, Father, please! Tell Detective Leung, so he can find who really did it!'

I found I was crying big babyish tears. I dashed them away, but they kept on coming. It felt so dreadful to think that my own father might not trust me any more.

'Hazel,' said my father. 'Hazel, look at me.'

For a moment I could not bear to, but then he leaned across the car, put his big square hands below my jaw, and tilted my face up towards him.

'I have been thinking about this,' he said. 'And I will not tell Leung anything. You did a stupid thing, but we have all done stupid things lately. The one thing I do not believe is that you could be part of this crime, not even for a moment. I know my daughter better than that. You have done wrong, and you will be punished. When we get home, you and Miss Wells will not leave the house for the rest of your time here. You will be confined to your room – Miss Wells must rest, after all. But I will not have you mixed up in this, not even for a moment.'

'Father!' I cried.

'Not a word,' he said. 'That is the end of the matter.'

'You have to tell Detective Leung about the pin!' I said. 'Please! If you don't – he can't help Teddy!'

'I think I know what will help Teddy,' said my father. 'Do not argue with me, Hazel.'

'You don't!' I said. 'You don't know how upset the other servants were with Su Li, when she became his maid. And you didn't even ask her if she minded – or if I did! She died because she was in the lift with Teddy. Don't you feel guilty about that?'

'ENOUGH!' shouted my father. 'Wong Fung Ying, never speak to me that way again. Never question me again. That is an order.'

May and Rose were gasping, wide-eyed. Daisy was open-mouthed. I could feel myself shaking.

Everything had gone wrong. How could we solve the case now? How could we prove that Sai Yat was innocent? How could we get Teddy back?

'Yes, Father,' was all I said.

# 8

'This is all terribly unfair,' said Daisy, sitting up with a bounce. We were at home, in our bedroom, leaning out of the window and watching the sun as it dropped towards the horizon over the gardens with the shocking speed it does in Hong Kong. 'I cannot believe we've been confined like this! It puts a terrible crimp in our investigations.'

'It could have been worse. At least you're not dead!' I said.

Daisy snorted elegantly. 'I do think it's terribly amusing that you thought I really was dying. You have known me for two years – heavens, that's ages – and you have surely seen me eat plenty of fish-paste sandwiches. Why on earth would you think that I'd suddenly developed an allergy to prawns?'

'You looked very convincing,' I said weakly. 'And I – I really didn't want you to die.'

'I don't want me to die, either,' said Daisy. 'But you must remember, Hazel, that heroines do not die. We are both perfectly safe.'

'We're not in a book!' I cried. It would be quite lovely to know that, no matter what happens, everything will turn out all right in the end, but Daisy and I can never be sure of that. 'And this murderer is terribly ruthless. They've killed two people, and kidnapped Teddy. And he's just a *baby*.'

'Very true,' said Daisy thoughtfully. 'Talking of which, you don't think there's any chance that—'

'No!' I said. 'Don't even think it. We'll get Teddy back.'

'Fair enough,' said Daisy. 'Now, I've heard all about your exploits, which were extremely interesting and, I quite agree, answer several questions we had. But you haven't let me tell you what *I* discovered yet, and it's terribly important. I did an absolutely wonderful job of pretending to be dying. Everyone was quite taken in.'

'All right,' I said, making a face at her. 'Go on, then.'

'I will,' said Daisy happily. 'So. There I was, pretending to be deathly ill. I held on for as long as I could, and let Dr Aurelius prod me and look at my tongue and things. Then he said he wanted to give me some medicine, so I had to stage a miraculous revival, sharpish. He was very pleased about my recovery, especially when I told a story about it being in the family – passed down from Aunt E – so it sounded very plausible. I thought it was rather clever of me.

'I got him talking about the afternoon of the murder, then pretended to realize where I was, and cry a bit, and say I was frightened. Of course, people are so talkative when they're trying to reassure you. He told me not to be giddy, that the body was never in his office, that he made sure his patients were far away from it. He didn't know anything about it until we arrived. Remembered his receptionist coming in to say that his twelve o'clock patient hadn't turned up – that was Teddy, of course – and so she was sending his twelve fifteen in early. His face went serious and he said, *A bad case. Terminal – he doesn't have very long left.* Then he suddenly looked very worried that he'd said too much. Doctors aren't supposed to talk about their patients' illnesses, you know, it's meant to be very private and secret.

'So then, while your father was talking to the doctor, I went and stood next to the reception desk. Your little sister May was being a terrible nuisance, and Ping and the receptionist were trying to stop her ripping pages out of the magazines on the table. So while they were busy I flipped back through the appointment book, looking for Monday. And I found *this*.'

She held out a scrap of blotting paper that had been scribbled over lightly with a pencil. It showed the marks the receptionist had made, pressing down with a pen.

11:45 - Svensson
12:00 - Wong
12:15 - Wa Fan

'Mr Wa Fan!' I said. 'He's the twelve fifteen. He's seriously ill! That fits with what the lift operator told me: that he looked sad, and seemed weak. It makes sense if he'd been told that he was dying.'

'Yes!' said Daisy. 'Look, Hazel, if we add your evidence to mine, we reach some interesting conclusions. Wu Shing left the building by the stairs, but, according to the fruit seller, not with Teddy. So he must have given Teddy to his employer *on the eighth floor*, in the empty room you found. Mr Wa Fan arrived on the eighth floor some time before twelve, and then was with Dr Aurelius from just after twelve, to – about twelve ten. That fits with what the lift operator said, and when Wo On saw him at twelve fifteen. Remember what Wo On said – that he saw Mr Wa Fan hurrying away looking upset? It fits with him being ill; so ill that he decided to go to a Western doctor and is ashamed of it.'

'That's the key to everything he's been doing!' I said. I remembered how I had thought Mr Wa Fan looked tired and thin. 'Daisy, if Mr Wa Fan is dying, I don't think he would have planned to kidnap Teddy. I know he's cross with my father, and thinks he's not being dutiful, but Mr Wa Fan and my grandfather were friends, and Teddy is my grandfather's future. Mr Wa Fan wouldn't try to hurt that future, not when he knew he was dying as well. I think that him hiring Detective Leung for my father makes perfect sense. He really was just trying to help.'

'You truly think so, Hazel?' asked Daisy, frowning. 'You know, people do some dreadful things. You ought to be prepared by now.'

'Yes,' I said, 'but in Mr Wa Fan's religion – and my grandfather's – you're supposed to pay all your debts and settle your arguments before you die, see? And that's what he's doing.' I got rather a lump in my throat at that. 'And remember what the lift operator said, that he held Mr Wa Fan's bag? If Mr Wa Fan had taken Teddy, he would have had to hide him in that bag. The lift operator would have noticed him. We can rule out Mr Wa Fan, Daisy!'

'But what about the person the operator took up in his lift, just before Mr Wa Fan came down?' asked Daisy. 'Mr Svensson! His appointment was at eleven forty-five, and we saw him back out and in the bank at ten past twelve. So why was he going upstairs at eleven minutes past, unless it was to meet Wu Shing and get Teddy? He could have – I don't know – put him in his attaché case?'

'Perhaps,' I said. 'Daisy, do you think—'

There was a knock at our door. I went and opened it and there was May. She was scowling with concentration and clutching something in her small grubby hands. 'I got something for you from the garden,' she said. 'It's from that handsome pirate boy with no arm.'

'Give it to me!' I said.

'Promise to give me your egg waffles for a week?' said May, squinting up at me.

'Monkey!' I cried. 'All right, I promise. Give it here!'

May pouted, and stuck out her fists at me. In them was a crumpled packet. It was dog-eared and dirty and covered in rips, but when I tore it open I found more betting stubs and a note, in shaky writing.

Wu Shing part of betting ring. Gave tips. Mrs Fu one of his clients.

'Daisy!' I gasped. 'Wu Shing *was* working for Mrs Fu! They knew each other, just like I thought! What if – what if kidnapping Teddy was all part of it, to give them more money to bet? And what if she killed him, so she wouldn't have to split their winnings with him?'

'Oh! Yes!' cried Daisy. 'Those betting stubs you found will prove it!'

I pulled the stubs from Mrs Fu's rooms out of my pocket and looked at them. Were we about to discover who the person behind Teddy's kidnap really was?

# 9

I squinted at the smudged, rather grubby characters. Daisy, peering over my shoulder, said, 'Oh, they're all in code!'

'It's Chinese!' I said. 'And I can read it. Hold on, let me see.'

My Deepdean training did not matter now – this case might truly hinge on my Hong Kong childhood. I began to read.

And then I stopped. 'Daisy,' I said. 'These stubs – they're for the one o'clock race at Happy Valley on Monday. They've been put on a horse called Fet Lock, and it was a winner. Look, you can see the stamp. Remember what we know: that Mrs Fu went into Wu Shing's lift just before twelve, and then went into the bank to withdraw money? We thought that she met him to give him the pin, and his final orders. The money didn't make sense – but it *does* if he gave her a tip, and she went hurrying off to place it. And, Daisy, she would have had to hurry terribly. We saw her heading out of the bank at ten past twelve, and it's almost forty minutes across the city to Happy Valley from Queen's Road. Remember how long it took us to get to Wan Chai, last night? It's even further. I don't think she would have had time to take Teddy and then bet on Fet Lock – and besides, if she knew Fet Lock would win, she wouldn't need the money from Teddy's kidnap. She had another money-making scheme in place!'

'Hazel, your reasoning is good,' said Daisy. 'And if Mrs Fu can't have done it, I think we may have just solved the case!'

She ran to the window and leaned out, waving.

I followed her, and saw Ah Lan standing below our window next to a cart piled high with leaves and earth. He waved up at us and winked.

'I like him,' said May, behind us. 'When I grow up and become a pirate queen, I'm going to marry him.'

I took the packet May had brought us, and on the other side wrote:

We can rule out Mrs Fu with these stubs if someone saw her at the racecourse. We think it was Mr Svensson! Watch him!

Then I stuffed the stubs I had found into it and threw

281

it down into Ah Lan's cart. Ah Lan nodded at me and winked again, and then trundled his cart away.

We shooed May out of the room (though she protested mightily), and then Daisy and I looked at each other. We thought we were getting close to knowing who had done it. But how could we prove it?

## SUSPECT LIST

1. The lift operator (find out his name!) Wu Shing. The simplest explanation is that he committed the crime. But why? We think he and Su Li knew each other, and she was afraid of him, but we must find evidence to back this up. So was this his motive, and he kidnapped Teddy almost as an afterthought, or was he simply interested in making money by kidnapping Teddy, and Su Li got in the way? Was he working on his own, or did he carry out the crime for someone else? (The pin makes it very likely that he was working with another criminal.) If so, who hired him, and why? NOTES: We know from the photograph that he knew Su Li! He was her ex-boyfriend. So was he paid to kill her, or did he kill her because he didn't like her? RULED OUT. Although he may have agreed to kill Su Li because they were once in a relationship, he did not plan the

282

crime on his own – he talked about this to his neighbours in Peking Mansions. He has now become the second victim! Someone killed him in the room he rented on the day of the kidnapping, after he had arrived back and changed out of his uniform. They gave him money, and then took it back off his body. We do not believe Teddy was ever at Peking Mansions – Wu Shing must have handed him over to the person who hired him just after Su Li's murder.

2. *Sai Yat's Triad gang.* ~~MOTIVE TO KIDNAP TEDDY: Money, plain and simple! The pin stabbed into Su Li's throat is the calling card of a Triad gang (we heard someone say this, and Hazel confirms it) – but it is odd that they chose to use Hazel's pin. Were they trying to frame her? Was it just a mistake? NOTES: We heard from Pik An that she believes some of the servants are indeed Triad. Could this be Ng? But he says that Sai Yat had nothing to do with this – is that just a blind?~~ RULED OUT. We have Sai Yat's word that he did not take Teddy or kill Su Li. He swore it in a sacred place, so we believe him. Also, Wu Shing's murder was carried out in a way that does not fit with Sai Yat's gang method.

283

3. *Mr Svensson.* MOTIVE TO KIDNAP
TEDDY: He needs money, and Mr Wong will not
give him any. He is also angry with Mr Wong — might
this give him a motive to frame Hazel for the crime?
NOTES: He was seen at the bank at the time of the
crime in a strange mood, and there are ten minutes where
his movements cannot be accounted for. He was also at
the party the night before, so could have picked up
Hazel's pin and given it to the lift operator! He knew
that Teddy was due to be at the doctor's the next day,
because he heard Mr Wong mention this. Ng confirms
that Mr Svensson is in need of money! He has offered
to help pay Teddy's ransom, but we have heard from
Mrs Svensson that he is in fact having money troubles
and cannot afford to pay. Is his offer a ruse — and does
his lack of money give him a motive? He is the least likely
to have killed Wu Shing, as he is big and strong, and
would not have had to worry about Wu Shing
overpowering him. TIMINGS: He left the bank at
12:10, but did not leave the building until 12:20. Highly
suspicious! He was on the appointment list at
Dr Aurelius's office at 11:45 — but he went up in the
left-hand lift much later, at 12:11.

4. *Mrs Fu.* MOTIVE TO KIDNAP

TEDDY: She also seems to need money — and she was talking angrily with Mr Wong at the party.

NOTES: She was seen at the bank at the time of the crime by Hazel Wong and Daisy Wells, so could have given the pin to the operator. She was also at the party the night before, so could have picked up Hazel's pin and overheard about Teddy's appointment! We have found a letter from her to Mr Wong asking him for money to save her teahouse! Daisy and Hazel overheard her saying that she was about to come into money — could this be Teddy's ransom payment? And could her restaurant be the source of the rattling sound Mr Wong heard? Wu Shing was shot in the back — this method fits someone who is weaker than he was, like Mrs Fu.

TIMINGS: She was by the lifts at 11:55, and then in the bank at 12:10. We now know she was working with Wu Shing, and withdrew money to bet on a horse at 1 p.m. on the afternoon of Teddy's kidnap. We must discover whether she was seen at Happy Valley. If she was, it means that she did not need to kidnap Teddy — and also did not have time to!

5. Mr Wa Fan. ~~MOTIVE TO KIDNAP TEDDY~~: He is angry at Mr Wong because he thinks he is not being dutiful. But is this a good motive for kidnap? He was at the party, so could have taken the pin and heard about the appointment. But he was not seen at the bank, and we do not know if he is a patient of Dr Aurelius. ~~NOTES: Wo On the chauffeur says that he saw Mr Wa Fan leaving the bank with a bottle of medicine just before the murder was discovered. He was on the scene, and in a hurry! He has paid the detective, Mr Leung, to help find Teddy. But is this a kind gesture — or a controlling one? Wu Shing was shot in the back — this method fits someone who is weaker than he was, like Mr Wa Fan. TIMINGS: He left the bank building at approximately 12:15.~~ RULED OUT. We have discovered he is terribly ill. He was with Dr Aurelius from 12:00 until 12:10, and then took the lift down at 12:13. Wo On did not see him with a baby, and nor did the lift operator. And Hazel believes that if Mr Fan knew he was dying he would not have played a trick on the son of his friend. He is innocent.

6. June Wong. ~~MOTIVE TO HAVE TEDDY KIDNAPPED~~: She does not like him,

because he is the son of her husband's other wife. But, if she had arranged to have him taken, she must know that when he was recovered he would be more adored than ever. Hazel remembers her being friendly with Su Li — why would she arrange to have her killed?

NOTES: She was not at the bank on the day of the crime — she had a headache. And the pin implicates Hazel, her own daughter — why would she arrange a crime that did such a thing? Her bound feet would slow her down, though they do not rule her out.

RULED OUT. She did not leave the house during the afternoon after Teddy's kidnapping — she could not have killed Wu Shing, or taken Teddy from him.

## PLAN OF ACTION

1. Eliminate Wo On and Ping from our list of suspects.

2. Find out more about the lift operator Wu Shing — who was he, and why did he become a murderer and a kidnapper? Was he paid to do it, or was it a personal motive?

3. Find out more about the Triad gang who use pins as their calling cards.

4. Look into all motives of our suspects further.

5. Find out more about Dr Aurelius's office to understand how the crime was not discovered, and how Teddy was taken out of the bank building.

6. Find a way to investigate Sai Yat.

7. Begin to rule out suspects. Continue to rule out suspects – discover where they were during Monday afternoon.

8. Consider where Teddy may be hidden at the moment. Visit Mrs Fu's teahouse and see if it is the source of the rattling sound.

9. Tell Mr Wong about Hazel's pin.

10. Discover where Mrs Fu was on the afternoon of the killing.

11. Get Teddy back again!

# PART SIX

# A Prince's Ransom

# 1

On Wednesday night after I wrote all that up, I could not sleep. It is hardly even spring in Hong Kong, and the nights are still cool enough, but English living has made me forget what true heat is. I tossed and turned, sweating, and Daisy said from the other bed, 'Stop *flailing*, Hazel, it's awfully annoying!'

But there was too much on my mind. My head ached, and there was a crick in my neck, and I couldn't get comfortable, or find a cool place to rest my cheek. Tomorrow was Thursday, the day when we would get Teddy back – or not. I told myself that I had to be a detective, but at that moment I didn't feel much like one. I missed Su Li horribly. I even missed Teddy, though I told myself that it was impossible to miss someone I barely knew.

The handover was planned for noon, by the Kowloon docks. At breakfast, Jie Jie asked to come along, but my father said no.

'You will stay at home,' he said. '*I* will manage this.'

'Can't I go?' I asked, and my father glared at me. 'Certainly not,' he said. 'I don't want you near Detective Leung, Hazel. I will take care of this.' I flushed with shame and nervousness and annoyance.

Everyone was fretful after Father had been driven away in his big black car to the Star Ferry dock to meet Detective Leung. They would decide how to plan the handover to ensure that Teddy came back safely.

May went chasing around the house, whirling a large oil-purple beetle on a string that she had got from somewhere. The beetle buzzed miserably, and Rose burst into sobbing tears.

'Let it go!' she wailed. 'May, let it go!'

'Rose, quiet!' said Jie Jie, who was sitting on one of the chairs in the hall, staring straight ahead and squeezing her hands together until her nails dug into her skin.

My mother said, 'If you don't stop, I shall have your maid beat you.'

At that, Rose gasped and ran away upstairs, and May fled into the garden. 'I'm going to find another beetle for Teddy!' I heard her scream.

'I cannot be in this house any longer. I'm going shopping,' said my mother with a snap. 'Tell someone to bring a car round. I hope it's all over by the time I come home.'

She drove away, and I have never felt more useless. Daisy was vibrating with frustration at being so far from the action. She had come up with some hare-brained ideas, all of which were absolutely impossible: that we could get into the bank and inspect Mr Svensson's account to see if he had drawn out cash to pay Wu Shing, or we could go to his house and accuse him directly.

All I wanted to do was go after Father. I no longer cared that Detective Leung might accuse me. I simply wanted to be at the docks, waiting for Teddy's kidnapper. I knew that there would be many men there, but I also knew how busy it was, crammed with cross, hurrying people. Hong Kong is a city of business, and so everyone moves in their own world, rushing to get to the next place and not particularly bothering about looking around. There would be plenty of cover for someone to take a bag of money and leave a fat little baby without being seen, especially if they wore the ordinary servants' uniform of white jacket and black trousers. They could dodge behind a rickshaw driver or someone wheeling a cart piled with star fruit and leave no trace of themselves. If Daisy and I were there, we could at least help.

I looked at my wristwatch – it was ten minutes to ten. Just over two hours to go now. My heart hammered with each tick.

'COME OUTSIDE, HAZEL!' bellowed May suddenly. I jumped, and looked at Jie Jie.

'Go, go,' she said, wiping her hand across her face. 'Please.'

Daisy and I went out onto the steps. May was bouncing about, her beetle whirling around her head peevishly. It had been joined by another.

'The handsome boy gave it to me!' she said happily. 'Big Sister, he wants to see you.'

I looked at Daisy, and we both set off at a gallop round the side of the house. There, next to a pot of bright pink blooms, was Ah Lan, a rake in his hand and his hat on his head. He nodded at us casually.

'I've got news,' he said. 'You're right about Mrs Fu. Her alibi is good. She was seen by several people at Happy Valley just before one on Monday afternoon, placing her bet. I have also spoken to drivers who were at the bank that afternoon, and they confirm that when she left she was holding nothing apart from a slim bag. You might put banknotes in it – but not a baby. She could not have taken Teddy.'

'So it really is Mr Svensson!' cried Daisy. 'Golly! But what do we do now?'

'There are men watching his house,' said Ah Lan. 'If he leaves, we will follow. Mrs Svensson is out for the day, but he has not left yet.'

Daisy and I looked at each other. We were so close! Surely Mr Svensson couldn't escape. Surely he would be caught when he tried to hand Teddy back?

# 2

'Hazel!' called Jie Jie. 'Ying Ying! Come here!'

We rushed back into the hall and found her standing there, holding something in her hands. 'Rose's maid has just found this in the Music Room,' she said. 'It is one of your mother's files from her nail kit. You know where she keeps her things, don't you? Go and put it back in her room.'

I could have said no. I don't have to obey Jie Jie when she says something. But I didn't want to upset her any more that morning. I also understood what she was not saying – that she was afraid that if *she* went into my mother's room, and my mother heard about it, she would be punished.

'Yes, Jie Jie,' I said. 'Come on, Daisy.'

Up the stairs we went to my mother's door. As I stepped inside, I felt as I always do, as though I was five and ought not to be in there – but Daisy, of course, pushed past me boldly and began to sort through the perfumes and potions on my mother's dressing table while I looked about for the nail kit.

The kit is a pretty lacquered case with red butterflies chasing across it, very bright, and I ought to have noticed it at once. But I was in such a daze, my mind half on Teddy and half on what we had just learned about Mr Svensson, that I could not see it. Instead, I reached down and picked up another of my mother's magic boxes, twisting and pressing it in my hands as I tried to think where on earth the kit could be hidden.

Daisy looked at the box and said, 'She's moved that since we were here on Tuesday. Remember? It was over on that cabinet there.'

'Her maid must have done it,' I said vaguely, my fingers moving almost automatically. It was a box that my father had given to my mother when I was small. I remembered him showing me the solution and laughing as my little hands stretched to wrap around it, and then giving it to my mother, who sighed and opened it in five sharp movements. My mother never did much care for my father's games.

I used to think that, because I never saw her reading and never heard her speak English, she wasn't clever – but then I discovered that she could do both perfectly well, but simply chose not to. She can read Chinese too – her own father taught her when she was a little girl – but she will only do it if she is forced to. 'What is the point?' she said to me more than once. 'I have plenty of servants to read for me.'

I had felt sorry for her then, and decided that I did not want to be like her. I wanted to go to England, where girls could be clever. But now I know that it's not so simple. My mind drifted, and I thought of clever fathers, and clever daughters. We had heard about a clever father recently – who was it? I couldn't remember.

And, as I thought that, the box popped open in my hands, and I found myself staring down into the little wooden hollow.

I had heard something rattling inside, as I twisted it. It was a gold tag, the sort that usually goes with a key. On one side it said 213, and on the other (I turned it over curiously) PENINSULA HOTEL.

'Why does your mother keep a hotel key tag in a box?' Daisy asked me curiously, padding across the carpet and peeping over my shoulder. 'Where's the key itself? And where is the Peninsula, anyway?'

'Kowloon,' I said. 'On the waterfront. Just past the Star Ferry dock. Remember, I pointed it out to you? It's terribly posh. You can get a lovely afternoon tea there. It's where the Svenssons used to live before their house was ready. It's where – it's where the handover is about to take place.'

We both froze.

'Hazel,' said Daisy quietly. 'Hazel. Do you know where you might be able to telephone in peace, with no one wondering why you have a baby with you? A *hotel room*.'

'You think that Mr Svensson and my mother—' I said faintly. 'Daisy! They— Mother couldn't!'

'No,' said Daisy, wrinkling up her nose. Her face was paler than usual, but her eyes were glittering. 'I don't. We've never seen them speaking, have we? It's not *Mr* Svensson and your mother who are always forced together while their husbands talk business.'

She turned back to my mother's dressing table, and picked up the lavender scent that sat there among all of the others. She pressed the bulb, and the air was filled with a sweet, polite, purple perfume that smelled of England, and summer – and Mrs Svensson. She had been here – she and my mother were better friends than I had thought, if my mother had brought her to her room to talk. And I suddenly realized where else I had smelled it: Peking Mansions, in the room where we found Wu Shing's body.

'Hazel,' said Daisy. 'We've been thinking about this all wrong. This is a conspiracy between *two* people. Mrs Svensson and your mother.'

# 3

I reeled. I did not want to believe it – but there was the key tag, without its key, and my nose was still filled with Mrs Svensson's perfume.

'Listen,' said Daisy. 'We've been idiots. We knew the Svenssons need money, so we thought that gave *Mr* Svensson a motive. But of course it gives *Mrs* Svensson exactly the same one. And, in fact, we also know that Mrs Svensson is the more money-minded of the two. Her father was a famous mathematician. Mr Svensson is silly with money – we've heard lots of people say that he's always asking your father for loans, and we watched him come and offer your father help he couldn't afford to give. *Mrs* Svensson seems much more careful with money – and much more worried about their financial troubles. We heard her tell your mother so, didn't we?'

'No!' I cried. 'We heard them arguing. My mother hates Mrs Svensson! How can they be working together?'

'Yes, we heard them arguing. But, Hazel, consider what we overheard. They were talking about money, and Teddy. They could just as easily have been two people discussing their conspiracy, Mrs Svensson warning your mother to hold firm by reminding her that, if they were caught, their children would suffer. And in terms of character they complement each other excellently. Mrs Svensson is bold, and your mother is a planner.'

'Yes, but *why?*' I cried.

'Well, for Mrs Svensson it's easy. She needs money to save her family. And your mother – why, that's not hard, either. She hated Teddy being born. She's angry with your father.'

'But she wouldn't agree to have Su Li killed,' I said. 'She – she wouldn't. She *knew* her, Daisy. And she couldn't kill Wu Shing, she wouldn't be so heartless.'

'Of course she didn't kill Wu Shing,' said Daisy. 'She couldn't have left the house on Monday. Mrs Svensson probably did that— Oh, Hazel, think: that explains the ring. They gave money *and jewels* to Wu Shing as a reward for a successful kidnap. Then, when Mrs Svensson killed him, she took it all back, and gave your mother her ring when they saw each other on Tuesday. That's why she wasn't wearing it on Tuesday morning, but she *was* on Wednesday. But even if she didn't kill him, I bet it was your mother who thought of hiring him. Remember, he used to work here? She would have known him, and known he needed the money.'

'But the pin,' I said weakly. 'Ah Mah wouldn't frame me!'

'I do agree with you there,' said Daisy. 'She wouldn't do that. So what if that wasn't part of the original plan? What if Mrs Svensson found the pin after the party, and thought what a good opportunity it was? She gave it to Wu Shing that morning – somehow – and told him to use it in the murder. Then she'd have a way to make sure your mother didn't get cold feet and admit what had happened. Oh, remember Mrs Svensson mentioning your name? That was— Hazel, that *was* her warning your mother to keep quiet!'

'But it's such an awful thing to do,' I said, shaking my head as though Daisy was being idiotic. Except she wasn't. My chest was aching and my heart was sinking, because, although I didn't believe my mother could ever do something like this, I knew how long she could hold a grudge, and how elaborate her punishments could be.

'You know your mother, Hazel,' said Daisy. 'Would she do this?'

'She gets very upset with people,' I said. 'She hates it when they betray her. And that's what Father did with Teddy, I suppose, and Su Li too, by becoming his maid. But – she really wouldn't *kill* someone. She *couldn't*!'

'The more important question is how the kidnap worked,' said Daisy. 'Your mother wasn't at the bank, and neither was Mrs Svensson. How could they have been up on the eighth floor to take Teddy from Wu Shing as we know they must have?'

I thought. I remembered that patient list Daisy had found. *Svensson. Wong. Wa Fan.*

And I saw again that we had been thinking all wrong.

'Mrs Svensson *was* there!' I cried. 'We saw Svensson and thought *Mr*, but it could equally have been *Mrs*. She must have arrived before we did, at eleven forty-five, gone up in Wu Shing's lift, given him the pin and then waited in that empty room after her appointment. Then, as soon as Wu Shing climbed out of the lift with Teddy at twelve, he handed him to her in the room and she went back down in the right-hand lift with him, while Wu Shing escaped out of the side entrance. Then, later, Mr Svensson went up to the eighth floor because he thought his wife might still be there. That's what the left-hand lift operator said yesterday – that Mr Svensson was looking for his wife! That's why he was behaving oddly, because he couldn't find her!'

'Hazel, you're quite right!' cried Daisy. 'And I've just had the most genius thought! The best way to hide a baby is to disguise him as another baby. We know that Mrs Svensson likes to go about with Roald without her maid. So she could have got into the car that morning with a

302

bundle of clothes wrapped up like a baby, and said that Roald was asleep and she was taking him with her to the doctor. Then she could have taken Teddy from Wu Shing, wrapped him in the same bundle and clutched him to her chest. No one would have looked closely enough at the baby to see that he was Chinese, not European, not if they *expected* him to be Mrs Svensson's son.

'And then she took him to the hotel room at the Peninsula. She made the call from there that afternoon, making her voice low and quiet, like your father said. Then she left again to kill Wu Shing and went home to Mr Svensson— Oh, Hazel, of course! *He* was out because he spent the afternoon looking for her!'

'But what about Roald?' I asked. 'Wouldn't someone have noticed that he'd been left behind at the house?'

'Not if Mrs Svensson's maid was in on it too!' said Daisy. 'She would have had to look after Roald that afternoon, and meet Mrs Svensson just before she arrived home to hand him back to her. What if she's the person who's been looking after Teddy this week? And that's why your mother had a hotel room key too, just in case she wanted to look in on him.'

I swallowed hard as it all began to sink into place. 'But, Daisy – do we need to say anything? I mean – if we get Teddy back. If the handover works. Sai Yat – he'll be so angry, but—'

'Hazel,' said Daisy. 'Watson. No.'

She did not need to say anything else. Su Li and Wu Shing were dead, and I knew that nothing – not family loyalty, not all the desperate, hopeless love I had for my mother simply because she was my mother – mattered more than making sure that the people who had caused their deaths were caught.

My breath hitched, and I wiped at my eyes. Daisy threw her arms about me. Her chin dug into the top of my head – she really is very tall these days – but she smelled warm, of soap and a little of sweat. At least, I thought, I knew that even the Honourable Daisy Wells could sweat.

'Detective Society for ever,' said Daisy, muffled. 'Remember that, Hazel. No matter how everyone else may betray you, I promise to never die or murder anyone, and that is what matters.'

'I promise never to do either of those things as well,' I said.

'Don't be silly, Hazel, you don't even need to promise,' said Daisy. 'I know you never would. This is dreadful, but we shall face it together, all right? Because it *will* be all right. I shall *make* it all right.'

I stepped back and smoothed down my hair. I took a deep breath and I felt it go through me, head to toe.

'I'm ready,' I said. 'I know we're not supposed to leave the house, but we have to, Daisy. Ah Mah must have gone to help with the handover. So we have to make Jie Jie take us to Kowloon. We have to go to the Peninsula Hotel.'

# 4

It was raining as we stepped onto the Star Ferry, the drops pressing down the waves and turning the sea flat and scuffed looking.

Jie Jie had not been hard to persuade. 'We *have* to go,' I said to her. 'Don't you want to see Teddy as soon as he's rescued? Won't he want you there?'

Jie Jie looked up and set her jaw – and she suddenly looked very much like May.

'I *do* want to be there for him,' she said. 'You are right, Ying Ying. We will go.'

Wo On brought the car round, eyebrows raised but silent, Ping took us to the car and we set off, rain drumming thickly on the canvas roof.

Although we had not told my sisters, May decided during the car journey that we were going to find Teddy. She still had her beetles on their strings, and she wouldn't let go of them. 'I'm giving this one to Teddy,' she said stubbornly. She also had her stick in the belt of her trousers, in case she came across the kidnappers.

'I like your sister,' said Daisy approvingly as we stood at the railing and watched the dimpling water. 'One day she will make a fine detective assistant.'

One day, I thought, May would probably be the leader of her own Detective Society.

The ferry jumped to life, its rumble starting beneath my feet and shaking its way up my spine into my ears. I held onto the railing and squinted ahead, across the rain-shadowed bay, to the grey buildings of Kowloon. There was no time to even feel seasick, not today.

'Big Sister,' said a small voice. Rose had crept up behind me and was clinging to the rail, her face twisted with worry. 'Do you think Teddy's all right?'

'I hope so, Ling Ling,' I said, and she looked so small and sad that I hugged her. 'I think Father is going to get him back very soon.'

'I didn't like him much when he was born,' said Rose. 'I wanted another sister.'

'I didn't like him, either,' I said, and admitting it felt like breathing out. 'But . . . it's worse when he isn't here.'

'I know,' said Rose. 'I've been praying for him to come back. I saved some of my supper and set it out for the gods, only Pik An cleared it up, and I'm afraid today will go wrong because of that.'

'Don't be silly!' I said, hugging her. 'And I promise we'll find him. I know we will.'

'Good,' said Rose, nodding. 'And then – do you think Father will let me go to English school?'

'Do you really want to?' I asked. 'Or do you still just want to run away?'

'Partly that,' said Rose. 'But England looks nice. And I hate school here; it's stupid and the uniform is ugly. I want to go and eat buns and play games like in the books.'

I almost laughed. 'I'll speak to Father about it,' I said.

'Would you?' asked Rose blissfully. 'My English is getting *so* good. It's . . . spiffing!'

It was not *fair*, what my mother had done, I thought suddenly. It was not fair on May and Rose and me. It would hurt us all. Just like Daisy cannot get out from the shadow of Fallingford, we would always be the girls whose mother did something terrible.

We stepped off the ferry, the gangplank bouncing as the water sloshed below us, and then we were in the press and smell of Kowloon docks. This was where the handover would take place in less than an hour. Jie Jie looked around nervously, and pulled May and Rose to her. The maids stood over us with umbrellas.

'Let's wait in the Peninsula,' I said, my breath hitching. 'We can have tea.'

'Tea!' cried May. 'And then we see Teddy!'

Jie Jie's face screwed up, and my heart beat fast. We were about to arrive at the place where Teddy could very well be at this moment. But would we be able – would we be clever enough – to save him?

# 5

I always forget how very grand the Peninsula Hotel is, and what an odd mix of English and not English at all. Up the wide, sloping entrance we walked, the white-windowed expanse above us like an English palace. But, as we came up the low stone steps, we were greeted by a pair of snarling Chinese lions.

We stepped into the lobby, dripping water from folding umbrellas, into a world of high ceilings, white columns and green potted ferns, of buttery light and tasteful gold detail, of soft music played by a string quartet tucked away in a little alcove, and of tea in bone-china cups served by white-jacketed waiters. Everything was gentle and hushed – and heads turned to look at us, a most unusual family. Four girls, one of them European, three maids and one mother. Jie Jie shrank backwards shyly, automatically trying to look more like a maid.

'I WANT EGG WAFFLES!' shouted May, and was hushed by everyone.

'There aren't any egg waffles here, stupid,' Rose told her. 'But they have chocolate cake.'

'CHOCOLATE CAKE!' cried May. 'Is Teddy here?'

I saw the agonized expression that passed across Jie Jie's face, and the look on Daisy's. Jie Jie didn't know it, but Teddy *was* here.

We were guided to a large, round table beside a pillar, and a respectfully bowing waiter took our orders. Then there was a pause, a spreading pool of silence that no one seemed able to break.

'GOODNESS!' said Daisy suddenly. 'Is that— Look! *Surely* it's Constance Goring.'

We all turned in our seats in time to see the back of a lady proceeding out of the lobby up the stairs. I could not tell anything about her apart from the fact that she was European, and a grown-up.

'It *is*!' said Daisy in excitement. 'I must – will you excuse me? I simply *must* ask at the desk – she's a cousin, you know, I haven't seen her for *years*!'

Before any of us could stop her, she had leaped to her feet and was moving in a ladylike gallop across the lobby to the front desk. We all watched as she spoke rapidly to the receptionist, picked up the telephone and chattered into it. Was Daisy calling room 213?

But when Daisy turned and came back towards us, slower this time, weaving in and out of the tea tables, there was a rather cross expression on her face. I decided that the person she had called hadn't answered.

'It wasn't her at all!' she cried. 'How bothersome! There was a Goring registered, but when I called up to the room it was an old gentleman, not my cousin at all. What a pity.'

Jie Jie looked confused, and I could tell that she didn't understand why Daisy cared more about her cousin than a missing child. I wished I could explain to her.

The tea arrived, fat pots of it, along with four enormous slices of chocolate cake filled with rich dark ganache. It looked most inviting, and I swallowed mine hungrily. And then, as the maids were serving us, my mother stepped into the lobby.

I saw her before she saw us. Her earrings glinted in the lamplight and her lips were red, and she moved slowly on her bound feet. She was carrying a small shopping bag, and I had to acknowledge how good her cover was. She had made sure to really go shopping, to make the lie perfect. I looked at her, as beautiful and poised as ever – but now I saw the thoughts as they hurried through her brain, the calculations she was making. She showed no sign of fear, and I realized how very bold my mother was. I had always thought, when I summoned my bravery, that I was calling on my father's character. But now I was not so sure.

We had to move faster than her. In only a few moments, my mother would see us, and it would all be over.

'I have to go to the loo,' I said.

'I'll go with you!' said Daisy at once, bouncing up. She had seen my mother too, and her cheeks had gone pink with alarm.

'I'm going to eat your cake!' said May gleefully.

We wound round the tea-takers and the talkers, the pretty little upholstered chairs and the round white-clothed tables, the string quartet playing gently over the chatter. We walked past maids and ladies, gentlemen in robes and in suits. There was the grand central staircase, a carpet running up the centre. As we started to climb it, Daisy pressed her hand into mine.

'Get ready,' she whispered, as we stepped out onto the first-floor landing, into more hushed carpet and lamps and beautifully arranged flowers. 'We have to get there before your mother. When I say run – RUN!'

She surged forward like a deer, and I pelted after her up the stairs.

We hammered upwards, our feet muffled by the carpet, and then turned out on the second-floor landing. We ran past a maid who was walking the other way. She looked at us in surprise. She had her hair tied back, and I noticed a little scar on her neck. And I remembered her – this was the woman who had warned me all those days ago. 'Miss Hazel!' she cried. 'Stop!' Her face was horrified, and something at last made sense to me. Mrs Svensson's maid had known about the plot and had been trying to make sure that I wasn't drawn into it. Of course, she had failed.

But there was no time to think about that now. Rooms stretched away on either side of us, and I tried to make out numbers in our haste – 208, 209, 211 – and there was 213, a tall mahogany door with elegant gold trim. I fumbled at the handle. My fingers were sweating and my hands were shaking, but the door opened. There was no time to wait, no time to ponder what we ought to do. Daisy and I simply threw ourselves inside and slammed the door behind us.

# 6

The room we were in was pretty and light. There was a bed, curtained in floating white fabric. There was a window, closed against the rain, which looked out onto the harbour and the Peak. There was a desk and a chair – and sitting in the chair was Mrs Svensson.

She jumped and stood up as we came in. Her eyes were wide and confused, and they darted around the room – at us, then at the desk, and finally at something beside the bed. My eyes followed hers and I saw a little bassinet peeping out from behind it.

'What are you doing here?' asked Mrs Svensson. 'Did Mrs Wong—?'

'Yes,' said Daisy at once. 'That's right. She told us to come here. She wanted us to ask you – to ask you—'

I had begun to walk towards the bassinet.

'Hazel,' said Mrs Svensson. 'Leave him. Roald's sleeping.'

'Oh, is that your baby?' asked Daisy, starting after me. 'I love babies, do let me look!'

'Really, Daisy, there's no need. You'll only wake him. The maid's just put him down.'

'Oh, I really must!' cried Daisy.

'STOP!' shouted Mrs Svensson, a furious look on her face.

Daisy and I both froze, and from the bassinet came a fretful murmur – and then, a moment later, a wail.

Mrs Svensson darted forward. I was not sure whether she was moving towards us or towards the bassinet, but Daisy was moving too, throwing herself on Mrs Svensson and knocking her off balance. There was a strong smell of lavender in the air, and Mrs Svensson gasped and staggered backwards.

I rushed forward and peered down into the bassinet – and I saw, cuddled inside it, not one baby, but *two*.

One was blond, his hair so fine and pale that he looked quite bald. He glared at me out of bright blue eyes, screwed up crossly as he wriggled his body like a landed fish.

And the other was Teddy.

His silky dark hair was scruffy with sleep, but he blinked at me and raised his little fists in the air. Without even knowing what I was doing, I reached down and scooped his fat little body up, and Teddy beamed up at me, his whole face crinkling with joy. I told myself that this was how he was with everyone – but at that moment I suddenly felt as though he knew I was his big sister, come to find him.

'*Neih hou*, Teddy,' I said, smiling back.

'Put him down,' said Mrs Svensson. 'Put him down at once!'

'No, she won't,' said Daisy. 'And how dare you keep him here! We know all about what you've done. You were the one who plotted with Mrs Wong to have him taken, and Hazel's maid murdered, so you could get the ransom money. You smuggled Teddy away from the eighth floor pretending he was Roald, and you've been keeping him here, being looked after by your maid. You're about to hand him over for the ransom money – but we got here first!'

Mrs Svensson was looking from Daisy to me and Teddy, and back again.

'You girls are in terrible trouble,' she said.

'No, *you* are!' said Daisy furiously. '*You* killed Su Li, and *you* tried to frame Hazel for it to frighten her mother into keeping your secret! We know your game, *and* we've told Detective Leung about it. There will be police here any moment, just you wait and see.'

'You haven't done anything of the sort,' said Mrs Svensson. She sounded so calm, so ... grown up, I thought. She sounded like a mother talking to her silly children. 'You wouldn't dare, not after the pin.'

I squeezed Teddy to me, and he yelped.

'You can't blackmail us!' said Daisy.

'It was useful insurance to keep June in line,' said Mrs Svensson calmly. 'I don't care about those silly Triads. And I shall use it to keep you quiet too. If you say anything, I shall tell Detective Leung that you were the one behind the whole plan. I can find plenty of witnesses to say that you had a mysterious run-in with a maid, and you handed over your orders for Teddy's kidnap at that moment. Rest assured, I can destroy you, Hazel Wong, and your mother.'

My ears were ringing and my throat felt as though something was stuck in it. I swayed against Daisy, and she clutched at my arm.

'But why would she do it?' I whispered.

'Isn't that obvious?' asked Mrs Svensson. 'For *you*.'

And at that moment there was a knock on the door.

# 7

'Who is it?' called Mrs Svensson, her voice suddenly shrill. She *was* afraid, I realized – afraid that Daisy hadn't lied about Detective Leung. Daisy and I glanced at each other, and I knew she was thinking the same thing.

'Madam!' said a female voice in heavily accented English. 'I've come about the job!'

I jumped. I knew that voice. It was Ping!

'What job?' said Mrs Svensson. 'Go away at once.'

'But I have come to be maid to the baby,' said Ping. What on earth was she doing?

Mrs Svensson reached into the pocket of her dress and pulled out a small pearl-handled pistol. She pointed it at us. 'Get into that wardrobe,' she hissed. 'Keep the baby quiet. Not a sound, if you please. I shall deal with this.'

I looked at the pistol. I remembered Wu Shing, and I knew, sickeningly, that we had found our murder weapon, and confirmed the murderer of our second victim.

The wardrobe was light, thin wood, barely large enough for both of us, but Daisy and I crawled inside. It smelled of mothballs, hot and close, and we squashed up against each other, Teddy cradled between us. He wriggled happily against my stomach and sucked my finger. And I was terrified. Daisy and I could look after ourselves – but how could we protect Teddy?

We heard the door to the room open.

'Madam,' said Ping again. 'I have come about the—'

'Yes, the job, you said,' said Mrs Svensson. 'I don't need another maid. Who told you I did?'

'What *is* she playing at?' whispered Daisy.

I didn't know.

'My friend,' said Ping. 'Su Li.'

There was a metallic click. I thought I knew that sound – the safety catch of a gun being removed.

'If you say another word, I shall shoot you,' said Mrs Svensson. 'I've shot someone before.'

'You will not,' said Ping. 'Miss Wong and Miss Wells are here too, and you cannot kill all of us. Mr Wong will come looking for them, and he will find out that you are the person who had Su Li killed.'

I heard the door open again.

'Kendra?' said my mother in English. 'Where are you? I thought I saw—'

'Ah,' said Mrs Svensson. 'Hello, June.'

It was horridly absolute proof, hearing my mother's voice.

'Kendra,' she said, 'I have to talk to you. Where's that maid of yours? We're getting close to the handover; she should be on her way—' There was a pause. 'Why is Ping here?' she asked sharply.

'She knocked,' said Mrs Svensson. 'I thought you might have sent her.'

'Mrs Wong!' said Ping, shocked. '*You* are part of this too?'

'I ought to shoot her,' said Mrs Svensson.

'Ping, you stupid girl,' said my mother. 'Why are you here?'

'Because of Su Li,' said Ping, a wobble in her voice. 'Mrs Wong! How *could* you?'

'I never thought Su Li would die,' said my mother. 'That wasn't the plan. Her stupid ex-boyfriend went too far. We only told him to hurt her! She deserved to be punished, and so did my husband, but not like that. And I never would have made the Triads part of it. Kendra doesn't understand, she—'

'It may not have been part of *your* plan to kill the maid,' said Mrs Svensson, 'but it was always mine. No witnesses, you see. It was the same with Wu Shing. Better off dead.'

I couldn't catch my breath. This was too terrible.

'Where is Hazel?' my mother went on. 'Why aren't you with her?'

'June,' said Mrs Svensson. 'The girls. They're here.'

'What do you mean?' said my mother sharply.

'They've worked it all out,' said Mrs Svensson. 'It's terribly annoying. I put them in the wardrobe.'

'Dead?' cried my mother. 'You haven't— *Kendra!*' And in that moment I understood, for the first time in years, that my mother truly did care about me.

'Of course they aren't dead,' said Mrs Svensson. 'They're perfectly alive at the moment. Call them out if you like.'

'Come here, Wong Fung Ying!' cried my mother. 'Come here!'

I had no choice but to go to her.

# 8

Out of the wardrobe, the world seemed bright and very airy. I was still not breathing properly. I kept hold of Teddy, squeezing him close as though I could keep us all safe that way. He let out a small, disapproving yelp. Daisy stood by my side, our arms touching, and I was glad to have her there.

'Ah Mah,' I said desperately. 'Please. Help us.'

'You are not supposed to be here!' said my mother. Her face was flushed and her eyes glittered. 'Ying Ying, you are so stupid! I could have managed this, I could have kept you out of it! Didn't I *tell* you?'

'I was looking for Teddy,' I whispered. 'I'm sorry.' I suddenly remembered our conversations. I had thought that my mother was afraid I was guilty – but of course she had known that I was innocent.

'I was so *close*!' cried my mother. 'Another hour, Hazel, and the child would have been given back, and everything would have been over. You silly girl! I've been trying to protect you, but you can never do the right thing.'

'*This is your fault!*' said Daisy indignantly. I jabbed my elbow into her side in horror. Mrs Svensson still had the pistol raised, and my mother looked as though she might slap us. For once, Daisy had to stay quiet.

'How can you be part of this?' I said, staring at my mother. '*Why?*'

'I didn't want anyone to die,' she said, and I heard a catch in her voice. Her eyes were glittering still, but not with rage – with tears. Suddenly she looked small and weak and afraid. I realized that she had no more idea what to do than I did. 'I only wanted your father to suffer a little. He took my child away from me, so I took his. But only for a while!'

'I wasn't taken away!' I said. 'I *asked* to go to England!'

'You asked because he made you want it,' said my mother. 'He took you away from me. You think you are *his* child, not mine. And that is his fault.'

I felt my face go red. It was so close to what I *had* thought that I could not bear it.

'But I have you home now, and I was always going to give Teddy back to him. Kendra would get her ransom money, and I was going to have some too, so that when you are grown, whatever happens you will not be poor. You will not have to marry a man you hate, do you see?'

I suddenly remembered my mother saying, *Hazel will not marry*. I had thought that she meant that I was too awkward and bookish to be interesting, but it hadn't been that at all. It wasn't fair. I hadn't asked for this. I didn't want it.

'Father *wouldn't* leave me with nothing,' I said. 'And he wouldn't make me marry someone I didn't like.'

'You don't know anything,' said my mother. 'You are a child.'

'No!' I cried. 'It's you who don't understand. You've ruined everything!'

'I think I might have,' whispered my mother.

There was another knock on the door.

'Good grief, who is it this time?' cried Mrs Svensson.

And then the door was kicked in, in a crack and a burst of splinters, and Detective Leung rushed into Room 213.

Mrs Svensson dropped the gun and threw her hands in the air. 'You're just in time!' she cried. 'Hazel and June Wong have cooked up this kidnap between them. They were just about to kill me. It was Hazel's pin at the murder scene. She is to blame!'

'She's lying! She is the one who killed Su Li and Wu Shing!' cried Ping, pointing to Mrs Svensson.

It was a wealthy white woman's word against a Chinese maid's. I had to speak up – but would I be believed? And even if I did, how could I keep my mother safe? She was mixed up in everything. Daisy and I had faced this choice once before, and I had thought I understood the pain of it, but until it is *your* family you can only feel half the horror. But then—

'My employer had a telephone call half an hour ago saying that we would find Edward Wong in this room,' said Detective Leung. 'And I see that he is here. Someone in this room must be responsible. Although the caller said that Mrs Svensson was the kidnapper, I am not yet sure of that. I have spoken to Mr Svensson, who admits that he couldn't find his wife for much of Monday afternoon – he went to look for her at the doctor's office, but couldn't find her – and that he has been concerned about her behaviour. Mrs Svensson, I am taking you in for questioning. But, Mrs Wong and Miss Wong, because of what I have heard about *you*, I'm afraid that you must come too.'

Mrs Svensson went pink. My mother went white. I went limp, clutching Teddy.

'Hazel,' said Daisy quietly. 'It will be all right, Hazel.' For the second time that day she pulled me into a hug – and, just as I had all those weeks before at Deepdean, I cried as though I would never stop.

# 9

We all walked downstairs together. At the first-floor landing Mrs Svensson made a sudden dart to the left, but Detective Leung seized her wrist, and she yelped and desisted. 'Downstairs,' he said firmly. I caught his eye – and, if I had thought about trying to escape, the idea vanished.

I was still holding Teddy, even though his weight made my arms wobble. I found I did not want to let go of him. I held him until we came out into the foyer and found it full of people – not just Jie Jie and May and Rose, but my father and two police officers – along with Mrs Svensson's maid. When she saw Teddy, Jie Jie screamed and ran to me. She pulled Teddy out of my arms into her own, so roughly that he squealed and I gasped. My father bent over Teddy's dark head. Then he looked up at me.

'*Hazel!*' he shouted, and I saw what this must look like. I opened my mouth to deny it, to explain that I had only found Teddy, not stolen him. But my mother spoke first.

'Stop that at once, Vincent! Ying Ying has nothing to do with this,' she snapped, drawing herself up to her full height. 'It was Mrs Svensson, and me.'

My father stopped still. His forehead wrinkled. 'Don't lie, June,' he said. 'Not now.'

'I am not lying,' said my mother, sounding exasperated. 'You never listen to me! You never believe me! I planned to have Teddy kidnapped, to punish you. I chose Wu Shing to do it, and I helped pay him. I planned it perfectly. And then you put *our daughter* in harm's way. *You* sent her to the bank with that stupid baby. *You* ruined my plan – you and Kendra.'

She turned on Mrs Svensson, who was scarlet with panic. 'I certainly had nothing to do with it!' she blustered. 'It was all June. I only heard about it later. I came here to get the baby back, I swear. It was all June and Hazel. The pin! Look at that pin! It was Hazel's, I can prove it—'

'Be quiet!' cried my mother. 'You are a liar. You didn't tell me that you had paid Wu Shing extra to kill Su Li. You gave him Hazel's pin – to frame her and frighten me. You don't understand what it means to get the Triads involved, even though I tried to explain. And you told me . . . you told me you'd killed him, and you would kill her if I didn't stay silent.'

'They are guilty!' screeched Mrs Svensson. 'I am innocent! Don't believe a word they say—'

'SILENCE!' bellowed my father. 'June. How could you? I never . . . I never thought.'

'You never *do* think, Vincent,' said my mother.

'We need to clear this up,' said Detective Leung. 'I will question Mrs Svensson, Mrs Wong and Miss Wong. You' – he nodded to the police – 'may question the maids.'

'You can do what you like with Mrs Svensson,' said my father, folding his arms. 'But you will not take my wife or my daughter away from me.'

And that is how I ended up sitting next to my mother in another Peninsula Hotel room, with my father and Detective Leung opposite me, asking questions.

I talked and talked, explaining about the pin, and how I had lost it, and how afraid I had been. I said nothing about Sai Yat, or our night-time adventure (I was glad that my mother had already mentioned Wu Shing's death, so I didn't need to lead the detective to it), and I made it sound as though lucky chance, instead of detection, had led Daisy and me to the correct hotel room. I told them everything that had happened there, though, how Mrs Svensson had threatened us with a gun, and admitted to her part in the crime.

My mother was cold and to the point. Yes, she had plotted with Mrs Svensson to have Teddy kidnapped. Kendra needed the money, and my mother wanted to punish my father after Teddy's birth. 'I didn't want to kill the maid,' she said, again and again. 'She was a silly, proud little thing, but I knew Hazel was fond of her. She was only meant to be hurt. I swear it. And Teddy was always supposed to come home again. No one should have been killed. I only wanted to frighten you. You were all so smug about that baby!'

My heart broke as I listened to her, and then broke again as I watched my father watching her. My mother had changed – or perhaps we had just never really seen her before today.

At last, Detective Leung leaned back in his chair and took a deep breath. I stared at the dark fleck in his eye and tried to breathe calmly.

'Miss Wong, you are free to go,' he said. 'Although you are clearly not telling me certain things, I am at last confident that you had nothing to do with the crime. And, Mrs Wong – you may go home with your husband this evening, as long as you do not leave your compound.'

'Where would I go?' asked my mother bitterly. 'And what do I care any more?'

'Ah Mah!' I said.

My mother turned to look at me, and then she put out her hand very carefully and touched my wrist. 'At least you're safe, Ying Ying,' she said. 'I did one thing right, I suppose.'

And, for a moment, she did not look bitter at all.

# 10

Suddenly I was reeling with tiredness. I barely remember the journey home. I simply leaned against Daisy, utterly empty.

Jie Jie put Teddy back in his room, and then she and May and Rose and I sat around his cot and watched him. I think none of us wanted to let him out of our sight. Of course, Teddy behaved as though nothing particularly dramatic had happened at all. He lay there, sucking his toes and burbling at us. I couldn't help smiling at him.

'I do like him now,' whispered Rose.

'I do too,' I admitted, putting my arm round her.

Father came in then, looking somehow thinner and older than he had that morning.

'All of you except Jie Jie, leave,' he said. From the look on his face, I knew there was no arguing with him. I wanted to know whether he really believed that I was innocent – but I couldn't ask yet. I went back to our room and closed the door.

Daisy was there with Ping. Daisy was looking indignant, and Ping was blushing furiously.

'Hazel,' said Daisy, 'Ping has been telling me . . . well, I feel rather a fool. Do you realize that she *knew* what we were doing, all the way along?'

Ping ducked her head and flushed even harder. 'Of course I did,' she said. 'I knew it was important, so I listened in when you were having your detective meetings. I wanted to help you, because you cared about Su Li, as well as Teddy.'

'You were awfully good at the Peninsula,' I said, turning to her, because Daisy is rather bad at praising anyone other than herself.

'I had to do it, miss,' said Ping.

'You didn't!' I cried. 'You didn't have to do anything. You saved us, honestly you did. We are so lucky.'

'You did really,' agreed Daisy, grudgingly admiring. 'It was quite impressive.'

'Thank you, miss,' said Ping, and she stood up a little straighter.

'You ought to be a proper Detective Society member!' I said to her.

'Hmm!' said Daisy. 'Really, Hazel, that's a bit much.'

'It isn't!' I said. I found I did not care any more about Daisy and her rules for the Detective Society. 'We let

Beanie and Kitty and Lavinia in when they helped us, didn't we? This is just the same. Daisy, don't make that face. It's true!'

Daisy hemmed and hawed – and finally sighed and threw up her hands.

'Oh, all right, then,' she said. '*Assistant* member *only*, though, please.'

Ping beamed.

'All right,' I said. 'Ping, recite after me.'

'*I* say the pledge, Hazel!' cried Daisy.

'Not in Hong Kong you don't,' I said, smiling despite myself, because I knew that it was up to me now, not Daisy. '*I* can say it in Cantonese.'

The next morning Ping, Daisy and I went out to the fish pond to meet Ah Lan.

'Mrs Svensson is in prison,' he told us. 'She's going to be tried and convicted – and if she isn't for some reason, we have men watching her. She won't escape justice for Su Li and Wu Shing's deaths. But Sai Yat has decided that your mother *will* be allowed to escape prison. He accepts her statement that she was tricked, and he will allow her to remain in the Big House with your family under watch, mostly because she is the mother of the girl who helped us to clear Sai Yat's name.'

'Thank you,' I said weakly. I knew that my mother had done wrong, but she was *my mother*. She mattered to me more than justice, no matter how shameful that was to realize.

'And one more thing: Sai Yat has sent you a present, to thank you for your hard work.'

He put his hand in his pocket and pulled out something wrapped in red fabric. I unfolded it and saw that it was a jade pin. It was not my rooster pin, but a new one, a beautifully carved lotus flower.

'It is from all of us,' said Ah Lan, nodding at me. 'It's not a threat, I promise.'

I breathed out.

'And a reminder,' said Ah Lan, his lips quirking up in a smile. 'Sai Yat is grateful, and Sai Yat will be watching what you do next with interest.'

I closed my fist around the jade pin. It was cool and slightly slippery in my hand. It felt, somehow, like a last gift from Su Li, a reminder that family is sometimes about more than blood relationships. We were to bury her that afternoon, and I knew what I would wear in my hair.

'We wouldn't have been able to solve the case without you!' I said, coming back to myself.

'Why is there only one pin?' asked Daisy indignantly. 'What about me? We did solve the case together!'

'You can learn to share,' said Ah Lan.

'Thank you, Ah Lan,' I said hurriedly, because Daisy was puffing up with indignation. 'We have something for you too.'

'Hazel!' hissed Daisy, behind me. 'Not again!'

'We want you to be part of the Detective Society,' I said, ignoring her. I heard her huff in annoyance. 'It's all we can give.'

'As long as it doesn't interfere with my place in the Five Jade Figures,' said Ah Lan, winking.

I gave him the translated version of the Detective Society pledge, and Ah Lan recited it. His cheek twitched as he tried not to laugh at some of the words, but all the same I felt he was pleased.

Halfway through, May came running up and asked what we were doing.

'Boring grown-up things,' I said quickly.

'I think you're lying,' said May. 'Some grown-up things are interesting. When I grow up, I'm going to be a pirate queen.'

We watched her as she ran away, brandishing her stick.

'You have to look after her and Rose when I go back to England,' I said to Ah Lan. 'Don't let them do anything too dangerous.'

'I'm not sure I can promise that,' said Ah Lan, leaning on his rake. 'They're your sisters. I think it's in their blood.'

Detective Leung came back to the house one more time, with Mr Wa Fan. Now that I knew about Mr Wa

Fan's secret, I could see how his hand shook when he raised it, how the lines in his face looked as deep as cuts. He really had only wanted to help, and I felt so ashamed of myself that I bowed almost to the ground when I saw him.

'Thank you,' I said.

Mr Wa Fan put his hand on my shoulder. 'Your grandfather and I were friends,' he said. 'I could do nothing less. But I am sorry, Miss Wong, for what happened. I am sorry for the pain you feel now.'

Detective Leung stopped in front of me. 'Miss Wong,' he said, the little dot in his eye dancing as he spoke. 'I hope you will forgive me for suspecting you. I have to look into everything. It is my job.'

'It's – it's all right,' I said. 'You did have to.'

'Now,' he went on. 'You and Miss Wells have been very brave. Especially Miss Wells, with the hotel telephone. Without that, I wouldn't have known where to find you.'

Daisy glowed. 'No, you wouldn't, would you?' she said. 'I expect you want to give us medals now, don't you?'

Detective Leung looked at her askance. 'I do not give out medals,' he said at last. 'Pride in the case should be its own reward.'

And, despite everything, I nearly laughed out loud to see Daisy's cross face.

# 11

My father and Jie Jie were more wrapped up in Teddy than ever. They hovered around, my father's eyes straying to him halfway through a sentence, Jie Jie reaching out to touch him as he lay in Ping's arms – for Ping was to look after him when Daisy and I went home again. It was funny: a few weeks before I would have been furiously jealous, but now I understood that love is not a thing that can be cut up and doled out like a cake. It keeps on expanding.

And I also discovered that although I couldn't forgive my mother, I still loved her. That was why what she had done hurt me. The pain of it kept overwhelming me whenever I thought of it. It was not fading, like the pain of my grandfather's death, which had become a soft ache that I could look at and touch and put away like a lovely dress that has become too small now to wear. I tried to laugh and smile and be strong, but it felt as though I was fighting to be so all the time. My mother had done what she had done not just for herself, but for *me*, and that was dreadful.

Then, one afternoon, my father called me into the Library. He was sitting at his desk, without Teddy for once, and I saw how tired he still looked, and how sad.

'Father,' I said to him.

'My Hazel,' said my father. 'I am sorry. I'm sorry for what your mother has done, I'm sorry that I doubted you, I'm sorry that I was angry with you, and I am sorry that I ever made you feel as though I did not care for you.'

'No, *I'm* sorry!' I cried. 'I was awful, Father, I really was. I didn't behave like a proper big sister, or a proper daughter. I'm sorry I was angry with you about Su Li.'

'Hazel, be quiet,' said my father, and he smiled at me for the first time in what felt like weeks. 'As your father, I command you to be proud of yourself and what you have done. I made some mistakes, I admit it, and I'm sorry. It breaks my heart that Su Li is dead, and I think you are right that I could have done more to prevent it. But *you* brought her murderer to justice. *You* saved your brother and you brought him back to me. You are wonderful and brave and clever, and you are a credit to me. I ought to have said this to everyone, and especially to you, when you first arrived, but I will say it now: Teddy does not change anything. You are still my clever daughter, and I am proud of everything you do with that brain of yours. I am even coming round to your Miss Wells. I see that, although she is wilful, this can sometimes serve her well. You seem to have a talent for – for solving problems together, and this time I am grateful for it.'

I threw myself at him. 'I don't have to go back to England,' I said, my face muffled in his shoulder. 'I can stay. I can look after you.'

'I don't need looking after, Hazel,' said my father. 'You are my child. I look after you, and Rose and May and Teddy – and I will look after your mother. She is still my wife. This is hard to say, but for your sake she will always be part of this family, and she will stay in this house. I think that might be punishment enough.'

'All right,' I said in a tiny voice. 'Thank you. Father, about England . . . Rose wants to go to school there one day too. Can she?'

'Rose?' said my father. 'But – well, why not? She shall go, and May too, one day. If I have learned anything, it is that it is important never to underestimate anyone, no matter how well you think you know them. But it is also important to remember that you cannot take responsibility for what another person does. Hazel, no matter what she says, you are *not* the reason for what your mother did. Do you hear me? It isn't your fault.'

When I came out of the room, I bumped into Daisy, who had been listening at the door.

'You're a chump,' she said in a low voice. 'You know your father was telling the truth.'

And I finally believed her.

And then we were standing on the boat as it pulled away from the Hong Kong dock, water churning white beneath us and my stomach churning in sympathy. Father and May and Rose and Jie Jie and Ping and Teddy were all waving from the shore, and Daisy was standing beside me, waving back. I watched my life and my family become smaller and smaller, and I felt a tug in my chest, as though my heart was tied to them.

We were on our way back to England, and school, and friendships and arguments and foreign food and grey skies and cold and rain, Kitty and Beanie and Lavinia and George and Alexander, and I couldn't wait. I knew, more and more, that grown-up life was sometimes rather horrid, but I was learning that I could bear it. I squeezed Daisy's hand, and waved with my free one, waved and waved until the figures on the dock winked out and we were alone at sea. I was waving goodbye to my grandfather, and Su Li – and my mother too. She was at home today. She had not seen me off, and I was both hurt and glad about that.

'I'm rather looking forward to going home,' said Daisy. 'Aren't you? Hong Kong has been eventful, and adventurous, but also awful and topsy-turvy. I'm quite ready to go back to being the Honourable Daisy Wells again.'

'You always were Daisy Wells,' I said, smiling. 'Hong Kong just made you a different sort of Daisy.'

'You're quite a different Hazel in Hong Kong too!' said Daisy. 'I hardly know you any more.'

'Do you like the Hong Kong me?' I asked nervously.

'Oh, more than ever,' said Daisy, beaming. 'Only you're *far* more difficult to order about.'

'I like the Hong Kong Daisy too,' I said. 'Let's not change back again all the way, even when we get back to England.'

'All right,' said Daisy. 'But I'm still President, and you're still Vice-President. *Some* things will never change.'

'Some things will never change,' I agreed, and we did the Detective Society handshake as we leaned against the railing.

# Hazel's Hong Kong Glossary

Ordinarily, Daisy writes the glossaries at the back of my casebooks. But she has said to me, with rather an annoyed look on her face, that this time I might be the better person to do it. I think she is right. So this is my glossary, for Daisy's benefit, of some of the words and phrases that would be odd for anyone English reading this account.

By the way, Hong Kong dollars are not the same as British pounds. They are only worth about a tenth as much. If we had been in England, Teddy's ransom would have been ten thousand pounds (which is still a dreadful lot of money).

- **Ah Mah** — this means 'mother', but Rose and May also use it to mean my mother, June. I know this is very odd to Daisy, but it would be odd to hear my sisters call Jie Jie Mother!

- **Ah Yeh** — 'grandfather' in Cantonese.

- **bound feet** — wealthy little girls' feet used to be wrapped up tightly to keep them very small and pretty. It was done to my mother, and it means that she cannot run about, but only walk slowly. Often her feet hurt her, so I am very glad that it had gone out of fashion by the time I was born.

- **char sui bao** — a *bao* is a bun, and *char sui* is a way of cooking pork. *Char sui bao* are like dough pillows full of delicious meat. Even Daisy likes them.

- **cheongsam** — a tight silk Chinese dress, with slits up the sides. It is what women wear in Hong Kong if they want to look nice.

- **Ching Shih** — May is obsessed with Ching Shih. She was a pirate queen, the very best in history. She fought the British and the Portuguese and was absolutely fearless.

- **cloisonné** — a way of decorating a pot with gold wire and gems. It is beautiful to look at.

- **congee** — this is a sort of breakfast porridge made of rice instead of oats. I think it is very nice, but Daisy says it's gluey.

- **coolie** – a type of worker who is not paid well.

- **daan jeung** – soya milk (not cow's milk at all; it is a sort of bean paste) that is served in a bowl. It is a thing we eat for breakfast in Hong Kong.

- **dim sum** – a meal of small portions of lots of different sorts of food, including dumplings, savoury buns and cakes. You always have *dim sum* with tea, and you usually eat it in the morning.

- **egg waffles** – May's favourite Hong Kong bunbreak! These are sweet and shaped like fat little bubbles. You can get them from street vendors – they are not really the sort of thing you would have in the Peninsula Hotel.

- **eight** – this number is very auspicious in Hong Kong, which is why it's lucky to have offices on the eighth floor of a building.

- **four** – this number is very unlucky, the way thirteen is in England.

- **fung tsao** – a way of cooking chicken feet! Daisy doesn't trust them, but I think they are delicious. The trick really is to start with the toes and work upwards.

- **ginseng** – a sort of plant that is used in Chinese medicine.

- **har gau** – prawn dumplings: little parcels of dough with prawns inside them.

- **junk** – a sort of large Chinese ship with a beautiful crest of triangular sails that can be red or white.

- **koi** – a sort of fish that we have in our ponds in Hong Kong. They are big and speckled white, red and black. When they all swim together, they're beautiful.

- **lions** – lots of Chinese places have lions outside the main doors to guard them from ill will, I suppose.

- **lo bak go** – turnip cakes. They are small and square and white, and they taste rather gluey, but in a very nice way.

- ***mah lai goh*** – a sort of very soft, very pillowy yellow cake, much lighter than even the lightest Victoria sponge in England.

- **the Monkey King** – this is a Chinese myth about a monkey who annoys the gods and goes on a journey to the West.

- **mooncake** – my favourite Hong Kong bunbreak! They are made for the mid-autumn festival, so we couldn't eat any this visit, but they are made of rich pastry filled with sticky red bean or lotus paste.

- ***mui tsai*** – the easiest way to explain this is that it's just another word for 'maid', although that isn't quite it. *Mui tsai* are younger than maids. They began as slave girls, and so lots of people, including the governor's wife, are understandably cross and want to outlaw them. Of course, my father pays his *mui tsai* just like the maids and sends them to school too, so they aren't *mui tsai* at all in the proper sense. We only call them *mui tsai* out of family habit.

- ***Neih hou*** – this is just hello in Cantonese. I did try to keep Chinese out of this account, for Daisy's sake, but some things are important.

- **pi-dog** – the poor mangy dogs without owners who run about in Hong Kong.

- **pith helmet** – rich European men wear these when they go to hot countries, or into places they think will be dangerous. They are the sort of hat you wear if you want to look like an explorer.

- **queue** – another word for a braid of hair at the nape of your neck.

- **sampan** – a small Hong Kong fishing boat, rather like a barge.

- **sewing amah** – our maids do not mend our clothes. That is the job of the sewing *amah*. An *amah* is just a nanny, so she is the nanny who sews.

- **siu lung bau** – these are dumplings that have soup inside them as well as meat and herbs. You have to be very careful when you bite into them!

- **thousand-year eggs** – thousand-year eggs are preserved, but only for a month or two, not a thousand years. It turns them a funny grey colour, and they taste salty and strong. Daisy doesn't like them at all, but I do.

- *tsaa leung* – these are fried dough sticks wrapped in rice noodle rolls.

- **Triads** – a group of Hong Kong gangs. Hundreds of years ago they were monks who wanted to get rid of the dynasty who ruled over China, but that happened a few years before I was born. Now the Triads spend their time making money by doing illegal things.

- **Tung Wah** – a group of Chinese men who are a sort of unofficial local government. They run things like hospitals, and if you want to be important in Chinese society, you join the Tung Wah.

- **wife cakes** – small flat cakes with flaky pastry outsides and melon and almond paste insides.

- *yum cha* – this is what you say when you go to get *dim sum*. It is a little like saying *teatime* in English.

# Author's Note and Acknowledgements

This book was both a joy to write, and extremely difficult. This is mostly because I became aware, as never before, how wide the gap between Hazel and me really is. We share a love of books and mysteries. We both have large, blended families. But a British-American upbringing is not a Hong Kong Chinese one. I'm very lucky to have a group of school friends who have become more like family, who I've known since we were Hazel and Daisy's age and who have, over many years, introduced me to Hong Kong culture. When I told them about this book they were very willing to help me with it. Alison Wong and Scarlett Fu read drafts, and Scarlett took me out for the *dim sum* meal that Hazel and Daisy eat. Thank you to both of them, and also to Zara Un and Sarah Fok, Alice Shone and Sarah Warry, for seventeen wonderful years of food-based friendship.

I took a research trip to Hong Kong in September 2016. This was in fact supposed to be the beginning of our honeymoon, so I have to thank my husband, David, from the bottom of my heart for the time he spent following me around as I went into raptures over small bits of paper in Hong Kong history museums.

We really did go to the Peninsula Hotel, and the Peak, and several teahouses, and many of the other places Hazel and Daisy visit in this book. We even took a night-time hike down from the Peak and almost walked into a spider. But what we did not do was visit a house like Hazel's, for one simple reason: they no longer really exist. Old Hong Kong houses were built of granite. They were built to last – but today, almost none of them have. Going hunting for buildings from the 1930s was incredibly difficult, because Hong Kong is constantly changing as land changes hands. To recreate the Hong Kong Hazel knew would have been nearly impossible without the help of a woman who grew up in Hong Kong in the 1940s, in a household very like Hazel's. Details of the Big House and Hazel's family, as well as the bank setting and the idea of a lift-based murder, came from her recollections, and interviewing her was truly one of the greatest honours of my life. I hope I have done her and her memories proud – thank you, OB, for giving your time and your knowledge to this project.

I met many kind and helpful people in Hong Kong who influenced this story. Special thanks to Professor David Fauré at the Chinese University of Hong Kong, who was so generous with his time and answered all my questions about 1930s Hong Kong life, Professor Simon Haines, and Associate Professor Eddie Tay, who allowed me to speak to his students about publishing and took us for a wonderful campus lunch. John Millen at the *South China Morning Post* has been wonderfully helpful from the outset of this project, and I was delighted to meet Karly Cox, Miuccia and Sebastian for a very noisy *dim sum* interview in the traditional 1930s teahouse that has become the Luk Man.

Although this is a novel, and therefore full of things that are inevitably not as correct as a history book, I have tried to use the truth as much as I can. The history of Hong Kong is an incredible one – if you're interested in finding out more, I think Steve Tsang's book on it is very good. The Triads as an organization are absolutely real, and very much a part of Hong Kong society then and now (although there is no such thing as the Five Jade Figures, and I have not drawn on any real people in my portrayal of Sai Yat and his gang). *Mui tsai* are also real – as Hazel says in her glossary, they were originally slaves, rather than paid servants, and because of this they were (quite rightly) being outlawed in the 1930s. However, I decided to keep them in my story by name on the understanding that the fair and generous Mr Wong would have been paying his, and also educating them!

Wealthy Hong Kong children like Hazel and her siblings really did live in fear of being kidnapped, and they were always carefully watched for that reason. The lift to the doctor's (yes, doctors' offices really were above banks) would be one of the only times a child like Teddy would have been without a guard of some kind. And, by the way, the Hong Kong and Shanghai Bank building is both a real place and a real bank – if you or an adult you know bank with HSBC, you use it every day.

All the food in this book has been recommended to me by various Hong Kong friends and readers. I have eaten (almost) everything I describe here, including thousand-year egg and chicken feet. I liked them both a lot! If you live in England and you want to try them too, I'd recommend visiting Chinatown in London. Unsurprisingly (given its history as a British colony) a lot of London's Chinese population are of Hong Kong descent, and so the food available there is close to what you'll get in Hong Kong itself.

Mrs Svensson's name is Kendra because of Kendra Gilbertson, whose generous bid in the Authors for Refugees auction won her the right to see her name in one of my books. My research into Hong Kong reminded me how its history (just like that of every city and country in the world) is a history of migration, sometimes forced. Hazel and her family do not know it, but the Japanese invasion of Hong Kong is just round the corner, followed swiftly by the Second World War. Anyone can become a refugee, and during those years even Hong Kong's wealthiest families did. To those of us currently happy and safe in our homes, remember how lucky you are. Treat today's refugees as though they matter just as much as you know you do.

And now, on to the proper thank-you bit.

I am enormously indebted to the generosity and wisdom of my early readers, without whom this story would be not nearly as good or as true: Miuccia Chan, Sebastian Wong, Karly Cox, Scarlett Fu, Alison Wong, Kwan Ching Yi Angie, Cerrie Burnell (who gave me invaluable advice on Ah Lan), Charlie Morris, Anne Miller, Kathie Booth Stevens, Wei Ming Kam, Viki Cheung, Katherine Webber and the Tsang family. Anything that is correct is down to them. Anything that is wrong is absolutely my fault.

Thank you to my endlessly brilliant Puffin team: Nat Doherty, Tom Rawlinson, Naomi Colthurst, Harriet Venn, Sonia Razvi, Francesca Dow, Jane Tait, Frances Evans, Jan Bielecki, Wendy Shakespeare and everyone else who has worked in-house on this book. My name is on its cover, but it wouldn't mean much without their support. Thank you also to my agent, Gemma Cooper, who has adored and fought for this series for many years, and to Jenny Bent, who has tirelessly worked to send Daisy and Hazel around the world. Thanks to Nina Tara for a beautiful cover and maps, and thanks to the woman who brings Hazel's voice to life in my audiobooks, Katie Leung.

Thank you to my family and friends, who have supported me through this weird process once again. Special shout-out to my partner-in-crime, Non Pratt, and to Team Cooper. Thanks to my wonderful parents, who would love me whatever I did (but are especially proud of the book thing), and my wonderful husband, who once again has lived with me every day of this book and remarkably still enjoys my company. And thank you to my brother and sister, Richard and Carey Stevens, who are absolutely nothing like Rose, May and Teddy but who I thought of often while I was creating Hazel's siblings.

And, finally, thank you to my fans. Your letters, your drawings, your reviews, your stories, your costumes, your plays, your lessons, your parties, your events and your Detective Societies have brought my characters to life in the most extraordinary ways. I am astonishingly lucky to inspire you, and you are the reason I wrote this book.

London, August 2017